# Goat

## Jordan Elizabeth

Published by CHBB Publishing, Inc.

Cover by Rue Volley
Edited by CLS Editing

Published by CHBB Publishing, Inc.

## Dedication

For my grandmother, Vivian Mae Clark Hatfield (1920-2015), who wrote down my stories for me before I was old enough to write them myself.

# Early Reviews

Manhattan teen Keziah is in for big changes when she moves to rural New Winchester to take care of her grandmother. Already concerned with complicated family relationships, she finds dementia sometimes steals the Oma she had always loved. Most frustrating is the old woman's instance about her relationship with the Goat Children. Frustrating, yes, but also intriguing? As the veil between past and present, real and unseen, begins to fail for Oma, Keziah fears she may lose herself in the rift as well. – Danny Kuhn, author of *Fezziwig: a Life*

Keziah is torn between the loving, nurturing woman Oma was in the past; and the raving, sick old woman she has become. Each chapter ends with a sweet and touching memory of Oma in her prime, which helps the reader parallel the woman's two sides as Keziah struggles with the irrational old woman. The story mixes dramatic scenes of Keziah's hopelessness with touching scenes of love and promise. There are funny moments and moments of sheer dread. But there is hope. The Goat Children are mythical warriors that Oma invented, and if Keziah plays her cards right the Goat Children could be her saviors. Goat Children is reminiscent of Pan's Labyrinth with our main character escaping from the harsh reality of life to a mystical world of fantasy and intrigue. It's an enjoyable story that will have you staying up late and reading into the night, rooting for the main character…a terrific read. - James McNally, author of the *Immortal Trilogy*

This book allows the reader an honest, no frills, not romanticized story of the real heartache of Alzheimer's Disease. The author does a wonderful job of showing just how hard it is to live with someone when their mind is so unreliable. Cruel words are said, but can't be believed as truth. Unexpected actions will occur that can't be prevented. Good descriptions, excellent attention to detail, and good family drama. Highly recommended! – Ann M. Noser, author of *How to Date Dead Guys*

# Chapter 1

Bodies crushed against each other, a blur of hair and clothes, in the mad dash to exit the subway. The air smelled of the greasy restaurants above and felt stuffy, despite the bitter cold that rattled through the damp subway tunnel. My mouth watered as I sniffed roasted chestnuts. *You haven't eaten dinner yet*, my rumbling stomach scolded.

I slipped past a man speaking rapid Spanish to board the train, grabbed a pole, slid on to a seat, and pulled my green bag higher towards my chest. The two paperbacks inside jammed into my ribs. With a groan, I shifted into a new position, wondering what glorious worlds awaited within the glossy covers.

"Whoa ho, ho, *ho*."

More people ranting on the subway. It could never be a quiet ride. I opened my bag to peer at the fantasy novels. I'd chosen thick books because they lasted longer and made the reading more rewarding.

"Ho, little one."

A face shoved into mine from the aisle, and I jerked back, squeaking. Oily black hair hung over a scarred forehead. The man swayed, braying a laugh. I glanced at the woman with bright pink hair sitting on the next seat. She read a newspaper without looking up.

"So much to you." The man licked his lips and slurred the words.

His pungent odor clawed its way through my nose; no escaping the invisible fumes. They washed over me with groping draws until my eyes watered. I cringed, my craving for chestnuts gone. Anyone on a diet would be thankful to have him around.

He stood, clinging to a pole with one gloved hand. Threads poked from the torn seams in the gripping brown leather. Two duffel bags, stained with mud, rested near his feet, bulging with contents.

I lowered my gaze, clutching the bag tighter. *Please go away.* I shouldn't have taken the subway, but I'd done it to save time. Even though I was seventeen, Mama said it wasn't safe to ride alone, and now, I agreed. *I'm not gonna be home by my seven o'clock curfew. Mama's gonna freak. I can't believe I forgot my phone.*

"You don't belong on this world." He smacked his lips. Behind his head, a large sign told the public not to smoke, or they'd get lung cancer and die. It far preferred to stare at the anti-smoking sign than at him.

"Yes, thank you," I mumbled as he leered at me. Even if he lacked a home and suffered from insanity, he didn't deserve rudeness.

"You like fantasy?"

I stared at my lap, but when he repeated the question louder, I nodded.

"What would ya do if fantasy became your life? What would ya do if it wasn't fantasy anymore?"

"Fantasy isn't real." I shifted my gaze to my knee-high black socks. The right sock had a tiny hole near the knee. I'd have to sew it when I got home. If I studied it, maybe he'd grow bored and mosey on elsewhere.

"Are you happy here? Don't you want more, little one? I can take you to another world." His deep breaths made snot rattle in his nose.

8

I gagged, hiding my mouth behind my hand. The woman with the newspaper glanced over. I pleaded silently for her to make the man go away, but she moved to an empty seat down the car, wrinkling her nose. I still had five more stops before I could get away.

*Do I dare follow her?*

"Don't you believe in destiny?"

*What if he sits next to me?* I slid my bag onto the empty seat, clutching the handle. As the subway curved around the corner, it screeched, the sound echoing through the metallic enclosure as if screaming, "*Doom!*"

"I've been to other lands. I've seen my future, and I spit at it." He turned his head to hack on the floor. The saliva bubbled with a yellowish hue.

The subway squealed to a halt, and some of the passengers stood to exit. I removed the bag in case someone new sat down, someone safe, but no one came near or looked at us as they found seats. The doors slid shut, and the train moved again. Four more stops to go.

"Don't shun fantasy. I've made mistakes and don't want you to make 'em too. Take the chance and see what you can do. Take it!" He pumped his fist, revealing grease stains on his coat sleeves.

I scanned the other passengers' faces. They ignored us, although the ranting man filled the car with his voice. Only the smiling stock photo faces on wall advertisements watched. Ever-smiling, ever-trapped in their realm of sales. I fiddled with the zipper on the front of my gray hoodie, heart racing.

The subway halted at the next station. Again, people exited and entered, and no one sat beside me. Three more stops to go. I drummed my fingers against my thigh.

"I know all about the ones they call the Goats." He drew a ragged breath. "I'm not supposed to, but I know. My wife was one. She told me all about them. Oh, yes, she did. She wasn't supposed to, but she did. They don't let them take over the world. They won't!"

*Why do crazies always go for alien invasions?* I twirled my brown curls. I'd get off at the next stop and walk the rest of the way, even if I arrived home later.

*What if he follows me?*

"The Goats!" He flapped his arm.

*Alien goat invasion. How awesome.* I clutched my bag like a shield. The subway screeched as it approached the next station. He waved both arms, repeating the scream.

The doors swished open, but if I stood to escape, he could attack. Two more stops to go. *What if I can't escape at my stop, either?*

As soon as the subway started, he lowered his arm and drew a few breaths. He reeked of alcohol, overpowering the sweat stench; the stench made my head swirl.

"Beware of the Goats." His chest heaved. "Help the Goats. Save the Goats!"

*He really is deranged.* I'd ever seen goats in New York City.

"Yes, I will." *Go away.* "I'll … I'll watch out for the goats."

"The *Goats*," he corrected, as if I'd mispronounced the word. He picked up his duffel bags and waddled to the back of the car, where he dropped onto a seat. He took a small paperback book from the pocket of his trench coat and flipped it open.

When the doors swished open at the next stop, I exited in the crush of bodies. People coughed and spoke, heels clicked and wheels on backpacks rolled, and the sounds echoed off the stone walls.

I slid through the turnstile and bolted up the cement steps two at a time, the edges cracked and crumbled, and graffiti decorated the walls with images of fire and obscene language. The brightness of the paint, and the harsh edges that curved and sang were beautiful. The scrawls seemed to leap off the stone, suddenly alive.

At the top, I grasped the railing. Cold, dented metal bit through the fishnet of my fingerless gloves while I gazed over my shoulder. The people emerging didn't spare me a glance. I was lost in the crowd, a stationary fixture.

The man wasn't following. I ducked my head to push into the crowd. People bumped into me, jostling with elbows and bags. I almost walked into a tourist, who snapped a picture of the taxicabs.

"Hey," called a stout vender from the corner. "You okay?"

I tucked back a brown curl. "I'm fine, but thanks." Wind whipping between the skyscrapers stole the power of my words.

"Wanna dog?" He held one out, nestled in a white roll.

"No, thanks. I don't eat meat."

"Good," I thought I heard him whisper. "Your kind shouldn't."

He couldn't have spoken. It must've been someone else. It wouldn't make sense for a man who made his living off people scarfing down meat-in-a-tube to agree with my vegetarian lifestyle.

I ogled the sea of metal vehicles washed in the afternoon sunlight like sharks swarming for a fresh kill. I shook off the thought and ran, an empty Styrofoam cup crunching beneath my foot. I didn't have a watch, but the sun hung low in the sky. A thought raced through my mind as the sun made windows wink and flash.

*Beware of Goats.*

\*\*\*\*

"Long line at the bookstore." I dropped my bag on the marble table beside the door to my family's condo. Instrumental Celtic music wafted from the living room as I left the small foyer, and I almost tripped over my sprawled little sister.

"Phebe, you shouldn't lie on the floor."

"Why are you home so late?" Phebe dragged an orange crayon over the page of her coloring book. Her ponytail bobbed as she tipped her head. "You should've taken me with you. Mommy said so."

"I'm sure she did." I rolled my eyes.

When I'd left earlier, Phebe had still been doing her mathematics homework. We were home schooled, so even in the summer, we had work to do. It sucked because other home schooled students I knew had summers off. That was our penalty for having a mother with a Master's degree in elementary education.

"Where're Mama and Dad?"

Phebe sat up on her knees with her eyebrows knit together. "Mommy's crying."

My heart sunk and dropped clear out of my stomach. Mama never got *that* upset when I came home late. *Did she find out about the party last weekend at Tiffany's?* I'd lied and said it was only going to be Tiff, her parents and siblings, and me. I hadn't mentioned her parents were in Vancouver on vacation or that Tiff had invited *all* of her friends, not just me. Regret stabbed my gut.

"Mama, I'm home! Mama?"

The family photographs glared at me from the wall, none so reprimanding as the face of my Reverend Uncle. I kicked off my flats and hurried into my parents' bedroom. With the lamp off, only a little light slipped through the closed venetian blinds covering the single window.

Short brown hair fanned over the plaid pillowcase, and Mama lay sideways on the king-sized bed, a crumpled tissue pressed against her nose. Dad sat beside her, stroking her shoulders. He still wore his suit from work—an even worse sign. Dad always peeled off his jacket and tossed the tie onto the table as soon as he got home.

"Mama?" My voice cracked as my throat constricted.

"Your uncle called." Dad tugged on his green silk tie that should've been lost in the pile of mail, not still fastened around his neck.

"Uncle Tom?"

The Reverend in Massachusetts, Dad's younger brother, only called once a month, on the first Friday. Even though we called him Uncle Tom around the house, we all referred to him as Pastor Thomas to his face.

"No, Uncle Jan."

Mama's brother, the one who called less than Uncle Tom did.

"What…what did he want? Has someone died?" *Oh no, is it my grandmother?* Uncle Jan lived upstate, in the same town as her.

"Keziah, it's your grandmother," Dad continued.

*Oh no, oh no, oh no.* When I'd been younger, we'd lived down the street from Mama's mother. She had taken care of me while my parents worked, and we'd often picked violets in the yard. Sometimes, I imagined I could smell their perfume years later and hundreds of miles away.

I'd always called her *Oma*, which meant grandmother in Dutch. I could still remember the way I'd cried and screamed, begging to stay with Oma when we'd moved to New York City. The hours separating us seemed like an eternity.

"She has dementia." Dad removed his tie and knotted it around his fingers.

I blinked at him. "Dementia?" *Demented, like the man on the subway?*

"She hasn't been officially diagnosed, but the symptoms are there. Uncle Jan doesn't feel she can live on her own anymore." Dad dropped his tie onto the alarm clock.

"So…she's moving in with Uncle Jan?" I pictured waking up from a sleepover at Oma's house with fresh squeezed orange juice waiting in the kitchen beside a bowl of cream of wheat cereal, steamy and sweet.

"Good morning, sunshine," Oma would sing. She'd pull out the chair, the seat hideous and green, leftover from the 1970s. It had been an honor to sit at the kitchen table with her.

Dad rubbed his chin. "Your aunt won't let her do that."

I grinned. "She's moving in with us? That's amazing!" I only saw Oma on school holidays, and that summer, we'd had to pass because Mama had taught a summer school class.

"You know that wouldn't work." Dad gazed at the dresser across the room, a fog coming over his eyes.

I pulled at a loose thread on my black skirt. If Oma moved in, then Dad would have to move out or risk family war. The yelling would never stop. She hated Dad with a roaring passion I'd never understood. That anger had contributed to the reason why we'd moved, and when we visited Oma, Dad never went.

"Your uncle wants to put her in a home." Dad leaned over to rub a spot on the wall's blue paint as if that space was the problem, and he could make it disappear.

I licked my dry lips. "You mean like a nursing home?"

"No!" Mama rose on her elbows. "I'm *not* putting my mother in a nursing home. Do you know how they treat their patients? It's horrible. All those people. Oma would hate it. She's so antisocial these days. Really hate it."

"What are we going to do?" My question made Mama cry harder, and I flinched.

"We'll think of something," Dad whispered.

**** 

*I am six years old. Oma washes and curls her hair with pink sponge rollers. She ties a black ribbon with white lace around my forehead and dresses me in a blue velvet gown. We walk around the block. Many people are outside, doing yard work or sitting on their porches. She stops to talk to them and knows them by name. They know her, too.*

*"This is Princess Keziah," Oma says.*

*I am shy, so I hold her hand and keep quiet. She tells them about the wonderful things I do—painting, reading, knitting.*

*One of the neighbors snaps a photograph of us. Oma keeps it in a plastic frame on the piano. Her and me in the bright summer afternoon.*

# Chapter 2

Sirens whirred in the distance, clashing with the honking horns and screaming voices. The glow of streetlights splashed through the window and across the brocade comforter, reflected off the glass on the photograph resting on my dresser. Oma and me, arms linked, in the middle. Mama stood behind, holding a laughing Phebe, and Dad hovered to the side near solemn Uncle Tom. Five years ago, we all looked so happy, so healthy. Dementia-free.

Phebe nestled in the crook of my arm. Her head of brown curls matched mine and rested against my shoulder. *Phebe, darling Phebe...* I pressed my lips against her smooth forehead. Phebe had been a baby when we'd moved and another reason why we'd left. Oma had disliked Phebe beginning the day Mama had announced she was pregnant—a fact she'd kept from Oma until her belly became too round to hide.

I recalled sitting in the living room of our old house, the carpet soft and tangerine-colored, always smelling like garlic for a reason we'd never discovered. Phebe had been lying on a blanket, kicking her legs, gurgling and cooing as babies do. Oma had strolled in, wearing a knit hat as always.

"Look what I taught Phebe how to do," I'd called over, which made the baby fuss. The trick had been having Phebe grab my finger, something silly most babies do, but I'd been thrilled. *My sister is the smartest baby in the world.*

"Hello, Keziah." Oma had looked only at me. It hurt me to see Phebe treated like that. I remembered the time Oma had spent with me when I was a child, her love and care, her willingness to drop everything to make sure I was happy. One time, she drove out in a blizzard to buy me garlic knots because I was home sick.

Cruelty to Phebe must have been one of the first signs of dementia. All this time, poor Oma had suffered alone. My heart ached, and I squeezed my eyes shut.

I left Phebe asleep, curled around a worn-out stuffed pig. The hardwood floor chilled my bare feet as I plodded into the hallway. I nudged my parents' bedroom door open with my shoulder.

The bed creaked as I sat on the end. Mama slept, lost in the throes of unconsciousness, dragged down by heartache mirroring mine.

Dad sat up, rubbing the corner of his eye. "What's the matter, hon?"

I shook Mama's leg. "Mama, I'll go move in with Oma."

****

"I'm fine," Oma yelled over the phone. "I don't need anyone living with me. How dare you even suggest such an outrageous thing?"

I didn't know how to tell Oma she needed me. If I wasn't around, she'd go in a nursing home. Those words sounded too final, and they dried on my tongue.

Mama cleared her throat. "The city's a bad influence on Keziah, so we think it best if we send her away for a little while." A lie from us for Oma's betterment, to ease the pain.

That earned a nasty, "I told you so. The city is no place to raise a child."

I winced, and Mama pursed her lips.

Phebe wept as she clung to me. "It's not fair! You can't go."

I held her tighter, willing my tears not to come. As the oldest, I had to be stronger.

I stayed home with my sister while our parents worked, and in the afternoons, we were home schooled. Even though Mama taught in the district, she didn't want us attending public schools where metal detectors were used to keep out weapons.

"I don't want my girls growing up to think they're better than everyone else," Mama had said when Dad brought up the option of private schools.

I only had one friend to say goodbye to, and Tiffany shrugged it away.

She lifted one brow, so waxed it seemed to be nothing more than a pencil line. "You'll be back. It's all farms and cows upstate."

I'd show her. I'd prosper. Yet, I knew I'd miss her, the bowling parties, late night sleep overs, and yelling at her for rolling quarters to the homeless just to watch them scurry for money.

I stood on the street in front of our condominium, the blur of faces passing by. The people lived on my street, yet I' never knew their names or remembered what they looked like on a day-to-day basis. Pigeons pecked at garbage strewn across the sidewalk. One swooped away with a scrap of moldy bread.

Dad hugged me goodbye in the ornate entranceway to our building. "Be good. I hope public school isn't too awful. If things don't work out within two months, you'll have to come back, and we'll look into nursing home options."

I nodded, unable to answer without crying. *Bye, Dad. I'll miss you more than I can say.*

He nudged Phebe forward, but she hugged her stuffed pig and stared straight ahead. I kissed her anyway, and she ducked behind Dad's legs. He rested his hand on her head.

"Farewell, my little love," I said. Life was unfair to split us up. Phebe should come help with Oma too. They could finally bond.

The bus took me away as my stomach churned with trepidation. This wasn't a vacation with a deadline. I couldn't back out. Oma needed me, just as I'd once needed Oma.

Usually when we took the Greyhound bus to visit Oma, Mama and I played games along the ride. Mama brought game books, or we made them up spur of the moment. Sometimes, we told each other fantastic stories, taking turns telling bits and pieces.

This time, neither of us spoke.

Mama sat in the plush seat, her teeth clenched and hands clasped in her lap.

"At least the air feels good. Circulating. We won't catch other people's germs," I rambled.

Mama shrugged and handed me a sandwich from her canvas tote.

"Thanks, this is really going to help."

I took out my iPod and slipped on the earphones to listen to Lacuna Coil. The bus seat had never felt so uncomfortable. I fidgeted, sweat from my nerves breaking out across my brow. People didn't get better from dementia. The medicine didn't cure it, just slowed the progression, and Uncle Jan said Oma wouldn't go to the doctor anyway.

*When will I get to return to the city?*

The man behind me leaned against the back of my seat. "Good morning, ladies. Where are you heading?"

Mama smiled. I wondered how she could appear so calm. My teeth chattered from those stupid nerves, so I let her answer.

"New Winchester for a vacation," Mama said.

*Vacation, yeah.* I stared at a diner out the window. The bus's air conditioning caressed my face, and I removed a miniature notebook from my purse and scribbled observations to use up time. *This four-hour bus ride equals torture.*

**** 

I peered through the dirty window of Uncle Jan's white car while he spoke to a man at the bus station. *Ew.* What looked like chocolate pudding streaked the window. The back seat contained a plastic bucket, filled with moist leaves and twigs, as well as newspapers, magazines, and a dog's leash.

"Where are we supposed to sit?" I glanced at our bags. "Or put our stuff?"

Mama twirled her watch. "He always finds room for us."

"It's never *this* messy." *Please don't let this be a sign of worse things to come.* My stomach knotted.

"Hey, sorry about that." Uncle Jan swaggered over, waving the car keys. "I used to work with him. A great guy, really feel sorry for him. His wife left, took the kids, got a restraining order, and all that stuff. Got really messed up, was homeless for a while, and then he met this other girl. He got back to work, and then she ran off with all his money." Uncle Jan slid the key into the lock, turning it, and opened the driver's door. He nodded at the backseat. "Here, I'll clean this off for you."

He grabbed a pile of magazines and tossed them to the other side of the backseat, where they slid against the newspapers. Two of the magazines plopped into the bucket of wet leaves. They sloshed as he pulled them out and threw them onto the floor.

"Don't worry, you can step on those."

I dug my fingernails into my palms to stop a grimace, and shuddered at the blue material, streaked with mud and gum. Holding my breath, I slid in while Uncle Jan popped the trunk.

"Well," he said, "guess we'll have to be moving some stuff around back here."

I shut the door and gagged. The leaves and twigs reeked of mold. Mama squished into the front passenger seat. "Kez, your face is bright red. Are you okay?"

*Okay* didn't begin to describe how I felt. "It smells worse than the city in the summer."

"Put down the windows," she suggested as Uncle Jan jumped in, slamming his door. The whole car shook.

As he pulled into traffic, I realized I couldn't find the seatbelt, so I sank into the stiff cushion that stuck to the back of my t-shirt. *I swear this car is a deathtrap on wheels.*

"This is real nice, what you're doing." Uncle Jan snuffled.

Who wouldn't have allergies in a dump like this?

"How bad is Oma?" Mama asked. "She was fine last time we were here. She forgot things, sure, but she's almost ninety. Forgetting things is natural at her age."

"Her eyesight's gotten bad." He rambled.

I should've listened so I'd know what I was getting into, but I didn't want to. Oma needed to be as I remembered. I could bring her back to that state. Couldn't I?

Sometimes, Mama would look through the photo album of New Winchester and sigh. "Too bad you were too young to remember," she would say to Phebe. "New Winchester put on the best events, like a spring ice cream social."

Would Oma remember who we were? Sure, Mama spoke to Oma every day, but on the phone, Oma pulled it together. According to an Internet site, that was something a dementia sufferer could do. I shuddered, fighting back tears.

I needed Oma to be as she'd always been, smiling and laughing. We'd sit on the big living room chair and eat potato chips while watching cartoons. Years ago, we'd tied dolls to the rocking chair to see who could knock them off the fastest by rocking it harder.

The world of New Winchester sputtered by outside the window. A pudgy girl rode her scooter with a calico cat following. The big houses had small front yards, and siding in white and blue, a few greens, and a purple. Everything was so different from the brick and concrete buildings of New York City.

I saw front porches, trees, and garages. Tiffany might think everything upstate was farmland, but there weren't any farms in New Winchester. I'd never even been to a farm.

Uncle Jan swerved into a driveway and slammed on the brakes. Without a seatbelt on, I crashed into his seat, a stench of rotten banana peels assailing my nostrils. Filth rained over my lap. I bit back a retort aimed at Uncle Jan as I peeled myself off the cushion.

*Don't make him mad. You need him on your side.*

Outside the window, Oma's house loomed above us. The roof was black trimmed in metal to avoid ice buildup, and the siding was blue, framed in white. The wooden front porch spread from the front door to the garage, and a magnolia tree sprawled in front of the bedroom window.

The home looked the same, and a sudden bitter taste of hatred welled in my mouth. It should look different. If Oma wasn't okay, the house shouldn't pretend to be.

A truck in John Deere green drove by. Maybe Tiffany wasn't all wrong about the farms. She'd throw a fit if I ever showed up at a party with a farmer on my arm.

Mama took the luggage from the trunk while I stared at the house. A cement walkway led to the porch, lined in rose bushes, the weeds among them the only odd thing. Oma never allowed weeds to grow amongst her roses.

"Call me if you need anything." Uncle Jan patted me on the shoulder before hopping into his car.

He waved as he drove away, so Mama waved back, but I couldn't move.

"Get your suitcase," Mama said.

Weeds grew underneath the magnolia tree, and we had to duck beneath branches to get to the porch. Moss spread over the creaking porch slats.

Mama pressed the doorbell and frowned. "Did you hear it ring?"

"No." My stomach flip-flopped. I dragged my gaze away from a blue jay perched in the tree.

Mama opened the screen. It whooshed and creaked. I listened to the rapping of knuckles on the stained glass panes of the door, depicting trees and reindeers, a project Mama had done a few summers before.

"Go knock on the bedroom window. Maybe she's sleeping." Mama kept rapping her knuckles to beat out a tune.

*Where's Oma? Is she injured and unable to get up and come to the door? Has she fallen?*

I climbed over the porch railing to avoid stepping on the rosebushes and tapped on the bedroom window. Behind the glass, the curtains were drawn. I didn't see any shapes, so I knocked harder.

"Come on back." Mama searched through her purse for the key. Usually Oma opened the door on one of the first knocks.

Mama fiddled with the lock and stepped inside. I grabbed the screen door, the luggage left on the porch.

"Hello?" Mama called.

*Is Oma lying somewhere?*

\*\*\*\*

*I am four years old. Oma buys me a kitchen set and keeps it in her living room.*

*"This way, she will have something to do at my house," she tells Mama.*

*I set up my dolls on the carpet. "What do you want to eat?" They don't answer, but I pretend they request pancakes. I spread out the plastic food and dishes, but the set doesn't include pancakes.*

*Oma sits with me on the floor. "What are you making?"*

*"I was going to make pancakes, but there aren't any." I set a plastic chicken leg on a plate and hand it to my stuffed monkey.*

25

The next day when I return to play more, Oma surprises me with new food. She crocheted pancakes, eggs, candies, and cakes.

"Let me know what else you want," she says as we sit on the floor to play.

"Hmm." I think for a minute, considering foods Oma enjoys. "Ice cream cones."

She makes those for me, too.

# Chapter 3

"What?" Oma snapped as the bathroom door banged against the towel rack. "What's all that screaming for?"

I closed my eyes, silently saying a prayer of thanks that Oma was all right. The phrase *'don't scare me like that'* flashed through my mind as my heartbeat raced.

Mama grasped the wall, knuckles turning white. "We didn't know where you were."

"Where'd you think I was? You think I'd go out shopping?"

"I called and asked you to leave the door open."

Oma snorted. "Why would I leave the door unlocked? Somebody could come marching in."

Mama yanked her hand away from the wall as if afraid she'd crack the plaster. "That was the idea. We needed to come marching in."

Oma harrumphed and stormed past us into the kitchen. I blinked. My grandmother looked the same as ever, pale with dark circles under her eyes. Her nose was more of a beak, with a tiny wart on the end, giving her a Halloween witch look. Mama had been after Oma to get that taken care of, but Oma believed in castor oil treatments, which still hadn't worked. She'd looked that way for as long as my memory served.

She wore a thin blue shirt and black sweatpants. That was a little different. Before, she'd tended to wear ankle-long dresses.

"Keziah, get the bags." Mama followed Oma into the kitchen.

The air smelled of burnt toast. The hardwood floor had a gray rug spread over it, caked with mud, and deep gouges covered the floor. The walls had once been pink, but had faded to peach, and some of the paint peeled to reveal white underneath. The original shade still vibrant was only around the doorframes.

I dragged the luggage into the living room, and curls slipped free of the single braid to tickle my cheeks. The living room walls were the same faded pink, with a huge dark square over the fireplace where a portrait had once hung. My blood warmed with a sense of home.

Beside the spot were two sconces, postcards from my cousins on the mantle. I stepped over an assortment of birdseed bags and newspapers to sit on the familiar cushion of the rocking chair, the creak of its metal a soothing rhythm. I braced my legs to start rocking.

The chair moaned, and the back pounded against the wall. The jolt sent my teeth into my tongue, and I swore.

"You okay?" Mama called. "What was that bang?"

"Sorry, the chair hit the wall." When I stood, the rocking chair smashed against the wall again. I winced from the ringing thud before hurrying into the kitchen.

Mama closed the refrigerator door, and Oma held her cup to her lips, taking a sip.

"I guess the chair's broken." How were we going to sit in it together and watch cartoons?

Oma lowered the cup. "Yeah, that's cute. Real cute."

My heart thudded at Oma's bitterness. "What?"

"What's the matter?" Mama asked.

Oma pushed past us for the hallway. Mama rolled her eyes. Oma had always been moody, but was this dementia? Before, I would've assumed Oma was having a bad day.

We followed Oma into the bedroom. She sat on the end of her bed, cradling the cup of water in her lap and glaring at the window. In the glass, I noticed the hole from a toy BB gun Uncle Jan had once owned.

Mama touched the foot of the bed. "Oma?"

*Great, what's wrong?* I folded my arms to suppress a shudder.

"Go take her side on the matter." Oma's knee bumped the bedside table and knocked a pair of tweezers onto the floor.

"Oma."

"No, go. You aren't needed." Oma swung her gaze to me. "What did she do? Get on drugs or steal?"

Mama frowned. "What're you talking about?"

"Why else would she be coming here? I told you the city's a bad place."

My stomach cramped. "I don't do drugs!" I could say I'd never touched the stuff thanks to Oma. Whenever Tiffany had offered me pot, I'd pictured Oma's frown and refused.

Oma took a tissue from her pocket and rubbed her nose. When she put it back, the Kleenex missed her pants and fell onto the carpet.

Mama picked it up. "It isn't like that. You *know* Keziah's a good girl."

"Right," Oma snapped.

"Oma ..." I began, but my grandmother stiffened.

"Just go away. No one wants you here."

"Go back into the living room, Keziah," Mama whispered.

I looked from their faces, one stoic and the other crumpling in tears, before I retreated with a spinning mind.

This house had once felt like my own. The rooms had been familiar, with memories of laughter, but now they seemed cold and empty. She didn't want me. What if Oma stayed mad? What if I had to go back to the city? Oma would still be alone.

I rubbed my hand over my face. Pressure built behind my nose. For a distraction, I crossed to the fireplace to pick up one of the postcards—a picture of the Eiffel Tower that said 'Paris' in the corner. I turned it over to decipher my cousin's handwriting. The first line might've said, "Dear Grandma," except it looked more like, "Face Burning."

"Kez?"

I jumped, turning to find Mama in the doorway.

"I think I calmed her down. You know she doesn't mean it. She's just stressed out and frustrated. She knows she can't live alone anymore. How do you think that makes her feel? Let's go get something to eat. It's almost lunchtime."

"It's after four."

"Okay, we'll get dinner. I just want to get out of the house."

I grabbed my purse, echoing the goodbye Mama called to Oma. Mama took the car keys off the table beside the front door.

"Lori, hello!" The high voice with a southern accent shattered the quiet of the front yard as Mama locked the door.

Mama smiled at Oma's neighbor and waved.

An elderly woman retrieved her mail from the box attached to the siding beside her stoop. "Is this little Rebecca?"

Before we'd moved, the woman had always given me a Christmas present. They'd been silly plastic dolls, but Oma had always fawned over how nice it was, since the neighbors didn't have much money.

"Keziah," Mama corrected. "Her name's Keziah."

"Look at how big she's gotten. How old are you now, Rebecca? Fifteen?"

*Great job listening.* Mama poked my shoulder, so I called back, "Seventeen."

"She's gotten so big. I didn't know y'all were visitin'."

"I am, but *Keziah* is staying for a while." Mama clicked the keychain to unlock the car.

"Enjoyin' your time in New Winchester?" The woman swatted a bee with her mail.

"Yes, but we have to go now. Nice talking to you again." Mama nudged me around the car.

I slipped into the passenger's seat. Usually, I would make a joke to Mama about still remembering how to drive a car, but I didn't feel like humor today. Mama didn't speak until she headed down the road.

"Oma really doesn't mean it. You know that, right? She loves you."

"I know." Houses passed by. People mowed their lawns. Two little girls drew on the sidewalk with chalk, and a woman hung a sign in front of a building: *Apartment for Rent.*

"You're going to really like living here again, you'll see. Did you know Oma wanted to write? She had all these ideas for a cute little series about goats, but I don't think she wrote any of it down. Maybe you can get her to tell you some stories. You're probably old enough now."

"They're bad stories?" *Goats.* I shivered. The man on the subway had talked about that. *Beware of the goats.* Maybe the

31

stories were going to give me paper cuts. My skin crawled at the thought.

"Not bad, just complex. Actually, she used to tell them to me like warnings. The morals were deep. She could have made it with those stories, I think."

I glanced at Mama as the tone of her voice shifted. A question hung unspoken between us. *How long will Oma still remember her tales?*

\*\*\*\*

The New Winchester grocery store sat in a shopping center, nestled between a dry cleaner's and a dollar store. I'd forgotten how much stuff they packed on the towering shelves. They didn't have big markets in the city near our apartment, just corner shops. Stepping inside a supermarket was like entering a new world. I snapped my jaw shut to stop gaping.

Mama pushed the silver cart around a table of cookies. "You better start stocking up on supplies now. I'm not sure how often Uncle Jan is going to take you shopping."

"But ..." *Since when have I stocked up on groceries?* "I don't know what to get."

"I'll help you make a list once we get back. You can keep track of what you need every week, like toilet paper and soap. We'll get through this. You're doing a wonderful thing for your grandmother." Mama paused beside the potato stack. "I'll make sweet potato pie for dinner."

I shivered. *Who are we kidding?* This was a game of playing house, only with more at stake than who got to play with the kitchen unit.

\*\*\*\*

When we finished filling the trunk with groceries, I walked the cart back to the cart return. A red convertible with two guys in the back was parked near it, and a girl leaned against the trunk. With cigarettes in hand, they turned to look at me. I kept my gaze on the pavement, stepping over a Styrofoam coffee cup. These teenagers might be my new classmates.

I'd gone to public school before we'd moved, and I had gone into Mama's classroom in the city to help out. I wasn't completely in the dark, but that had all been in elementary school. I'd heard horrible stories about high school. Sure, there were fights in the city, but none I'd ever seen. Then again, my only friend was Tiffany, and her friends usually ignored me. I didn't smoke or guzzle beer as if it was water. I didn't go to clubs. *Much.*

I glanced at the teens. One of the boys lifted his hand in greeting. He kept his hair long and bleached blond where it wasn't dyed purple. When I climbed into the car, I looked back and saw they spoke amongst themselves again.

"Really?" Mama spoke on her cell phone, fiddling with the car keys. "No, Oma is fine. I was just getting dinner. No, there was just a little incident earlier, but nothing too big. Sure, put her on. Hi, sweetie, what's the matter?"

I fastened my seatbelt, scanning the parking lot. The cars all looked clean and new, except for one rusty junker. At the far end of the parking lot, a local farmer had set up a wooden stand. A large white sign, painted with bold red letters, let the world know they sold fruits, vegetables, and flowers.

"Sure, here's Keziah. Phebe wants to talk to you."

I held the phone to my ear, the casing hot from Mama's palm. "What's up?"

"I hate you," Phebe whined. "You know what Dad gave me for lunch? One sandwich. That was it. It didn't even have any mustard on it. He said mustard doesn't go on PB and J. What's PB and J? Dad won't tell me."

"Peanut butter and jelly." I chuckled. "He just doesn't understand mustard."

"I'll be right back." Mama opened the car door.

I nodded.

"But he wouldn't let me put any on." Phebe's voice rose.

"Did you tell him you don't like peanut butter and jelly?"

"He didn't listen. When are you coming home? I don't like it when it's just Dad here. He doesn't *get it.*"

In the background, our father yelled, "Hey, I heard that."

"I like how *you* make lunch and breakfast."

"And I like how you'll eat anything I make."

Mama returned from the produce stand with two boxes of purple pansies, and I ended the call. Mama set the boxes on the floor in the backseat.

"You're going to put pansies around Oma's house?"

"Yes, except for two."

Mama backed out of the parking space and headed for the shopping center's entrance. Instead of turning left, she maneuvered right, heading away from Oma's house.

"Where're we going?"

"You'll see."

We passed a veterinary hospital, a Jewish temple, and a Subway. She turned the car down another road. *Oh, that destination.* Mama pulled through the wrought iron gate of the

New Winchester Cemetery. The path curved, made of dirt and gravel with deep ruts from the press of car tires.

"This was built in the early 1700s with the village's first settlers buried within the sloping hills," I read off a large plaque.

The grass was lush and green, and sunlight filtered through the trees to dapple across tombstones, the marble glistening. It felt as if a thousand pairs of hollow eyes turned their direction to me.

Mama stopped the car at the top of a knoll and turned it off. Without speaking, we unfastened our seatbelts and snapped the car doors open. The air seemed cooler there, yet with more sunshine than in the hot parking lot at the grocery store.

My foot sank into the moist ground, blades of grass curling around my Converse sneakers. When I pushed the door shut, the echo of it danced through the graveyard, weaving between the graves. I imagined dead eyes flying open beneath the soil. Hands reached up, skeletal fingers scraping the insides of coffins.

Mama slammed the trunk, and I jumped. Leaving her purse in the car, she carried a box of pansies in one hand and an ice scraper in the other. I followed a few steps behind. Oma used to call the names written on gravestones "people who'd soon be forgotten." The gravestones would ruin, the words weathered away, and no one would remember. The grave occupants would fade as if they had never existed.

Mama crouched in front of a grave near the fence, far back from the path. I hovered over her shoulder, hands sliding through the belt loops of my shorts while I stared at my grandfather's tombstone. The space alongside it for my grandmother already had her name and birth year.

"Hey, Daddy." Mama jabbed the ice scrapper into the soil near where a few flowers grew alongside the marble marker. The dark earth parted beneath the force

"Hi, Grandpa." I shifted my stance. I didn't remember him; he'd died of a heart attack when I was a baby.

Mama sang as she continued to plant, lost in her own world, the same one she always retreated to when we visited the cemetery.

I wandered to the next grave, grass crunching beneath my feet.

"Thankful Brooks," I read aloud. Interesting name. No one had planted a flower for Thankful, the dirt hard and uncared for around the stone.

"Can I have an extra flower?" Thankful deserved one as Grandpa's permanent neighbor.

Mama knelt beside me in the grass. Side by side, we planted for the dead.

****

*I am six years old. My father's uncle dies from a heart attack. He wants to take me to the funeral, so I can see my family, but Mama doesn't want me to see a dead man. They argue but finally decide I will wait in the car until afterward and then meet people.*

*Oma goes too, so she can watch me. The funeral is three-hours away, near Vermont. When we get there, my parents go inside the church, but Oma and I walk to a park nearby. She*

*buys a bag of peanuts from a grocery store on the way, so we can feed the squirrels.*

*We return to the car and wait, playing with crossword puzzle books. Oma writes the answers, but we both discuss them. When the funeral ends, my father drives us to the cemetery. Oma keeps me in the car.*

*"Why can't I go too?" It must be something scary if I have to stay behind.*

*"It's a gathering for adults," she says.*

*I notice there aren't any children in the dark-clad crowd.*

*Afterwards, Mama fetches us from the car and people come over to see me.*

*"Isn't she pretty?"*

*They poke me, ask questions, and giggle when I don't reply. I don't recognize anyone, so I run back to Oma. She holds my hand and answers for me.*

# Chapter 4

The air was thin, the sky blue, and a woman soared, one arm extended. Her face was tranquil, dark eyes solemn. Short black hair curled around her ears, shifting from the force of wind. A slow and melancholy harp mingled with a violin.

The woman plummeted towards the ground. I wanted to scream, but my lips froze together. I couldn't look away, nor could I close my eyes. The woman sped up as though determined to crash. She was going to strike.

*... Now.*

Instead of smashing, the woman landed on a white garbage bag filled with fluff.

A man loomed over her, smirking. His hair was short and blue, and he wore thick glasses made from prisms. Rainbows danced across his high cheekbones.

More people lounged amongst white garbage bags, women of crystalline skin and curling blue hair. A hulking man lifted a brass horn to his lips and blew, the sound like a needle piercing into my skull.

I grabbed my blanket, sitting up so fast my abdomen hurt. Next to me in the queen size bed, Mama snored. Warm sunlight streamed through the windows, sending a pattern of lace spilling across the yellow comforter. Random holes littered the cotton, and some of the seams were held together by safety pins.

I pushed off the comforter. The digital clock on the dresser said it was almost eight in the morning. The numbers seemed huge, red, and angry, and I dropped a t-shirt over them.

The upstairs master suite we used during visits was divided into two rooms. One room was the bedroom, hence the large bed and walk-in closet, and the other, smaller room was used for storage. Boxes covered the floor and bookshelves consumed the walls. A large attic laid across the hallway.

I entered the storage room. The space contained one window with lace curtains. Above it, a wooden shelf stretched from wall to wall, filled with old hardcover books. Parting the curtain, I stared at the house with green shutters next door. A birch tree grew between the two houses. The gnarled branches reached for the sky.

The white and black bark had always intrigued me, a maze of mystery. There were pictures to be found in the pattern, faces laughing and screaming.

If I opened the window, I could touch the tree. When I was younger, I'd always wondered what it would be like to climb onto it. Would the thin branches hold beneath my weight, or would I plummet? I'd never gathered enough courage to try.

I dropped the curtain so it settled over the glass. Sunlight blinked through the lace.

Water ran downstairs in the kitchen. Leaving Mama asleep in the bed, I crept out the door and down the stairs. Black and white photographs of Mama and Uncle Jan followed my descending path

Oma stood in the kitchen, washing her pink mug. She didn't turn around until after she'd turned off the sink and plucked a paper towel off its roll.

"Good morning," I sang to be chipper.

Oma jumped. "What are you trying to do, scare me? Can't you make some noise to let people know where you are without creeping along like that?"

I blinked. It wouldn't do to contradict Oma by saying she was just having trouble hearing because of the running water. "Why don't I find you a dish cloth? Using paper towels to dry dishes is kind of wasteful and expensive."

Oma huffed, crumpling her paper towel to throw onto the counter near the toaster. She set the mug down and opened the refrigerator. I didn't remember the kitchen ever looking so chaotic. There were usually things sitting around, but it just looked filthy. Used paper towels formed mountains on the countertops, and dirty dishes overflowed from the sink.

"Mama's still sleeping upstairs."

Oma removed a bottle of water from the fridge. I squeezed past her to get to the cupboard and removed another mug, white with a huge yellow daisy on the side.

Oma bumped the water bottle against the counter. "If it's time for *you* to be in the kitchen, just say so. I'll wait my turn, even though I was here first."

I shut the cupboard door with a click. "But I'm over here. I'm not in your way. Here, I'll just go into the living room for now, okay?"

"So where's your *dad*?" Oma spat. "Is he there?"

"You mean in New York?"

"No, I don't mean in New York. Is he at the hospital?"

I frowned. "No. Why would he be at the hospital?"

"With your mom," Oma growled as if I was being the difficult one.

"She's not at the hospital."

"You just said she was at the hospital."

"I never said that. She isn't at the hospital." I clenched my fists, trying to keep my voice calm.

Oma's face crumpled, her cheeks reddening. "How can you scream at me like that? Don't you love me? You told me a lie. You did. God is watching you!"

She slammed the mug down so hard I winced, expecting it to shatter. It didn't, but water sloshed over the edge. Her face bright red and eyes glossy, Oma stormed out of the kitchen and down the hall.

*I hate you, dementia.* Balanced on the verge of tears, I forced up an inner wall, banishing emotion.

****

Still massaging my shoulder from a mad kitchen cleaning spree, I went to the public school with Mama to register for classes. Later in the week I would have to take a tour of the building, but I tried to block that out. It made my stomach churn and gurgle. I didn't want to imagine what high school would be like.

"You'll be okay?" Mama asked as we left the school. "It won't be that bad. This is a great school system, and you went to elementary here." The New Winchester Public School consisted of the high school, junior high, and elementary, divided into different wings of a single building. "I'm sure it'll seem familiar."

I kicked a stone off the sidewalk.

"I went to school here, too," Mama continued. "Maybe you'll find an old yearbook in the library and look me up? Actually, my old yearbooks are probably still in the attic. You know how Oma never throws anything out."

I nodded, kicking another stone. A car drove by, and up ahead, a woman walking a German shepherd approached.

"Hey, can I have Phebe?" I asked. "Can she come live here, too?"

"Keziah …"

"Come on, please? It would be perfect." The words spilled out. "She can even help me with Oma."

We stepped aside to allow the woman and her dog to pass.

"Keziah." Mama increased her pace as we resumed walking. "The high school starts earlier than the elementary. How would she get to school? She'd have to walk, and I don't want her walking alone."

"I'm sure other kids do it, and this isn't like the city."

"So? Oma or I always walked you to school and picked you up."

Hand in hand, strolling down the street. Sometimes stopping at the ice cream parlor in the spring.

"Oma can walk her then."

"Oma is older now. I don't want her walking around here in the winter with ice on the sidewalk."

"Mama, please!"

"No."

A squirrel darted up a maple tree and I envied its freedom. "Just because Oma hates her? Why doesn't Oma like Phebe?"

"Oma doesn't hate Phebe! They just … They don't get along. Stop it, Kez. Phebe is going to stay with me. You're not an adult yet, sweetie, and you're already taking care of one woman. That should be more than enough." Mama stopped walking. "Don't you want to stay here? Just say it and you won't have to, you know that."

I blushed. "No, I'll stay. This is the only way to keep her out of a nursing home." *She needs me.*

\*\*\*\*

Oma was still fuming about the confrontation in the kitchen when we returned.

"Where were you?" she snapped.

"We went to the school. I had to register Keziah."

"You were gone for hours."

"No, we've only been gone forty-five minutes."

I slipped past them as they argued. In the living room, I checked my cell phone for a message from my sister. How was I going to put up with Oma if she always acted like that?

"Look, what do you want for lunch?" Mama raised her voice.

"Steak and bacon."

Mama lifted her eyebrows. "You don't eat meat."

Oma snorted. "I know that. I'm not that old yet. I don't want you sleeping upstairs anymore."

I slid my phone into my purse, joining them in the hallway.

"When you leave and Keziah's here, I don't want her up there all alone. I won't know what she's doing up there."

"Am I going to get drunk or something?" I muttered.

Oma must not have heard, but Mama glared.

"I need to be able to keep an eye on her," Oma continued. "I want her in the living room. She can sleep on the floor."

"Wait, I have to sleep in the *living room?*"

"She can't sleep on the floor, and she can't sleep on the couch, either," Mama said.

I envied her calmness.

"Keziah will be fine upstairs," Mama said.

"Teenagers should not get rooms with doors." Oma pursed her lips.

"I did. Jan did."

"And just see what happened." Oma threw her hands up. "There are two beds in my room. She can sleep in there with me."

"What? No," I yelped. "I don't get my own bedroom?"

"That's because after Daddy died, you didn't want to sleep upstairs anymore," Mama reminded Oma. "You cleaned out my room and put my bed in Jan's room. What if we put the bed back into my room?"

"She sleeps in the living room or in with me."

"But that's not fair," I yelled.

"Override me," Oma snapped. "Argue it out with your mother *right in front of me.*"

"Oma, please." Mama set her purse on the table near the door. "When we moved, we put Keziah's old bed in your attic. What if we set that up in the living room?"

"That would work fine." Oma brushed past us for the kitchen.

"I guess we'll go get that down after lunch."

"Mama, this isn't fair! Why can't I have my own bedroom?" *First, I come here, and now I don't even get my own space? I want to go home, but I can't, I have to stay with Oma.*

"Kez." Mama met my gaze. "Maybe this is better. Oma needs help around here. What if something happened in the night? If you were upstairs, you wouldn't be able to hear."

"Thanks a lot. What did you do that was so horrible Oma doesn't trust me?" I hissed, turning away for the living room. I ignored the paleness on Mama's face, and the way she gulped.

****

*I am five years old. Oma takes me to the summer fair in the park. It happens every year, right after school ends.*

*Oma and I go on a few of the rides. She orders fried dough with lots of powdered sugar, and we share it on a picnic table. When we finish, she orders us each a candied apple. I enjoy eating the junk food, since Mama will not let me eat it at home.*

*Before we leave, Oma buys me a huge balloon. It is as big as I am and bright pink with purple swirls. The balloon maker put glitter inside, so when I shake the balloon, it sparkles.*

*I store it in the backseat of the car until we get to her house. I pull the balloon out and dance to the front door, too happy to remember the briar bush by the stairs. My balloon snags on one of the thorns. The pop startles me. Glitter rains over the porch. For a moment, I stare at my shredded toy.*

*I start to cry, but Oma hugs me. She herds me back into the car and drives back to the fair, so she can buy me a new one.*

# Chapter 5

The mattress and boxspring from my old bed rested towards the front of the attic, leaning against the wall and a giant orange cooler.

Mama yanked the protective sheets off. Dust clouds plumed into the air, tickling my nose and throat and burning my eyes. Mama coughed as I sneezed.

"It's going to work out better this way." Mama let the sheets fall in a crumpled mess over a cardboard box.

I folded my arms, feeling a bit like a child in a china store. I wasn't allowed in the attic, and neither was Mama, unless Oma followed, but she pouted downstairs.

Everything seemed exotic, fascinating, and fragile, as if it might disappear at any moment. I picked up a paper from the top of the vanity and wiped the dust off on my thigh. The particles clung to the fibers of my jeans to reveal a black and white photograph of my grandparents on their wedding day.

Oma wore a white dress, probably satin, since it shone. The tight collar made her neck appear long, her head tipped to the side, and a small smirk on her lips. Her hair was pinned in tight curls beneath a hat that curved like a crown, the veil spilling down her back.

My grandfather stood more stiffly, his suit a sharp contrast of black when compared to the pale gazebo behind. He had his hands folded in front of him, and his head tipped forward, so his eyes were cast in shadows.

"Why don't you take that down and show Oma?" Mama called. "She'd be happy to tell you about the wedding."

*Probably.* The word hung huge and heavy in the air. Dust particles danced in the sunbeams spilling through the windows. I poked at one.

"Your grandfather loved you." Mama coughed into her arm and wiped her mouth on the back of her hand. "He would come down to our house every morning, pick you up, swing you around, and call you his little Bumble Bee. You two were really close."

I squeezed my eyes shut, which made them itch, but I didn't want to rub them with my filthy fingers. Sometimes I recalled sitting in a rocking chair in the living room with a man who was soft, big, and warm as a cartoon about bees played in the background.

We lifted the mattress, my muscles screaming in protest. Mama faced backwards, and I pressed against the wall. A wind chime hung from a rusty hook near my head; I bumped the hummingbird figurine dangling from the bottom and the lawn ornament rattled at me. We maneuvered the mattress through the attic, avoiding the large obstacles, and only a Christmas ball met its doom beneath Mama's sneaker. We got the mattress past the doorframe and down the stairs.

"Took you long enough," Oma growled. "What were you doing up there?"

"It was hard to get out." Mama wiped her hands on her jeans, dirty handprints streaking her buttocks. "We'll have to move the living room table from there over to here, so we can put the mattress up against the couch. Here, let me clean these off." She picked the trinkets off the table to relocate them to the piano.

"I'm going to go get that picture." I ran back up the stairs before Mama could make me help clean off the table. The door to the attic gaped open like a mouth.

I stepped over the clutter for the picture, but then I curled my fingers into a fist and paused. The picture wasn't resting on the vanity's top, although the rectangular spot where I'd picked it up from remained, dust particles settling over the mahogany finish.

"Crap." Mama must have put it somewhere. I peered along the left side at a cardboard box of wrapping paper rolls, but no photo. On the right side were white boxes, the kind stores pack clothes into for gifts. I lifted the top of the box. Porcelain plates and tissue paper. No photograph.

A flash of light made me look at the mirror. Beneath the layer of dust, my face stared back, and beneath it another face shimmered, distorted by depth and the spider lines from a crack.

The second image looked to be a man. His face was round, with pale skin and shadowed eyes. His brow creased in a frown. *He's way too similar to the homeless man on the subway.*

"Whoa!" I dragged my fingers across the dust to see what it looked like under the thick layer.

Beneath the marks I made, the mirror was still dirty. I grabbed a hunk of tissue paper from the floor and rubbed clean a circle. Nothing except glass reflecting my face and the attic beyond. There was no giant picture of a man to have reflected in the glass. I licked my lips tasting dust and a chill crept up my spine.

Now I was seeing things. *Great.*

When I shut the attic door, a breeze stirred my hair. One of the windows must have been open.

Downstairs, Mama had the card table cleaned off.

"I couldn't find the picture."

"What?" Mama pushed the table against the fireplace.

"The wedding picture. It wasn't there."

Mama glanced at the doorway. "Don't tell Oma you lost it, or she'll have a fit. Come help me put the bed together. Maybe we won't need the boxspring."

It wasn't much of a bed with the height lower than the couch. Mama went back up into the attic and found old linens, plus cartoon character comforters from my childhood folded on the couch for use once winter came.

Oma hovered in the doorway while we put cases on the pillows. "I don't see why she can't sleep with me. I don't snore. She just doesn't want to be here, that's all. Go take her home with you." She muttered something about Saint Agatha and walked away.

"Who's Saint Agatha?"

Her mother shrugged. I gazed around the living room and sighed.

\*\*\*\*

I sighed again as we went outside, but more in relief. Since Oma still pouted in the bedroom—her lips pressed together while she stared at the wall above the television— Mama decided we would spruce up the front yard. She seized the handle of the garage door and yanked it up, the hinges squealing.

Mama stepped over a gas can to reach the rake hanging on the wall. "Oma likes the car in the driveway so it looks like someone's here. It should stop a robbery."

"But what if she tries to, you know, *drive*?"

"She apparently doesn't remember how."

"Apparently?" I accepted the rake and a pair of gardening gloves.

"Don't worry. She won't drive."

I had to have faith like that, but it nagged at my mind. Something dire could happen if Oma tried.

Mama pulled on the second pair of gloves and fished through a cardboard box of lawn ornaments. Plastic birds with spinning wings on long metal sticks glared at me through painted-on eyes. I shivered.

Mama handed me items, and I set the padded kneeling stools on the sidewalk, dropping the trowels next to them. *Does Uncle Jan do nothing in regards to yard work other than mow?*

Mama returned from the garage swinging a small plastic bag. "Sidewalk chalk, Kez. When you were little, we would sit here for hours drawing pictures."

I laughed. "For real? I don't remember that."

Mama set the bag on the sidewalk. "Come on, we're going to draw stuff. I'll look for a photo of you sidewalk chalking later. I'm sure Oma has one around here somewhere."

I lifted off the cushion, wincing as my knees cracked. For a cushion, it wasn't very soft.

Mama sat cross-legged on the sidewalk, picking through the bag. Her short tresses gave her an elfin aura. Crouched over the sidewalk like that, drawing with a piece of bright blue chalk, Mama looked like a teenager. I couldn't help but smile. She never looked that carefree in the city. Maybe it was because she'd grown up in New Winchester that she let go of her worries. Oma, for one. She was a big worry.

I pulled out a red piece of chalk and moved to the sidewalk square above Mama's. A spot of bird poo marred the upper left corner. I drew a circle and stared at it. *So now what?* I had a wobbly circle. I could make it into a smiley face, but that seemed cliché. I looked over my shoulder at Mama's square, where she had drawn a cat. Okay, my square was going to be a sunset with many lines of color, and it was going to look amazing. I leaned back on my heels, chewing my lip.

A car pulled into the two-family house next door. The driver turned the engine off, opened the door, and stepped out. Shaggy blonde hair fell around the young man's face; he lacked a shirt, and his shredded blue jeans hung low on his hips.

The guy grinned and waved. Mama waved back. My face heated. He was gorgeous, and I was sidewalk chalking with my mother. I dropped the chalk and rocked onto my bottom. Great, the guy walked toward us. Mama stood to greet him, so I did, too.

"Hello there." When he smiled, his teeth looked perfect and white.

"Hi," Mama said and began telling our life story.

She explained how she was a teacher, how we had once lived in New Winchester until moving to New York City. She told him, a complete stranger, about how I was moving in with Oma to help her out, leaving out that Oma had become different. I wanted to melt into the cement.

"That is quite a story," he said with a sarcastic whistle.

*He made fun of Mama, the jerk.* I ground my teeth.

"My name's Michael."

"And what do you do, Michael?" Mama smiled.

"I work over at the library."

"Don't you go to college?" she pressed.

"I graduated a few years ago." He chuckled. "I'm older than I look, *ma'am.*"

How "ma'am" could sound sarcastic, I would have never guessed, but he succeeded. My face turned redder.

"Now," he drawled, "I had best be going. Welcome to the neighborhood … Keziah." He lowered his voice as he said my name, the word a caress.

I scowled to hide the tingle that coursed through my body.

Mama waved as he walked away with a saunter in his step. "He's a nice young man. If you ever need anything, you should ask him for help. He's closer than Uncle Jan. That's what's so great about these little neighborhoods. There are people who really want to help."

"Yeah." I picked up a piece of chalk to draw a skeleton hanging from a noose and labelled it Michael.

\*\*\*\*

*I am twelve years old. Mama and I visit Oma on our summer vacation.*

*"I want to cut my hair," I tell Oma. We sit on her front porch and feed peanuts to the squirrels.*

*The one with the bushiest tail takes a peanut from her hand. "How come?"*

*"Because everyone on TV has short hair." I try to give the squirrel a peanut from my hand, but the critter jumps onto the railing. "Mama said I can't."*

*"You do look very pretty with long hair."*

*"So I'll be ugly with short?" I know that's not what she means, but I want to hear her call me pretty again.*

*"It will look different on you. It will take a long while to grow out if you don't like it."*

Very true. *"I still want to try it."*

*"Come here then." Oma leads me into the house. She takes bobby pins from her dresser and fastens my curls to my scalp. She pins some sections, twists others, and when she finishes, my hair only hangs down to my shoulders.*

*I do look different. Not ugly, not pretty, just unusual. I don't recognize myself.*

*"Do you like it?" she asks.*

*"Maybe." I glance at her reflection next to mine in the dresser's mirror. "You have short hair."*

*"It is easier to manage." Oma pats my head. "So, would you like me to take you to the hair dresser's now?"*

*"No. I don't think I would like it short all the time, but this, for now, is nice."*

*"I'll do it anytime you want," she says, even though we both know I will return to New York City in a few days.*

*I leave my hair short for the rest of the evening, and Oma snaps some photographs, but I never ask her to pin it for me again.*

# Chapter 6

The day Mama deserted me with Oma dawned sunny and warm, but it should pour buckets of rain from a cloudy sky to better fit my mood. Uncle Jan arrived to drive her to the bus station. As I joined them by the car, Oma barked harsh laughter.

"What's this? You *all* have to go take her back?"

"You can come, too." Mama hugged Oma. "You know I'm going to miss you, right? Take care of yourself. Come on now, we'll all go to the station."

"Me? Go? I'd rather not," Oma snorted. "I'm old. Do you think I want to ride in the car forever?"

"It's not that far."

"Don't lie to me. I know you too well for that." Oma stormed up the porch steps to the front door.

"Why don't you stay here instead of going with us," Mama said to me. "It might be better this way." Mama gazed at Oma with furrowed brows. "She seems upset. Uncle Jan would just have to drive you back here, anyway."

I wanted to beg her not to go and leave me with Oma, but I only nodded.

Then, Mama was gone with Uncle Jan. I was alone with Oma. *Okay, time for me to take responsibility. I can do this.*

I locked the screen door, but left the wooden door open to allow the summer breeze into the house. A mirror hung over the hallway table, framed in carved wood engraved with roses and thorny vines. I leaned over the marble table to trace the engravings.

"My friend had a mirror just like that one." Oma rubbed her finger across her nose. "It hung in the parlor, and whenever her mother wasn't paying attention, we would sneak in to look in it. We would primp our hair and pinch our cheeks. Sometimes, we pretended the girls looking back were from somewhere far, far away. We imagined we could join them."

The mirror reflected the top of my head and the staircase. For a second, I thought I saw feet running up the stairs, yet it was silent in the house.

"Her name was Celia Wein," she continued. "Her mother was French and never spoke a word of English as long as I knew her. They had a cook, but Celia's mother made the most delicious biscuits."

"Don't you mean croissants?"

"What?"

"Croissants. They're French, and kind of famous for being French."

"What are you talking about?"

"The French food Celia's mother made."

"Ah, yes. Celia." She braced her hand against the wall and crouched, winding her finger through a dust bunny.

Footsteps sounded outside. A woman with a clipboard strolled down the sidewalk, turning at the pathway. Her face broke out in a smile.

"Good morning," the woman called.

"Oma, someone's here."

My grandmother straightened from the crouch with a groan, the dust bunny in her hand. Instead of acknowledging the guest, she walked to the kitchen.

"Oma, there's a lady here," I said.

She paused. "You don't have to yell. I can hear you just fine."

"Someone's here." I pointed at the door.

The woman lifted her fingers in a wave. "Hello, can I just have a moment of your time?" The stranger wiggled her clipboard.

"What are you talking about? There's no one there," Oma snapped.

"But...but there's a lady right there." I pulled Oma over. "See?"

Oma rolled her eyes. "There was a glare off the screen. What do you want?" The last sentence she directed at the stranger.

"Hi, my name is Lauren. I'm selling Avon products." She unclipped a catalogue.

Oma turned to me. "Why's he just standing there? Why doesn't he say anything?"

The woman, Lauren, blinked, parting her bright red lips.

I said, "*She's* from Avon. *She's* selling make-up."

"What?" Oma asked.

"Do you have a regular Avon seller?" Lauren spoke with fake exuberance.

"She's selling make-up," I raised my voice. "She wants to give you a catalogue."

"Feel free to look through it at your convenience, and I have my number written here." Lauren pointed to words scrawled in Sharpie on the front of the catalogue. "I would love to become your Avon sales representative."

Since Oma didn't answer, I explained, "We don't want any, but thanks anyway. We'll take a look." I unlocked the screen door and opened it.

"Aren't you going to invite him in? A polite gentleman would come in," Oma stated.

I took the catalogue. "Thanks, Lauren."

"Him!" Oma pointed at Lauren. "He's a handsome gentleman."

Lauren's blush showed through her foundation and fake tan. She looked nothing like a man with her face covered in cosmetics, and wearing a white summer blouse and black pencil skirt. Her hair might have been pulled back in a ponytail, but her huge bosom made up for that.

"Oma, her name's Lauren. She isn't a guy."

"Of course this is a man." Oma waved the dust bunny at Lauren. "Don't make me think I can't see. You're mean, you know that. You are a mean little girl."

"Sorry about this." I shut the door and followed Oma into the kitchen. "*Her* name was Lauren."

Oma threw the dust bunny into the garbage and shook her head. "What happened to my little Keziah?"

"I'm still your little Keziah!"

"Yeah. Right." Her expression blank, Oma wandered into her bedroom.

I figured the anger over Lauren would fade eventually, so I walked into the living room. Mama had set the card table in the corner of the room for my laptop. I flipped it open, turning it on.

As I checked my Facebook page, Oma called from the bedroom. Images of Oma fallen to the floor filled my mind, and I ran.

"Are you okay?"

"Now look at that." Oma sat on the edge of the bed, nodding out the window. "Isn't that a nice young man? Why don't you go out and talk to him?"

*Michael?* I leaned over the bed to see who she meant. A little boy stood on the sidewalk, picking at his shoe.

"You want me to go talk to *him?*" My heart thudded extra hard to learn it wasn't Michael. "Why do you want me to go talk to him?"

"You need a boyfriend."

"*What?*"

"You heard me. He looks just your type. Go out and talk to him."

"No way. He's like ten years old. I'm almost eighteen."

"No, he's your age. Go talk to him."

He must have heard us through the open bedroom window, for he looked at the house.

"I don't see why not. Don't become antisocial," Oma said.

"I'm not antisocial," I exclaimed.

"You don't already have a boyfriend, do you?"

"No, I don't have a boyfriend."

"Then go talk to him."

He finished picking at his sandal and continued down the street.

I racked my brain for an excuse to leave the bedroom. "I have to go to the bathroom."

"That costs a quarter," Oma yelled.

In less than an hour, Oma called again. "Get in here!"

I dashed in, gasping. "What is it?"

"Look at that nice young man." Oma pointed out the window. "Why don't you go talk to him?"

I ground my teeth. The same boy from before now had a basketball, bouncing it on his way. "Now, you listen here, I want you to go talk to him. That's what you need, a nice boyfriend."

He moved without haste, concentrating on bouncing the basketball. *How comical it would be if he missed and it rolled down the street. He probably lives around here. Now I'm going to have to see him walking by a lot.*

"Okay, that's a great idea. Let me go ask him out." I ran to the door, waiting until I heard Oma follow before going outside.

"Hey," I called.

He paused, still bouncing the ball. I glanced over my shoulder, spotting Oma in the doorway.

I sauntered over to him. "Hey," I repeated loud enough for Oma to hear.

"Um, hi." He stopped bouncing the ball and held it under his arm.

I lowered my voice so Oma couldn't hear. "Have you seen a brown cat?"

"No, sorry." He shrugged. "I hate cats."

"He said no," I yelled to the house. "The answer is no." To him, I said, "Okay, thanks. Have a nice day."

"Yeah, sure." He rolled his eyes, continuing up the street. A car pulled into the apartment building next door. I turned to face it, folding my arms. Maybe it would be Michael, that jerk. Why I wanted to see him, I didn't know, but it irritated me when it was the elderly woman who lived downstairs.

"Hallo, Rebecca," she called. "Nice day, isn't it? Say hi to your grandma for me. Is your mom around?"

"No, my mom went home." *Where was my home now? Back in New York City, or here?*

"Okay. Good to have ya here with us, Rebecca." The woman might have winked, but I couldn't be sure.

\*\*\*\*

*I am eleven years old and want to see the new Disney movie. Dad is away on business, and Mama doesn't want to take baby Phebe. Usually, Mama, Oma, and I go to the movies together, but now we have Phebe.*

*Oma takes me to the movies alone. The theater is in the mall, so we arrive early to have dinner in the food court. We eat bean burritos. Afterwards, Oma still buys popcorn and sodas.*

*We sit in one of the middle rows, on the aisle, and laugh throughout the movie. Later, we go shopping, and Oma buys me a new pair of shoes.*

*I show them to Phebe when I get home. "When you're older, you can come with us, too. Then, Oma will buy you some shoes, and we'll eat lots of popcorn. You couldn't come this time because you're a baby, and you'd cry a lot."*

*"Someday." Mama doesn't look up from grading papers at her desk.*

*I carry Phebe out to the backyard and describe the movie to her, so we don't bother Mama.*

*Oma never cares if I'm loud, but sometimes too much noise gives Mama a headache.*

# Chapter 7

Oma shook me awake on Labor Day morning. "We're going out to breakfast. Get up."

I groaned, sitting up on my elbows to see the clock. The red bubble letters announced it was eight-thirty in the morning.

"But, Oma..."

"When you were little, we always went out to breakfast on Memorial Day. We always went to Ann's."

*It's Labor Day, not Memorial Day.*

"Ann's? Who the—" I caught myself on the swear word, "heck is Ann?"

"Come on, get up." Oma stumbled around my sneakers to get to the picture window and grab the curtain cord. She pulled it, the plastic hangers squealing against the curtain rod. Light poured into the room, making me blink. My nose felt stuffy, itching, and I snuffled. *Stupid, dusty living room.*

"When you were little," Oma grabbed the edge of the card table for balance, "we would always go out to eat at Ann's. Your mother never went. It was just you and me." She stepped over the sneakers again. "So get up. It's time for breakfast."

"This isn't Memorial Day. It's Labor Day."

"What?" Oma paused in the doorway.

"You said we have to go out for breakfast because it's Memorial Day."

"Yes?"

"Oma, this is Labor Day."

"So?"

"So why are we going out to eat?"

"Because it's Memorial Day. What's taking you so long? Get up."

I kicked off the blankets and snuffled again. *Allergies suck.* Being allergic to everything didn't make bearing Oma's dementia any easier. I never had to worry about being allergic to plants when I lived in the city.

I unzipped my suitcase and sorted through it for clothes. *Wish I had something to put them in. A closet would be great, but even a trunk would suffice.*

The T-shirt from Greece that Dad had brought back went fine with a red and black striped skirt. With the clothes in my arms, I set off for the bathroom. All too fast, I had learned not to undress in the living room. Oma was apt to walk in at any moment with a mundane question, like the temperature. The thermometer could only be seen through the picture window, and no matter how many times Oma looked at it per day, she never remembered.

Oma puttered in the bathroom. I leaned against the wall, closing my eyes. It was going to be torture having to get up at seven for school the next day. Classes started at eight o'clock sharp. I couldn't remember the last time I'd gotten up before ten in the morning more than one day in a row.

*I wish there was someone here to teach me so I could continue home schooling.*

Oma left the bathroom, combing her thin hair. "You're not ready yet?"

"I need the bathroom."

Oma muttered under her breath when I emerged.

"Okay, I'm ready."

"Help me get money together." Oma waved a purse. It wasn't her normal purse, which was white, but a brown Louis

Vuitton knock-off I'd given her for Christmas a few years back.

"But that's not your purse."

"Who else's purse would this be?"

"No, I mean that's not the purse you normally use."

Oma snorted. "You don't take your normal purse with you when you go out to breakfast. Now help me find some money to put in."

She stormed into the bedroom, so I followed. Oma's regular purse sat at the foot of the bed, unzipped and gaping open. Envelopes of money poked out.

"How much do I need?" she asked.

I licked my lips. *We need to pay at a friend's house? Would Ann even expect money since this isn't Memorial Day?*

I felt like smacking my forehead. Ann's was the restaurant down the street near the firehouse. Surely, breakfast there was cheaper than in the city, but then again, I rarely went out to eat in the city.

"A twenty?"

"Here." Oma pulled an envelope out of her purse and fished a fifty-dollar bill from it. "This will work."

"Oma, that's a fifty."

"Fine." Oma pulled out two twenties and a ten, stuffing them and the fifty into her knock-off purse. She zipped it shut. "Okay, let's go. We're wasting daylight."

Stepping outside, I had a strong feeling there would be a lot of daylight left, even if we did dawdle. A squirrel ran across the yard with a walnut clasped in its jaw. It bolted up the tree while Oma locked her front door and pocketed the key in her jacket. We headed down the street, Oma clutching her purse, and her arm looped through mine so she wouldn't fall on the uneven, cracked sidewalk.

"This is a Goat Children kind of day."

"What?" I kicked an empty soda can.

"The Goat Children. I never told you about the Goat Children?"

"No."

"They live up there." Oma swept her hand towards the sky. "They watch over us."

"Like angels?"

"They're not like angels," Oma whispered. "They come when you are so alone you can't fight."

"That's a good time to come, I guess."

"Yes, a good time." A glaze spread over Oma's eyes. "They know because it is obvious. It is so obvious that you have to wonder how you didn't know before. Yet, later on, you wonder how you learned at all."

That made zero sense. "What?"

"It is just how it is with the Goat Children."

"That's a cute fairy tale." *I have no idea what you're babbling about.* Haze clouded my memory, images of the homeless man on the subway.

A gruff voice teased me. "*...Beware of the goats.*"

"There aren't any fairies in it."

"So what are they? Ancient warriors?"

Oma chuckled. "You make it sound silly. No, they're not so old. Sometimes, when one of the Goat Children wants to retire, she must find someone else to take her place."

"Always a girl?"

"Of course. A Pegasus will only accept a girl. A *pure* girl," Oma emphasized.

*Of course there would be a Pegasus with a Goat Child.*
*Maybe we should throw in some leprechauns and pixies, make*
*it an all-out myth party.*

"I was a Goat Child," Oma said. "Your mother should have been one, but she's too flighty. Not *pure* enough."

"Right."

"You could be a Goat Child."

*Aren't baby goats called kids? This whole thing makes no sense.* "Sure. Maybe someday."

"Someone must first retire, but even when you do retire, you can always go back. Your Pegasus waits."

"It would be kind of cool to have a Pegasus. Watch out for that." A tree root caused the sidewalk to heave at the corner. "Was your friend Celia a Goat Child?"

"Celia? No, she died." Oma touched her throat. "She never got to be one."

****

*Ann's* sported a floral theme, with pink pansies on the curtains, plastic roses decorating the tables, daisy print on the tablecloths, and menus shaped like giant tulips.

The waitress led us to the table in front of the window. While Oma searched through her purse for her glasses, I studied the other customers. An elderly man sat at one table, reading a newspaper, and three elderly women occupied another table. A sheepish man and a peevish woman drank coffee without looking at each other.

"My glasses. Where are they?"

I glanced at Oma. "I don't know. What part of the purse did you put them in?"

"How should I know?" Oma flung the purse at me. "I can't find them. You look."

I unzipped each of the compartments, but only found the money. "I don't think you brought them."

"Then how am I supposed to read the menu?"

*Wow, I am the best caregiver in the world. I didn't make sure she brought along her glasses.*

"Here, I'll read it to you." I opened my menu. "What do you want?"

"Don't you remember?"

"No."

"I guess I'm not the only forgetful one around here, am I?"

The waitress raised her eyebrows at the noise. I tried to shrink behind the menu as my cheeks flamed. Every morning, Oma had a dish of blueberries, a glass of orange juice, and cereal.

"You want eggs?" I asked. That seemed like an out-to-breakfast meal.

"Yes."

"One egg over medium?" Mom always had those in the morning.

"No, two eggs. I always eat two eggs."

"Okay. Two eggs, then."

The waitress approached the table, her heels clicking against the tile floor. "What can I get for you today?" She wore khaki pants and a floral top. Did everything have to be floral at *Ann's*?

"She'll have two eggs, both over medium."

"What kind of toast?" the waitress asked. "Wheat, white, rye, or raisin?"

"Oma, what kind of toast do you want?"

Oma stared out the window.

"She'll have wheat."

"I hate wheat," Oma snapped.

"Okay, white." *I officially hate going out into public with you. All you do is embarrass me.* "Orange juice, too."

"No, apple." Oma groaned. "What happened to my little Keziah?"

The waitress fidgeted. "Do you guys need a few more minutes?"

"No, I'll have the veggie omelet. There isn't any meat in that is there?"

"No." The waitress laughed. "That's why it's called the *veggie* omelet. What'll you have to drink?"

"Hot chocolate, please." I handed the menus over and the waitress strutted off. *She must think we escaped from the loony bin.*

"We're going to the parade tonight," Oma said.

"Huh?"

"They always have a parade on Memorial Day. I always go with Muriel, but this year, she'll just have to go alone. I'm going with you."

"Okay." *Muriel?*

As if reading my mind, Oma elaborated. "Muriel Dwyer. The neighbor."

Right, the one who always called me Rebecca. "She could come with us."

"Of course not. I'm going with you. She can just find someone else to go with."

That sounded mean. "Won't she feel bad?"

"That's not my problem. She's a thief. She takes things from the garage, says she's only borrowing them, but then she never gives them back. When I ask her for them, she says they are hers. The nerve."

"That's not right."

"It's because," Oma leaned forward, "she's a Dwyer. You can never trust a Dwyer."

*So if she's a thief, why do you go with her? I wish I could have an actual conversation with you, like in the olden days.*

The little bell over the door jingled upon Michael's entrance. Maybe he was a Dwyer, too, since he rented the top apartment next door, and Muriel's family owned the building.

I ducked my head, hoping he hadn't seen us, but he strolled over with a swagger that made my heart flutter. I gnashed my teeth. *He's an arrogant idiot. I shouldn't like him at all.*

"Good morning," he sang. "You must be our Kezy's grandmother. I'm your neighbor, Michael." He held out his hand to Oma.

She played with a loose thread on her sleeve.

He had to have met her before. Either he was reintroducing himself because of her dementia, or he poked fun at her over it.

"My name's Keziah." *You imbecile.*

"Sure, Kezy. Nice jewelry." He grabbed my earring, a cameo with dangling silver chain.

I froze as his finger brushed against my throat. "Thanks."

He stared at me with brows lifted, then turned to Oma. "Nice meeting you." He walked toward the counter of baked goods in the back of the restaurant.

"Is that a friend of Jan's?" Oma asked.

"He lives next door."

"No he doesn't. A lady lives next door. He must be a friend of Jan's."

"Sure." The cameo suddenly felt heavy. The waitress arrived with our food dishes, and by the time she walked away, Michael had left.

"What's this?" Oma snapped.

I stood up to look at Oma's plate. "Eggs and toast. Why?"

"There are *two* eggs."

"You asked for two eggs."

"I never eat two eggs. I'm only eating one. Do you want me to be fat?"

The couple at the other table glared over Oma's outburst. I stabbed my spoon into the whipped cream dotting the top of my hot chocolate. *What foods do the Goat Children eat?*

\*\*\*\*

When Oma and I walked home from *Ann's*, we found Michael washing his car in his driveway. The sight of him shirtless made my heart flutter, and I snapped my mouth shut when I realized I was gaping.

He dropped his scrub brush into a bucket of suds and turned around, his cheeks flushed with sunburn. "How was breakfast?"

"Michael wants to know how breakfast was," I translated for my grandmother.

She stared ahead, her arm linked through mine.

I called over to him, "It was good."

"Probably not as great as what you get in the city, huh?"

"What?" Oma squinted at me through her sunglasses.

"Michael says hi." I pointed. "See. Michael, our neighbor."

"Humph." Oma kept walking, so I waved goodbye to him.

When he wiped his arm across his sweaty forehead, his muscles tensed. "Want me to help you clean your car?"

"Really?" I glanced at Oma's Buick in our driveway.

"Sure. I don't suppose you've washed a lot of cars, huh?"

"Never." I fiddled with my earrings, recalling the way he'd studied them.

"Come out in ten minutes and I should be done. We'll even wax it." Michael wiggled his eyebrows.

I laughed even though it wasn't even funny, earning a scowl from my grandmother. "Michael's gonna wash your car," I told her.

"Isn't that nice of her," Oma said.

I changed into jean shorts and an old *Sailor Moon* T-shirt. Complete with sandals and a ponytail, I ventured outdoors for my first car wash to find Michael screwing his hose into the faucet by Oma's garage. When he pressed on the nozzle, a stream of water bombarded the Buick.

I couldn't think of anything to discuss besides the weather. *Wow, mundane topic, Keziah.*

"Do you like stories?" I asked while he filled a bucket. Soap sprayed into the air. A few bubbles stuck to his jeans.

"What kind?"

"My grandmother has a story she made up. It's called the Goat Children."

"Cool. I tried writing a romance once. I wanted to be different. I mean, how many males do you know who pen love stories?"

I laughed as soap bubbles now hit my legs. "I can't think of one."

"Exactly. It never went anywhere, but I had fun, and I had a copy printed for my mom." He handed me the brush. "You start washing, and when you get tired, I'll take over."

"Okay." I slapped the soggy bristles against the side of the car. Soap ran down the door. "What's the goat book about?" Michael folded his arms and leaned against the porch railing.

"The Goat Children are magical warriors who ride Pegasuses."

"Cool." He didn't laugh. "What else?"

"Not sure. She hasn't told me much."

"When she does tell you more, feel free to pass it on." He sprayed me with the hose.

Ice cold water soaked through my clothes to nip at my skin. I squealed, lifting my hands against the stream. "A Goat Child would get you for that."

He sprayed the hose again, this time into the air, and a cold mist rained over us.

\*\*\*\*

*I am ten years old. Oma finishes reading the complete* Little House on the Prairie *series to me.*

*"I want to write a pioneer story, too," I say. My handwriting is atrocious, and my parents won't let me use their computers, so Oma writes it for me.*

*We sit on her bed. She keeps a notebook open in her lap and listens while I tell the story aloud. When I have to go*

71

*home, she gives me her tape recorder, and I finish telling the story into that. Later, she listens to the tape and keeps writing. After a week, the story is complete. She tapes blank paper to the cover of the notebook, and I draw a picture of the main character. Underneath it, I write the title,* Prairie Parents, *and sign it,* By Keziah and Oma. *I put the notebook on her bookshelf.*

*"Someday, we'll show your kids," she says.*

# Chapter 8

"Take two chairs instead of one to the parade," Oma said. "You'll want to use mine, and I'm not sitting on the grass."

"No, I don't need a chair. The ground isn't wet."

"Ha! I know how kids are. We're taking two chairs," Oma said.

I folded the two lawn chairs with their hideous, neon green print and heaved them over my shoulders. "Oma, isn't it awful early? The parade doesn't start until seven."

"Don't you want a good place to sit?"

Sure, why not sit down the street for half-an hour?

I leaned the chairs against the porch railing while Oma locked the front door. Squirrels frolicked in the front yard.

"You didn't tell me it was hot out."

I stifled a groan. "It's really not that hot. Come on, we better hurry before all the good spots are taken." I didn't actually believe that, but the chairs were hard to hold.

"I can't go. It's too hot."

"What?" I hated the anger that crept into my voice. What happened to the old Oma who would go out in any weather, be it the middle of a heat wave or the aftermath of an ice storm?

"It's too hot out. You should have known that. I can't go out in this. It is way too hot."

"Oma—"

"It's too hot! I'll die."

"You won't die," I snapped. "Come on, we'll go down there, and I'll set up the chairs. It's only a street away, so if you get hot or whatever, I'll just bring you right back."

"It's too hot. I can't go."

I wanted to say okay, we'll go back inside. *I can read and block out your nonsense.* Oma had been so excited about the parade, though. It didn't seem fair to give up.

"No, it's okay. It'll be fun."

So began the bickering, and after what seemed like forever, Oma followed me down the street, her hand clenched around my elbow.

Other families walked along the sidewalk. Mothers pushed strollers. Fathers walked dogs. Children rode on scooters or roller skates, screaming to each other. One little boy dropped his lollipop onto the cement. He picked it up and stuck it back into his mouth. My throat clenched.

Oma's hand slipped off me, and she gasped. I turned to find her sprawled in the grass blinking at me, her eyes expressionless.

"Oma!" I threw down the chairs. "Are you hurt?" *I'm such a horrible keeper. I let her fall over.*

"Why are you screaming? I'm not deaf," Oma said. "Help me up, and don't you dare tell your mother, or she'll make me go to the doctor."

I grabbed the outstretched hand, shocked at how bony it felt. The loose skin slid as I tightened my grip. Oma grunted while I pulled, using her other hand to heave herself onto her knees. I released her hand to grab her under the arms. Oma had always been a few inches taller than me. Now, with my chest pressed against her back, I was the taller one by five inches.

"That was a nasty fall," a man said from behind.

I brushed off my skirt to have something to do with my hands.

"Hi, ma'am," the middle-aged man smiled at Oma.

She rubbed her hands together.

"He's talking to you." I turned her around by the shoulders to face the man.

"What?" Her eyes glowed with something when she saw him.

"It's good to see you out," the man continued.

"Hi," Oma said, emotionless. Blank.

*She doesn't know who he is.*

"Hi," I butted in. "I'm Keziah, her granddaughter."

"I know who you are." He offered me his beefy hand and I shook it. "I live next door." He pointed at the house beside the Dwyer apartment building. "Luke Thesman. When you were little, you used to come over all the time and play with my goddaughter." People emerged from the house he indicated. "That's my wife, my daughter-in-law, my son, and their daughter."

"I wanna go home," Oma said.

I grabbed her words as an opportunity to continue down the hill to Seashell Lane. Where the seashells were, I had no idea. New Winchester was hours from the ocean.

"I'm hot," Oma complained. "Where's my water? Did you bring me water?"

"You don't even have a water bottle at home." I'd forgotten to check if she was all right from the fall, and asking now seemed pointless. *Bad keeper. Bad!*

People sat on the grassy space between Seashell Lane and the sidewalk, some in lawn chairs, others cross-legged. A few had blankets. Children perched on the curb or ran across the street. A car drove by, and a man hollered, "Kids, get out of the way!" As soon as the car passed, the kids ran back.

"We're late," Oma said. "Now what? Where am I supposed to sit? You just had to make us late."

Wow, she really had meant it was best to get there early.

I wandered over to the family on a blanket. "Can we set our chairs up behind you? My grandmother really wants to watch the parade."

"Sure, if you want to. We don't need the space." The woman glanced at the sidewalk where Oma pouted. Her husband talked on his cell phone and ignored me.

"Thank you so much," I gushed, but the woman looked away, yawning. I tried to snap open the legs on one chair, but they stuck. I pulled harder, and with a gasp, the chair flew open, pinching my finger.

"Shit."

"Hey," the woman next to me said. "There are kids around here."

*Oops.* I got the other chair up and hurried back to Oma.

"I'm hot," she repeated.

I led her over to the chairs and sat next to her. The metal dug into my back and the seat pinched my thighs.

I sat in a lawn chair on someone else's lawn, waiting for the start of a parade that was going to suck. New Winchester was a small town, so the parade was probably going to consist of the high school marching band and some fire trucks.

Across the road, sitting on the curb, a boy smoked a cigarette. A woman filed her fingernails. A baby started to cry, and that made a golden-doodle bark. A Pomeranian left a smelly present on a driveway.

Too bad I couldn't have brought Phebe. My little sister didn't get to interact with other children enough, but then again, Phebe shouldn't be near the boy smoking.

"Excuse me," a soft voice came from behind my chair. Luke Thesman's granddaughter held up a knock-off purse like Oma's. The grandfather stood on the sidewalk waiting. He waved one finger in a lopsided hello, so I waved back.

"Excuse me," the little girl repeated. "You dwop dis." She flung the purse at me and ran back to her grandfather. My jaw dropped, and my heart skipped a beat. This was *Oma's* purse. When Oma had fallen, she must have dropped it, and I hadn't even noticed. My face flushed hotter than before, and I snatched the purse off the grass. I unzipped it and flipped through the money to make sure nothing had been stolen.

*Stupid, stupid. I'm so stupid.*

"Do the Goat Children ever have parades?" I asked to get my mind off my lack of keeper skills.

"The Goat Children?" Oma squinted into the evening sun. "No, they don't have parades." Oma had beautiful green eyes, but her lashes had faded and thinned with age. The green still appeared pure and deep, bottomless.

"You have amazing eyes," I blurted out.

"My eyes?" Oma barked a laugh. "They used to be brown like yours. When you become one of the Goat Children, your eyes turn green."

*Why not?* I tipped my head to the side, still studying Oma's eyes. They were deep set, sinking into her skull. Her skin was loose, but not wrinkled. Oma used too much Vaseline at night for her skin to consider wrinkling.

There was something else about Oma's expression. Something haunted, lost in the never-ending depths, but there, surfacing for a second. Oma had seen things. She had done things that still plagued her, but the memories had probably become foggy with age.

"I'm hot," Oma said. "I want to go home. I don't see why you dragged me here in the first place, and give me my purse. I'm old enough to carry my own purse." She snatched the purse, rising from her chair with her face growing red, be it from heat or anger.

"Okay. Fine. We'll go home. I only came for you."

Oma stormed up the slight hill to the sidewalk with purse in hand, hitting a little boy in the head.

"Hey," the child yelled.

Oma kept marching.

"You old hag!"

"Stop," I snapped at him. "You can't call her that. Didn't anyone ever tell you to respect your elders?"

"You have a funny accent." The boy rounded on me. "You talk ugly."

I couldn't think of a comeback for that, but the boy's mother chose that moment to push into the conversation.

"How dare you talk to my son like that? What gives you the right to upset him? That woman hit him."

"Yeah, and she has dementia. She can't help it." Too bad I couldn't whack the family with one of our chairs. It would hurt much more than the purse.

Band music played in the distance while I scurried to the sidewalk after her, our chairs slung over my shoulders.

*How can Oma storm up a hill at her age? Oh yeah, she's a Goat Child. Of course she's tough.*

\*\*\*\*

78

*I am five years old. Oma drives me to the shopping center. Mama is sick, so we are going to get her a get-well present from the card shop.*

*Oma pulls into a parking space and turns off the car. I open my door.*

*"I should stop putting my purse back there. I'm getting too old to grab it." Oma leans into the back seat.*

*I grab the purse for her and start to step out, but a convertible crashes into my door and rips it off its hinges.*

*A few second later, and I might have been there. I burst into tears.*

*The driver hurries out. She's an older woman, with long black hair.*

*"It's your fault," she yells at me in a thick accent. "Your fault!"*

*I cry harder. Oma hugs me, but she has to deal with the lady and swapping insurance. An onlooker calls the police. I sit in Oma's car crying so hard I can barely breathe.*

*Later on, my parents ask what happened.*

*"Keziah was so brave," Oma says. "She stood up to the lady and told her, 'It's your fault. You should have watched where you were going.' The police declared her drunk. Keziah knew exactly what to do to that bully."*

*I gape at Oma. I never said anything to the woman. Oma winks at me, and I swear to become that strong girl, just for her.*

# Chapter 9

When the alarm went off at seven on my first day of school, I pushed the snooze button until I only had half an hour left. *Getting up early sucks.*

Without time for my usual grits, I wolfed down a Greek yogurt.

"Bye, I'm leaving for school," I called into Oma's bedroom.

My grandmother laid curled on her side, the blankets tucked tight around her legs. The air in her bedroom always felt cooler because of the broken wood around one of the windows. The scent of the magnolia tree wafted in from front yard.

I shook her foot. She snorted in her sleep, twitching her shoulder. Since she was so asleep, I grabbed my key and locked myself out.

I ran down the hill towards the school until I slowed my steps to avoid the other students walking to class. They didn't try to talk to me, either chatting with friends or listening to iPods. I didn't know them, and trying to converse with a stranger made my stomach churn.

Buses unloaded more students in front of the high school section. No one looked at me - good. On television, everyone always picked on each other at school, In first grade, a classmate had scribbled all over my textbook with a marker, and I'd been the one scolded.

When I entered the main office, I had to wait until the secretary finished talking to a teacher. My schedule had been sent through the mail, and I'd already marked the classrooms on the map enclosed.

The secretary tapped a pencil against the corner of her desk. Her black suit coat pinched her body as if a few sizes too small. It pushed her silk shirt until it wrinkled over her bosom.

"Can I help you?" she asked me at last.

I jumped, turning away from the bulletin board of lunch specials. Nothing was vegetarian, but the students were allowed to leave for lunch, and I would go home to make sure Oma ate.

"I'm Keziah de Forest. I need my locker."

"Did someone steal it?" She smiled.

"Um… This is my first day, and I don't know where my locker is."

The secretary pulled open a bottom drawer in a filing cabinet behind her desk. Her fake nails, ugly and long, tapped against the metal, and I fought the compulsion to remind her it wasn't Halloween yet.

I received a padlock lock, and the secretary copied the combination and locker number onto an index card.

"Since you're a senior, your locker is on the first floor of the high school wing," she said in her nasally voice.

"Where's that exactly?"

"Take the first hallway on the left. The lockers go in numerical order. If you need help, ask someone."

As I wandered down the hallway toward the senior lockers, I couldn't help thinking how it looked nothing like the high schools on television. The walls were cold and dirty, plain white. Blue paint peeled off the dented lockers. Nothing shiny and new, or inviting.

Students crowded together, huge masses of them, a blur of faces lost in a sea of nonsensical chatter. Someone bumped into me, knocking my shoulder bag down my arm. A hunk of hair caught in the strap.

I looked for someone like Tiffany, with funky hair and punk clothes. If there was anyone like that, he or she hid. The boys all wore T-shirts with words, and jeans, hair cut short. The girls wore jeans or short skirts, tank tops or T-shirts, hair pulled back in ponytails or brushing their shoulders.

I ducked into the first classroom with an open door. A young woman sat at a desk in the back corner, twirling a lock of hair around her finger while she studied a paper.

"Excuse me." I crumpled the index card in my fist. "I can't find my locker. I'm new here."

"Your locket?" The teacher looked up, still winding her hair. The copper strands slid over each other in silky waves.

"Huh? Oh no, not my locket." I touched my neck self-consciously. I'd worn my Celtic cross necklace, and it was still there. "I can't find my *locker*." I held out the ruined index card.

"Of course." The teacher released her hair and took the card, reading the number and combination. "This way."

She shied away from the other students, whispering, "Excuse me," and "Pardon." I almost wanted to protect her from them, to stand in front with my arms akimbo like a shield.

She tapped a locker and wound her hair again. "Here's your locker."

"Thank you so much. I'm Keziah de Forest."

"You're welcome." The teacher retreated into the crowd with her head down.

I stepped toward the locker to squint at the number. Yes, locker number 312. I tipped the index card to read the combination. I turned the lock to nine, looked back at the card, turned it to four, twisted it to twelve, and tugged. Nothing.

"Shit." I tried it again, but the lock still refused to open. I glanced at the boy next to me,with his boyish cute charm and a diamond stud in his ear reflected the dim light. "Excuse me."

He continued to laugh with a group of other boys as they discussed dirt bike racing.

"Excuse me," I repeated louder and tugged on his sleeve, so far the only hoodie I'd seen.

"Hey, don't touch me." He jerked his sleeve away, rubbing the spot as if I'd torn it. His gaze trailed over my body. "Whatcha want?"

I gulped. "I can't get my lock open."

He rolled his eyes at his friends and accepted the lock I held out, along with the index card. "Hey, are you really showing me your combination?"

Mama always talked about students stealing from each other. I couldn't say no or yank the index card away without sounding rude, though, so I nodded, my face hot and red.

"You're cute, you know that?" He fiddled with the lock and tugged, opening it. "So what kind of problem were you having?"

*He thinks I'm cute?* My mouth felt so dry I recalled an Oma saying. *"It was so dry I could spit cotton."*

I wanted to say he was cute, too, and then wink because he really *was*. That earring was gorgeous.

"I mean, it worked for me," he continued, "so it's not like there's anything wrong with it." He passed the lock and index card back. "I swear I didn't memorize the combo or nothing."

I stared at the lock in my hand. "I tried it, and it…it just didn't work for me."

"Here." He snapped my lock shut. "Try it again."

"Okay." My fingers trembled as I turned the dial, cursing my nervousness under my breath. I got to the second number when he pressed his hand over mine, stilling me.

"You're not turning it enough times. See, it's more like this. You can't just keep turning to each number. You gotta spin it, too." By the end of his tutorial, I felt ready to melt into the floor from mortification. "Where you from? You're new, aren't you?"

"I'm from here," Yay, a change in subject. "I mean, I used to live here. We moved to New York when I was ten."

"New York? Like the city?"

"Yeah, but now … I'm back." I'd been about to say I lived with my grandmother, but that just seemed … weird.

"Cool. I'm Matt."

"Keziah de Forest." Now would be a good time to shake hands, but I held the lock, and he made no move.

"Keziah," Matt repeated. "I'll look you up in my old class pictures. Maybe we had a class or two together." He grinned. "De Forest is a cool last name, too. It means 'from the forest,' right? Anyway, see you around."

The bell rang. I tossed my jacket into the locker and snapped the lock on, stuffing the index card into my bag. According to my schedule, the first class was economics. That sounded exciting.

\*\*\*\*

Too bad economics class sucked. The teacher, an older man with a balding head, yelled as soon as I walked through the doorway: "Don't have your shoulder bag in class! All bags must be kept in lockers. Go put it away. Didn't you read the security measures?"

During roll call, instead of saying my name as "Kez-eye-uh," he said "Kaz-ee-yah." When I tried to correct him, he brushed me aside and went on to the next student.

Matt sat on the other side of the room. I tried to talk to him when we filed to the front desk for textbooks, but he turned his back before I could approach and started conversing with another boy.

The material mentioned in class confused me, and I had no idea what any of the terms meant. The class was an hour and a half, since the high school indulged in block scheduling. On the plus side, the day consisted of four classes. By the time the bell rang, I wished there were more with shorter times.

The next class was probability in mathematics, a topic Mama had never concentrated on during home schooling.

Lunch came after that. I ran home only to face an angry Oma.

"I woke up and had no idea where you were," she shrieked.

"I was at school!"

"I was going to call the police. How was I supposed to know where you were?"

"You were sound asleep when I left. I didn't want to wake you up."

"I was so worried. I can't believe you'd be so ungrateful." She burst into tears.

I popped a TV dinner tofu casserole into the microwave.

****

The next class, gym, followed the pattern of being far less than perfect. The other students had their uniforms from the year before, and went into the locker room to change, but no one had mentioned I needed one. The gym teacher gave me a locker combination, but made me sit on the bleachers while everyone else played basketball, since I didn't have appropriate attire.

"How long have you taught here?" I asked the instructor. "My mom used to teach at the elementary."

He blew his whistle. "You need to start paying attention to what's going on around you."

*Aren't you a ray of glorious sunshine? I'm trying to make conversation.*

Ten minutes later, a ball hit me in the side of my head.

The next and last class was English with the teacher who liked to wind her hair.

"Hello." I grinned at her, this familiar face, but the teacher stared back with puckered lips. She must have forgotten the locker assistance.

We watched a Shakespeare movie in black-and-white, *Hamlet*, and I almost nodded off.

Walking home, I listed the day's good points. My head didn't hurt so much from the accident with the basketball. English concentrated on Shakespeare, works I wasn't too familiar with, so it could prove fun. I'd learned how to use a padlock. Oma might not be so mad anymore.

A car pulled into my neighbor's apartment building as I drew near. *Michael.* My gut sunk long before he turned off the car and emerged. Last thing I wanted him to see was disheveled me with a tiny bruise on my forehead.

"Hey, kid-*oh.*" He tipped his baseball cap.

"Hi," My mind drew a blank when I tried to think of something sophisticated to say. "Thanks for helping wash the car."

"No problem. How are you?" He leaned against his trunk.

"Well. How are you?" I hoped he'd stop talking so I could wash the dirt off my hair from the basketball.

"You heard, didn't you?"

I shifted my stance. "Heard what?"

"You know the Dwyers own this place." He nodded at the building.

"Yes." *No, I'm stupid.*

"Muriel Dwyer died while visiting her brother."

My jaw dropped. "She did?" *If you're kidding, I swear I'll never talk to you again.*

"A sudden heart attack. Her husband's really broken up. Are you going to the funeral?"

*So you're not kidding. I can't believe the woman who always called me Rebecca is gone.* "I don't know. Oma will probably want to go. When did Muriel die?"

"Late last night, I guess. If you and your grandma are going, I'll walk down with you." He pointed his thumb in the direction of Seashell Lane. "Just thought you should know."

"Thank you for telling me." I finished walking home in a stunned daze.

\*\*\*\*

*I am eleven years old. On Monday, we will move to New York City, but today is Friday. Every Friday, since I was two years old, I have spent the night at Oma's house.*

*Mama walks me up the street after school. She pushes Phebe in the stroller. I bring a duffel bag with me to take home my extra pairs of clothes from Oma's dresser. I will need them in the city.*

*She microwaves macaroni-and-cheese TV dinners because she doesn't like to cook. We sit at the kitchen table and work on a lighthouse jigsaw puzzle. We're almost through, but now it will have to wait until I visit again. I pretend I'm not moving so I won't cry.*

*After dinner, we sit in the living room chair and snack on a bag of chips while we watch cartoons. When it is bedtime, we curl up together against her pillows, and she reads to me from* Uncle Tom's Cabin. *The copy belonged to my grandfather's grandfather. It is from the 1800s, so Oma is careful with the brittle pages.*

*When she turns off the light, we play a guessing game.*

*"I'm thinking of an object," I say.*

*"Is it bigger than a breadbox?"*

*"No." I snicker.*

*"Is it hot?"*

*"Sometimes."*

*We keep playing until she guesses correctly. I was thinking of a match. Then, it's my turn to guess. Her object is a refrigerator.*

*In the morning, Oma squeezes fresh orange juice. "Liquid sunshine."*

*I gulp it while she prepares a bowl of Cream of Wheat.*

*"I wish I wasn't moving." Tears make me blink.*

*"You'll be back." Oma trails her fingers through my hair.*

*"But what if I don't?" I press my face against her shoulder. Her clothes smell like a blueberry sachet.*

*"You have to because we belong together." Her voice drops to a whisper. "Family never abandons their own kind."*

*I wonder if she is talking about something she did in the past.*

# Chapter 10

I wore the dress I'd packed because Mama said boys couldn't resist a girl in a dress. Matt was going to adore me in it. The bright yellow fabric represented the color of happiness, and it had a full skirt like something from the Renaissance. The bodice laced up the sides in green velvet, even though the back had a zipper. I skipped eye shadow and stuck with mascara. Best to let the dress do all the talking.

Back in the city, Tiffany had a friend who always dressed in that style. Everything was lace and brocade, thick chokers and heavy corsets, layers of the Renaissance reborn purchased off the Internet. I puckered my lips in the bathroom mirror, imagining that girl with her fake accent and scrunched breasts. I could be her and work this look, minus the gigantic chest.

Everyone I passed in the school hallway stared and whispered. I clutched my bag to my chest and hurried through the crowds.

While I opened my locker, a girl walked by and tapped my shoulder.

"Are you going to a masquerade?" she asked. "Your dress is really unusual."

Back in the city, everyone did his or her own thing, and I ignored him or her, only concentrating on my own affairs.

"Yeah," I said. "Aren't you?" In my opinion, that was the greatest comeback in the world. Television worthy. The other girl should become flustered and thwarted.

She shrugged and walked away.

"Screw you," I muttered.

I finished my combination and opened my locker. The rusty bottom always smelled like vomit. Wrinkling my nose, I hung the bag on the only hook remaining in the locker. Someone must have stolen the others, unless they'd broken.

"Yeah, man, sounds great," Matt said from behind.

I ran my fingers through my hair. I'd found sponge rollers in the bathroom under the sink, so I'd curled my tresses the night before. Soft ringlets bounced around my shoulders. My heartbeat sped. Matt would be my first boyfriend.

I rested my hand on the side of the locker, leaning back with a smile. Matt clapped a high-five with another guy.

"Hey," I purred. "What's up?"

"Hey!"

His expression lightened and my heart skipped a beat.

"I looked you up in my old pictures, you know? We were in fourth grade together." He wiped his hand on the front of his T-shirt, black with a clown head on the front.

"Wow, really?" I couldn't remember much about fourth grade other than the teacher's name. Mrs. Long...or maybe Mrs. Longmire. Okay, so I didn't remember that either.

"Yeah." He tossed his backpack into his locker.

"So do you live around here?"

"Just over there a few blocks." He nodded behind him. "I walk. How about you?"

"Yes, me too." I opened my mouth to ask if he'd like to walk to *Ann's* for lunch, but another guy walked up behind him.

He rested his hand on Matt's shoulder and Matt turned around, his face blossoming as if it had its own sun. Matt wrapped his arms around the boy's neck and tilted his head, his lips parted, and the boy did the same. Their tongues touched, and then their mouths crushed together.

Blood drained from my head, and my hand tightened around the locker door. Matt, my heartthrob, had a boyfriend. A lover even, if how they were going at it in the hallway indicated activities they participated in outside of school.

My face burned as I yanked my books out of my backpack and slammed the locker shut. I hoped a teacher walked by and busted them for their make out session.

\*\*\*\*

"Aren't you going to tell me about your day?" Oma asked when I walked in after school. "You never tell me anything. It's like I don't even exist." She narrowed her eyes and her cheeks flushed. I got my easy blushing from her it seemed.

I tossed my bag onto the chair in the hallway. "It was good." *My heartthrob is taken…and gay, so I don't ever stand a chance.* "I've got a lot of homework. Did Mama call?"

"She never calls."

I noticed a piece of paper taped to the living room doorway. Oma's handwriting read Mama had phoned about Muriel. Oma had spelled "Muriel" as Meerall.

"Are you going to Muriel Dwyer's funeral?" I asked for the hundredth time since I'd told Oma about the death.

"Poor Muriel." Oma's face softened. "She was such a nice lady. It will be weird without her next door."

"So, do you want to go to her funeral?"

"No, oh no. You go. She'd like that. She always liked you. Go with Jan."

I peeled the note off the wall and a piece of paint came with it. "This says Mommy called."

"She wants you to get some nice clothes for the funeral. She said you didn't pack any."

I glanced at my yellow dress. It wouldn't do for a funeral, or school.

"There's a store near *Ann's*, down in the village," Oma said. "Go buy something. They have dowdy old things."

*Dowdy old things. Yay.* "Are you sure?"

"I won't have my granddaughter going down there looking like a rose." She waved her hand at my dress and departed for the bedroom. She returned with two fifty-dollar bills.

"Oma, this is a hundred dollars." The bills were crisp in my fingers, bright and friendly. They begged to be spent.

"Bring back the change. Pick up dinner while you're at it. Order it at *Vighesso's*, it's right next door. Then, you can pick up the take-outs on your way back with the clothes."

It made sense, impressive even, coming from the new Oma.

\*\*\*\*

*Vighesso's* happened to be a cigar bar, or so the awning over the front door read. Even though it was five in the afternoon, people filled the bar. There weren't any cigars, though, and *No Smoking* signs hung on the walls.

Everyone at the tables chatted and laughed. The people sitting at the bar watched a baseball game on a flatscreen. A man behind the counter read a newspaper. I wove between the tables towards him, and my skirt caught on a woman's foot.

"Woo hoo," she said. "It's little Cinderella. Where's your mice, sweetie?"

Laughter nipped at my back, but I had a feeling the woman wasn't being mean, only teasing. Why hadn't I changed out of the dress?

"Excuse me." I squeezed between two men to get to the bar. I touched the corner of it and cringed, pulling away from the sticky surface.

The bartender looked up and licked his upper lip. "What do you want, kid?"

"I'd like to place an order for take-out. If that's okay," I added when a bored look crossed his face.

"Want a beer while ya wait?" the man to my right asked.

I glanced at him, taking in his greasy hair and golf tie. He snickered.

"Okay, sure, you want to go to jail? I'm only seventeen."

That shut him up, and he muttered, "Smart ass teen," before his attention turned back to the television.

"You shouldn't be in here." The bartender pulled a notepad from his shirt pocket and scribbled on a page. "Go back there." He hooked his thumb at a dark hallway in the rear of the room. "That's the restaurant area. Somebody there will take your order." He tore out the notebook page and handed it over.

Stepping through the dark hallway, I emerged in a room lined in booths with long tables erected in the middle. An elderly couple sat near a window sipping from mugs.

The door in the corner swung open, and a waitress emerged carrying a tray of plates. One had lasagna, the other stuffed shells. She set them in front of the couple.

"Need anything else?" she asked. When they shook their heads no, she carried the emptied tray over to me. "You can sit anywhere."

"No, I need a take-out, for me and my grandmother."

The waitress shrugged. "It'll be, like, twenty minutes."

"That's okay. I have other errands to do." I fished one of the fifties from my purse, but kept it in my fist.

"What'll it be?"

"Can I see a menu?"

The waitress brought one over from a rack on the wall and I flipped through the pages. Oma wanted the spaghetti dinner, except I hated spaghetti, so it would be the eggplant parmigiana for me.

"It'll be twenty minutes," the waitress reiterated. When I held out the money, she rubbed her wrist across her nose rather than accept it. "You pay when you pick up the food."

"Okay." I stuffed the money back into my purse. Exiting through the bar, I kept my eyes glued on the floor.

Even though *Vighesso's* wasn't the cozy, Italian restaurant I'd expected, the clothing store was dowdy, just as Oma had described. Most of the pants had elastic waists, the coloring either drab or pastel. The air smelled of bad perfume.

No one came over to help, so it took ten minutes before I found a black dress in my size, with a Peter Pan collar and a wide skirt. "Forty-nine dollars," I read off the ticket. I winced as I paid the woman behind the counter.

Back in *Vighesso's*, I sat in one of the booths to wait.

"You should've just gotten TV dinners," the waitress whispered when she brought me the take-out containers. "That food's better."

"Oh." A sour taste crept into the back of my throat.

As I left the bar, passing a table, a man stood. He stumbled, and his beer toppled. The murky liquid rose in a sloshing wave, bubbles and droplets splattering across my bodice and dripping down the skirt. I yelped, scurrying backwards. The beer, cold and sticky, ran everywhere.

"Wow, geez, I'm sorry." He reached for a napkin from the table.

His companions laughed, their voices slurred.

Tears pricked my eyes. My beautiful dress I'd gotten for one of Dad's events last year was ruined. The back of my nose tightened and I pressed the back of my hand to my mouth, eyes burning, before I ran for the door. I pushed it open, the drunken laughter following me into the street.

\*\*\*\*

"It's your fault," Oma said. "You should watch out for your surroundings." She clicked her tongue. "This would have never happened to a Goat Child. We learned to pay attention."

"The Goat Children aren't real!" Her mythical warriors weren't going to save my dress or my dignity. I'd actually cried in public. Snot poured down my face from my nose.

Oma shook her head. "It's just a dress, Kezi. Here, take it off. I'll rub some ivory soap on it and see if it'll come out."

"It's ruined. Besides, it has to be dry cleaned." I blew my nose into a tissue.

"If it's already ruined, it won't matter if we try washing it in the machine, then. I'll see what I can do." Oma unzipped it for me and helped me step out. "It's just a dress, sweetie. It's not the end of the world."

I wasn't just crying about the dress. It was everything. It was Oma. This Oma, the one helping me get into my pajamas, was the Oma I loved, the one from long ago. What happened when this Oma was gone forever?

\*\*\*\*

Exhaustion drove me into a thick sleep. I dreamt of a woman with kinky black hair, garbed in a white dress and holding a pewter dragon. She tossed the item to me.

"I might be a Goat Child, but I still love dragons." She laughed.

I laughed with her, although I didn't understand the humor. "It's nice." I trailed my fingernail over the pewter carving.

"You could be a Goat Child."

I handed the statuette back. "I don't think so."

"Do you ever hear them scream?"

Ice coated my skin. "What?"

"Do you ever hear the screams of the people who need your help? If you were a Goat Child, you could save them." Her laugh transformed into a shriek.

I pressed my hands over my ears, but the noise wouldn't cease.

I sat up in bed, my heart racing. The scream continued, and then stopped, only to resume a few seconds later.

"Oma?" My voice shook. No, it was too muted, coming from outdoors. My legs wobbled as I tiptoed to the hallway. Darkness consumed the glass of the front door.

The floor creaked beneath my feet, and I held my breath. The scream became louder the closer I came to the door. I parted the sheer curtain and peered out to the porch.

The streetlight flickered out, so I could make out only dark shapes. I reached for the light switch, but paused. My hand hovered. Should I turn on the light? What if something, or someone, took that as a sign to attack?

I checked to make sure the door was locked and flipped the switch. The porch light flared to life.

Nothing except the blue recycling bin. The houses up and down the street were dark. Someone else must have heard the scream.

I frowned. The noise sounded as if it were coming from the cellar now. I grabbed the flashlight off the stairs and crept into the kitchen. I flipped on the cellar light fast and threw open the door.

Nothing. I closed my eyes. *Stupid, it might've been a killer.*

I laughed. *A killer. Yeah, right.*

The scream came again, this time as though from the garage. I turned on the garage light and peered through the window in the door. Nothing moved, or looked as if it had moved. Whatever screamed had to be an animal of some sort.

An animal stuck somewhere around the house.

I turned off the lights and returned to bed, but kept the flashlight next to my pillow. The screams persisted. I watched half an hour pass on the clock. The animal must really be stuck or injured. I could call Uncle Jan, but he didn't seem the type to come over in the middle of the night.

*Michael!* I used the flashlight to find his number on the Internet and called on my cell. I counted eight rings, my heart dropping into my stomach. *Great, he isn't going to—*

"Hello?" Michael rasped.

"It's me. Keziah. There's an animal outside. It's hurt. It's screaming."

"Keziah? It's two in the morning."

"Two-fourteen." My forehead throbbed. "Please, I don't know who else to ask. The animal won't stop."

"I don't even hear it." He groaned.

How could he not? The sound pierced through my skull like a nail.

"Please. It's been screaming for a while now."

"Okay, I'll come over and take a look."

"Thanks so much." I shut my phone. Maybe I should awaken Oma, but when I checked on her, she snored. I stood at the front door with my forehead pressed against the glass, frigidness soaking through my skin. The scream wouldn't cease, save for a few second's worth of pauses, yet nothing stirred past the porch light's glow.

"Keziah?" Michael called.

The scream diminished. I unlocked the door and stepped onto the porch. Air nipped through my Hello Kitty pajamas, making me shiver. He wore only a pair of plaid boxers. I dragged my gaze off his flat abs to his face.

"So this noise?" He combed his fingers through his mussed hair. "Where is it?"

"It," I licked my lips, "stopped."

He stared at me. "You don't hear it anymore?" Despite the cold, my cheeks burned. "No. First I thought it was out here, but then I thought—"

"I'll take a look around," he interrupted. "Maybe it got scared."

"Thank you so much." A corner of my mind said the scream wouldn't start again. Something wasn't normal about this.

"No problem." He pecked the top of my head.

The voice of the woman in my dream flitted past my ears. *Do you ever hear the screams of the people who need your help?*

\*\*\*\*

*I am four years old. Next year, I will start kindergarten, and then I will have to eat in the cafeteria with my class. For now, I stay with Oma during the day. When Mama has her lunch time, Oma prepares a meal, and we walk it down the street to the elementary school. Usually, Oma makes sandwiches with veggie cold cuts, or she spoons Mama's salads into Tupperware containers.*

*Oma signs us in at the office.*

*The secretary stands up to smile at me. "Keziah, you get bigger every day."*

*"That's because I water her." Oma takes my hand and leads me to Mama's classroom.*

*I know the way, but sometimes, older kids walk by, so I'm glad Oma is with me.*

*Mama sits at her desk, and Oma pulls a chair over from the computer table. I choose the rocking chair in Mama's story corner. It faces the window, so I can watch cars drive by in the road.*

*When Mama goes to pick up her class from the playground, Oma gathers up the supplies into the two lunch bags. Holding hands, we walk home.*

# Chapter 11

The calling hours for Muriel Dwyer were held on Friday. "Funerals are for families, not neighbors," Uncle Jan said. "We'll just go to the calling hours."

He parked at Oma's, and we walked down the street to the funeral home. A tall man in a black suit opened the door for us. I smiled up at him, but his face remained solemn, and I realized I shouldn't smile at this sad time.

I made my expression somber while I followed my uncle up the stairs into a hallway. Nerves nagged my body.

I'd never been in a funeral home before. I expected gray walls and hardwood floors, but instead, a lush carpet of maroon with dark green vines covered the floors. The walls were white with green wainscoting and a floral border along the ceiling. Landscape paintings resided over gilded chairs and matching tables. Victorian style lamps and tissue boxes covered the tables.

*Should I be crying?*

A plaque over the assigned door read, 'Muriel Dwyer'. A few people occupied the couches and chairs. None of the faces looked familiar. I'd wanted to be respectful and see what calling hours were like, but how little I'd known Muriel Dwyer.

Uncle Jan rested his hand on my back, leading me towards the casket in the back of the room. It was polished mahogany, and the fluorescent lights in the ceiling reflected off the smooth surface. Inside, Muriel Dwyer lay nested amongst roses on white silk. Her face was pale and firm, like wax. There was a small smile on her lips, her eyes were shut, and her hands were folded over her chest, clutching a rosary. She appeared so pure and unreal. Tears came to my eyes.

Muriel Dwyer was never going to call me Rebecca again.

I hadn't really known the woman, but looking down at her lifeless body made the reality all the more final. Before I could start crying, Uncle Jan led me to an elderly man standing beside the casket.

"I'm sorry about your wife," Uncle Jan said. "If there's ever anything we can do, just let us know. My mother wished she could have come, but it's hard for her to get out these days."

"Thanks for your respects." Mr. Dwyer nodded.

I couldn't meet the man's gaze. He'd just lost his wife, and I couldn't imagine his sorrow. Nothing I thought up to say sounded soothing.

Still holding my arm, Uncle Jan led me away from the casket.

"Jan," a man called. "It's been a while."

"Hey!" Uncle Jan released my arm to shake hands with the stranger. "How've you been?"

I stepped against the wall to provide my uncle with some privacy. My gaze wandered around the room to absorb the unfamiliar faces. Once upon a time, before I moved to the city, had I known these people?

"Keziah, right?"

I looked to the left as Michael approached. "You know my name."

"I thought we were going to come to this together." He leaned against the wall near me. "You going to the funeral tomorrow?"

"No." I shook my head. "Uncle Jan wanted to come today. I came with him."

"So, how are you holding up?"

"I really didn't know Muriel Dwyer. I feel really bad about that, but I just got to New Winchester, you know?"

A smile pulled at his lips. "No, I mean, how are you holding up with your grandmother?"

My cheeks burned, and I lowered my gaze. The carpet was really quite exquisite, like the kind to roll on and pretend to fly over Arabia. "It's fine."

"Have you always been close to her?"

"I was closer to her when I was younger. She always watched me while my parents worked."

"What do they do?"

He wiped the back of his hand across his mouth. It drew attention to the shiny buttons on the cuff of his black suit. My gaze flitted over the crowd. Only Matt wore a suit.

"My mom teaches elementary. My dad works for a magazine. He travels a lot, writes stories about his travels. Like, he goes to Australia and writes a long paper about everything he did there. He goes to a new place every issue." I rambled, and he smirked as if in placation. I snapped my mouth shut.

"That sounds exciting," he drawled. "Do you ever go with him?"

"No."

He lifted an eyebrow.

"Okay, sometimes," I said. "Not usually. I have to stay home with Phebe. She's my sister. My mom home schools us, but I can help Phebe with her work. Sometimes, like if our dad goes somewhere in America, he takes us along."

"How come only you came to live with your grandmother?" He took his cell phone from his pocket and tapped the screen.

For a second, I thought he didn't care about my answer, but then he put the phone away.

"She doesn't like my dad. It wouldn't have worked." A corner of my heart blossomed to know Michael didn't belong to the sect of people who ignore others for the joy of a cell phone.

"And your uncle? Why doesn't he live with your grandmother or her with him?"

"My aunt won't let Oma live with them." If I called her nasty, Michael might think me disrespectful. If I related a story—like how when we lived in New Winchester before, my aunt used to call up my mom at least three times a week to ask a favor, but whenever my mom wanted something, my aunt was "too busy," or said, "Not right now, dear"—Michael might think I complained too much.

"So how do you like high school? Is it everything you thought it would be?" He wiped his mouth again, opening and closing his hand, and I realized he wanted something to do, a drink in his hand perhaps.

"No, it's not what I expected." I watched his fingers. They were thick and sparsely haired, and they twitched. "I'd been expecting people to be really mean, but they aren't. Not really. Everyone pretty much ignores me now."

"No boyfriend?"

I pictured Matt and suppressed a sigh. "Nope, no boyfriend." At least Matt was happy with his man.

"Hey, you wanna walk home with me?" Michael glanced at Uncle Jan. "It looks like your uncle might be a while."

Two other men had joined Uncle Jan. One of them laughed, clapping my uncle on the shoulder.

"Let me just ask, okay?"

I worked my way to Uncle Jan. "Do you mind if I walk home with Michael?"

"Feel free." He turned back to his friends. Not introduction time then. Michael rested his hand on the small of my back to turn me towards the doorway, reminding me of how Uncle Jan had steered me in.

No one seemed to care Muriel Dwyer was dead. They flitted amongst each other, chatting and smiling. No one except me wore full black. These were calling hours, not a party. Where were the hollow eyes and solemn smiles I'd imagined? Was this how people would act when I died?

Once outside, Michael drew a deep breath, puffing out his chest. "Is it just me, or was it stuffy in there?"

Muriel Dwyer was going to be sealed into the Earth. *That* was stuffy.

Michael slid his hands into his pockets. "So tell me more about school. What are the classes like?"

"Hard. My mom never gave me homework or anything, and there's a lot of homework here. Every night I have almost two hours' worth, and then my grandma gets mad. She calls my mom and complains that all I do is sit at my laptop. Oma always says when I get home, it's going to be in the garbage, but I know she doesn't mean it."

"Oma?"

"It's 'grandmother' in Dutch. She's Dutch. I've always called her Oma."

We paused at the corner to watch the streetlight. Vehicles sped by, a breeze brushing over my face. New Winchester was nothing like the city. Now *that* was traffic.

The light switched to green, and he touched my back again to get me moving. It felt comforting to have him at my side, an adult who wasn't family, who wasn't even a friend. I could say anything to him and know it would go no further, even if he laughed at my words.

Michael ran his fingers through his long hair. "It must be hard watching her disintegrate."

I winced. *Disintegrate?* What an awful word to use, but was it the truth? Her dementia would keep getting worse, and Oma had no intention of going to a doctor for medication to slow the progression. I'd mentioned a checkup a few times, and Oma had announced doctors were evil, only out to make money in any way they could.

I counted the cracks in the sidewalk to keep my mind off her.

"How do you like New Winchester?" Michael's voice broke through my reverie.

A man stood in a yard playing with a push mower, cussing when it refused to start.

"It's fine," Oma lived here. She didn't belong in a nursing home.

"No, how do you *really* like it? I'm sure it's a one-eighty from New York."

"Have you ever been to the city?"

"I used to go a lot when I was younger. I grew up in New Jersey, but then my parents moved to Utica. I went to college at SU."

"SU?" I picked at one of my cuticles.

"Syracuse University. What are you going to do about college?"

"I don't know yet. I want to go for teaching, like my mom. I might go to Oneonta. That's where she went. It's supposed to be *the* teaching college."

"I could never teach. I don't like little kids."

"Really?" I'd always thought of them as cute and innocent. "How come?"

Michael chuckled. "I'm a guy. Guys don't like little kids."

I'd never heard that before. "My dad likes me and my sister."

"*Normal* guys like *me* don't like little kids. Your dad has to like you guys. You're his kids, and he has to pay for all your crap."

That didn't sound pleasant. Unsure of how to respond, I looked away. A woman sat on the front porch, rocking back and forth.

We were almost home. *Home...* Was this home?

"Thanks for walking me home." The words emerged robotically from my mouth.

Michael held out his hand. "No problem, kid. My mom taught me manners."

"Thanks, really." I shook his hand, and he kissed my knuckles. His scruff tickled my skin.

The mail truck pulled to a halt alongside the curb.

"Did you ever want to be a mailman?" I asked to get my mind away from the softness of his lips.

Michael pulled an elastic from his pocket and tugged his hair into a short queue. "Why would I want to do that?"

"Good exercise?"

The mail carrier stepped out of his mail truck, and I noticed it was a different man. This one had black hair, not red, like the mailman who had come every day since I'd arrived.

"*You* wanna be a mailman?" Michael asked.

"Me? Oh, no." I giggled. "I want to be a Goat Child!"

"A kid?" He wiggled his eyebrows. "I've never wanted to be anything that wasn't human."

"No, they're a warrior class. Tough mythical warriors. They battle evil in the twilight hour with the night swirling around in their wake."

"Sure, if you say so." We arrived at his apartment, and he held out his hand again. "It was nice talking with you, Kezy."

I clasped his hand, amazed that his wrist was nearly twice as wide as mine. "See you around." He laughed as he walked away.

I folded my arms across my chest. Something caught the corner of my eye, and I looked at the mailman. He held a packet of white envelopes in his hands, his head tipped to the side as he stared at me. His lips parted and he said something, but from the distance, but I couldn't hear him. It could have been a question: "Are you sure Muriel died of natural causes?"

\*\*\*\*

*I am five years old. Oma decides I shouldn't have to eat in the cafeteria at lunch, so she drives to the elementary school every day and brings me home. She heats me a TV dinner. I eat it in the living room while I watch the* Wizard of Oz *tape.*

"She won't make friends if she doesn't stay for lunch," Mama says.

"Keziah, where do you want to eat?" Oma asks me.

"At your house." I get a warm meal, rather than a soggy sandwich, and I can drink all the milk I want.

"You don't have to," Mama says, but she doesn't bring it up again.

# Chapter 12

"Okay now." The substitute gym teacher clapped her hands, the sound echoing through the gym. All up and down the woman's pudgy fingers glistened rings, the cheap kind from costume stores that turn skin green.

I wondered why she was allowed to wear rings, but we weren't. Homeschooling must have poisoned my mind against the unfair tyranny of high school.

"Come on, class," the gym teacher said in her deep voice. "Since it's raining out, we're going to pass on Ultimate Frisbee for a round of kick-ball."

The class divided into lines. After the first day of explaining line placement, the students seemed to have "forgotten" where everyone went. They sat next to friends, so none of the lines had an equal number of occupants.

"Lines two and four, you're up to kick first. The rest of you, out to the field!" She blew her whistle and punched the air as if we were about to play a national championship. A boy yelled with her, but it was sarcastic and everyone snickered, except for me. Should I tell this teacher that I didn't know the rules to the game?

Every time I'd tried before, our regular gym teacher had told me to stop fooling around. "These aren't complex, newfangled games. Get to playing!"

I followed a boy into the so-called field. The occupants of rows two and four lined up along the wall near the gym office. A boy kicked the padding and yelled a cuss.

Since everyone in the field faced that line-up, I moved to the back near the door to the boy's locker room. The gym teacher retrieved a ball from the office and tossed it from hand to hand, the whistle balanced on her lips.

"Hey," someone said.

I turned to the girl next to me. "Hello."

"How come you always wear stockings for gym?" she asked.

I wore green and black striped stockings, sagging a bit over my black high-tops. The gym uniforms consisted of a T-shirt and shorts, both in an ugly reddish-orange color, and *New Winchester* was printed across the front of the shirt with a man saluting dressed like a pilgrim.

"I like stockings." It was easier to wear stockings than shave, since other than gym days, I never bared my legs.

"You have really pretty stockings. I like the ones you wore last time. The ones with all the spider webs."

"Thanks." If Tiffany had said that, I would've asked if she wanted to borrow them.

The gym teacher blew the whistle and pointed to the kicker. "First strike!"

"My mom would never let me wear anything like that," the girl said. "My mom's really strict."

"The only time Mama's flipped out was when I got my tattoo." I pointed at my left ankle where a fairy perched, hidden now beneath the stockings. "I'd mentioned wanting one, but then I went with my friend Tiff, and my mom was mad because she didn't think the tattoo place was all that clean. Plus, it's like a law to have parental consent, and I obviously didn't."

"Yo," the boy standing in front of me shouted.

*Who says "yo" anymore?* I chuckled. Then, he turned around and chucked the ball he'd caught into my face.

Blackness. Stars followed, bright lights that flashed, falling in a waterfall of rainbow colors. The pain started in my ears when they popped then spread across my forehead, chin, cheeks, and then my nose. I stumbled a few steps backwards, lifting my hands. My fingers brushed against my glasses. They hung off my nose at an odd angle, and when I tried to fix them, they fell off. Silence filled the gym a second before they plinked against the floor.

The blurry world spun, and the pain spread into my chest. My nose hurt too much for me to leave my fingers against it. When I pulled them back, blood streaked them. A roaring began in my ears.

"Yo, I had no idea you were there," the boy who'd thrown the ball said. "Sorry about that. Where'd you come from, anyway?"

*Bastard.*

"Hey, are you gonna be okay? Your glasses are pretty mangled," another boy said.

The gym teacher blew her whistle as she crossed the gym. "You wanna sit this one out?"

"My nose is bleeding." When I spoke, it sounded like the words came from a mile away. My lips throbbed. Maybe those weren't the words I'd said at all.

"Why don't you go to the nurse then? You know where the nurse is, don't you?"

I'd never been there. "No."

"Someone take her to the nurse's office," the gym teacher yelled.

"I'll do it," offered the girl I'd been talking to when I'd been hit.

"Thanks. Hurry back." The gym teacher blew her whistle again. The sound pierced through my skull, eliciting a wince.

"You forgot your glasses." The girl picked them up.

"That's why I wear contacts for gym," someone called.

When I got to the nurse's office, my nose had stopped bleeding, but my glasses had dug into my skin during the impact, leaving a cut. The nurse washed it off and gave me an ice compress to take down the swelling.

"Can you go back to class?" The nurse peered into the little room in the back of the office where she'd let me.

Stretched out on a cot, I kept my eyes shut.

"Here, move the ice pack and let me see how it's coming along."

When I did, the nurse clicked her tongue.

"Dear, it looks like you've got two black eyes. I looked at your glasses, and they can't be fixed. You'll have to get new ones."

Maybe I could sue the school.

"I want to go home," I said for what had to be the hundredth time.

Instead of saying that ice and rest would help – again - the nurse headed toward her desk. "I'll give your house a ring."

I settled into the hard cot. Everything throbbed, and the ice only numbed my hand, not the wound. A glove to cover my palm with would be awesome.

"Keziah?" The nurse opened the door again and the hinges squeaked. "I called your house and no one answered. I also called your uncle. I got his voicemail."

Where was Oma? I sucked breath through my lips.

113

"I can't send you home without parental consent," the nurse said. "I'll try calling again in a little while. Maybe you will feel well enough to go back to class by then."

Oma never went out. What if Oma had fallen and couldn't come to the phone? She might need me.

I sat up. My head throbbed worse, the room spinning, and my stomach quivered. I set the ice pack down, eyes shut and breaths even. I blew through my nose, willing my stomach to settle.

When I stood, I had to grab the wall. *No, I will not throw up. I will not pass out.* I opened the door, pausing to catch my breath. The veins in my head tried to pound out through my skin, and my nose felt as though it was on fire.

It took everything in me not to stagger as I emerged from the room. The nurse sat at her desk tending to a little boy.

"I feel better." My face hurt too much to attempt a smile. "I'd like to go back to class."

The nurse smiled for me. "You don't have a concussion, so you should be fine. If you feel bad again, just come back. Here's your glasses." She lifted them off a manila envelope. She'd attempted to fold the arms down, but they stuck out at odd angles. "Let your teachers know so they can help you with notes."

"Of course." I curled my fingers around the glasses and didn't look back as I left the office.

I walked past the classrooms. No one tried to talk to me. I pushed open the main doors and stepped into the sunshine.

My purse and clothes were in my gym locker. I still wore the uniform.

*Who cares?*

The sun was too bright. I couldn't see a thing. Even squinting, everything was a colorful blur.

When I reached the first street corner, I folded my arms across my chest. Cars zoomed by, and down the street, a horn honked. Autumnal wind bit through the thin gym uniform. I had to look a sight, spots of blood on my shirt and my face swollen, complete with two black eyes.

The cars slowed. Had the light changed?

I ran, praying the cars would stop for me. They didn't start up, didn't approach, and then my foot caught on the curb. I sprawled across the sidewalk. The cement gouged one of my elbows and tore my stockings. My glasses shot out of my hand.

"Shit!" I felt around for my glasses and my palms scraped over the cement.

Someone approached from the right dressed in blue. I squinted. They carried something that reminded me of a harp, but it couldn't be one.

"Help me," I called. The stoplight must have changed because the cars sped again. What if my glasses had fallen in the road?

"I can't see. I lost my glasses," I said to the blue person as they drew nearer. "Can you help me find my glasses?" They probably thought I'd gotten in a fight or was having a Velma moment from *Scooby-Doo*. "I got hurt in gym class, and now I can't find my glasses." A tear slid down my cheek. "Please help me!" I lunged for their leg.

My hand passed through the leg. It felt like nothing, and smoke swirled before solidifying back into that leg, the person continuing down the street.

Impossible. The lights played tricks on my blurry eyes. There was no one there.

My legs shook as I stood up. I'd have to look for my glasses later. I had to get home before I passed out. The sidewalk wavered beneath my feet with its hills and dips, and everything tried to consume me. I gasped out my sobs and everything hurt more. By the time I got to Oma's driveway, I hiccupped so hard I couldn't breathe.

"Keziah? Oh my God, what happened to you?" Michael grabbed my arm, and I would've fallen if he hadn't pulled me against him. "Did someone beat you up?"

I couldn't see a thing from the tears. Sputtering, I pointed at my house and then my face.

"Your grandmother went for a walk. I don't know if she's back yet. I've been unloading groceries. Here, come on, I'll help you. Where're your glasses?"

I pointed down the street. Snot poured from my nose, but I didn't care.

"Did someone punch you in the eye?" He helped me walk towards Oma's front porch.

"Gym," I sputtered.

"There's your grandmother."

Oma never went walking by herself. It must be what Uncle Jan called a "good day."

"What an awful school." Oma pet my arm before Michael led me into the house.

I rested on the bed while he called the school. "Hi, this is Jan, Keziah's uncle. She won't be back in from lunch today. She's not feeling well." Michael left at some point and the real Uncle Jan came. He looked for my glasses, but didn't find them.

"I thought I saw a man," I muttered as Oma spread a cool washcloth over my face. "He was dressed in blue, and he had a harp, but then he wasn't there."

Oma stiffened. "Did he have black hair that looked green?"

Yes, because that made sense. "I don't know. I couldn't see." It felt good to be home, curled up in bed with the soft blankets tucked around me. My face still hurt, but wet cloths helped more than the nurse's ice pack.

"He was a Comaly," she said.

"Huh?"

"Those who watch the Goat Children. They wait for weaknesses. They spy and report. That's why you couldn't touch him. He wasn't here. He was hiding."

So much for it being one of her good days.

"I'm going home," Uncle Jan said. "Call me if you need more pain killers."

"I'm going to make dinner. We'll have spaghetti and pepper. You love that," Oma said.

Spaghetti mixed with green peppers was Oma's favorite, not mine. As soon as Oma went into the kitchen to dice the green pepper, I reached for the phone to call my mother.

I would have to get new glasses, but Mama could send my old pair. In the meantime, I would have to miss school until I could wear the glasses, which meant the swelling of my nose would have to lessen.

I shouldn't have let Oma go into the kitchen to dice vegetables with a sharp knife, so I dragged myself out of bed to tell Oma I'd rather have frozen pancakes for dinner.

\*\*\*\*

117

I am six years old and have a wart.

"When you touch other kids at school, this is what you get," Oma says.

"All kids get warts." Mama buys me medicine patches, but they don't help.

The wart spreads. Now I have eight across my fingers, and one on my wrist. Oma takes me to the pediatrician. The appointment is during school, so Mama can't go.

The doctor tells me to soak my hands in hot water every night for a half-hour. "They'll be gone in a week."

I do it, even though the water burns, and I have to keep adding fresh when it starts to cool. In a week, though, my fingers are wart free. The one on my wrist is still there, so Oma takes me back to the pediatrician.

"Stubborn thing," he says. "I'll have to burn it off."

I cry, but Oma holds me close. He cleans the area, numbs it, and takes out his tool. It stings, but the pain isn't too bad as he burns off the nasty wart. It hurts more once he finishes.

"Would you like a get-well present?" Oma asks as she drives me home.

I cry, so I can't answer. She cuddles with me on the couch, watching a Leave it to Beaver marathon until Mama comes home. Oma returns an hour later with a get-well card and a Barbie doll.

# Chapter 13

It took a week for the swelling of my nose to go down. During that time, I stayed home, enduring Oma's constant questions. They revolved between, "Why aren't you in school?" and "Where's your mother?" Once, Oma thought I suffered from the chicken pox. "Don't come any closer!"

Other times, Oma tried to teach me how to play the piano, even though I couldn't see the keys or sheet music. I couldn't have read the sheet music, anyway, but I loved listening to Oma play. She used to play whenever I had visited as a child. I would sit on the couch hugging a stuffed skunk and close my eyes, losing myself to the perky show tunes from musicals I'd never heard of, since they were from the 1950s.

My favorite song was one Oma said belonged to the Goat Children - their anthem.

Phebe called to read her children books to me over the phone. Dad's brother, Tom, called to see how I was. He hardly ever called, so it brought bitter tears to my eyes because it had taken a nearly broken nose to make him care.

Michael brought over *Bloody Jack* on CD from the library

Mama called the school and complained they should've been more concerned about my state of wellbeing. The substitute gym teacher stressed it was my fault. I should've paid more attention to the game instead of daydreaming and talking to my friends.

I'd wanted to pay attention, but I didn't understand the game. The gym teacher stuck to her story, though. I hadn't asked for help. If I had, the teacher would've been more than happy to explain the rules.

The principal was more concerned with my walking home, despite saying I was going to class. I hadn't been allowed home sick since Oma and Uncle Jan hadn't answered their phones. This meant a day of in-school suspension on Monday. I would have to go back to school then, even if I still had two black eyes and a swollen nose.

*Shit.*

On Saturday morning, Oma stepped in front of the television while I ate Rice Krispies for breakfast.

"I want to buy some half-moon cookies." Oma waved her purse. "Up and at 'em. It'll make you feel better to get out of the house. We're going to the bakery."

I might look like crap, but that didn't matter with no one to impress at the bakery.

I stepped outside, and the cold wind tingled against my face. The air smelled tangy, like rain. I shivered and held tighter to Oma's arm. Maybe the walk to the bakery wasn't such a great idea. Neither of us could see well, and Oma was becoming more apt to reach for the wall when she walked around the house.

The clouds parted to let sunlight soak the city. Oma fiddled with her sunglasses. "We're going to walk the cookies over to Lesley," she said.

"Lesley?" The name almost sounded familiar.

"My friend Lesley," Oma snapped. "We used to visit her all the time when you were little. Back before your mother dragged you off to who knows where with *them*."

I drew a deep breath before blurting out. "Why don't you like Phebe?"

"Lesley never learned how to drive." Oma ignored my query. "I always used to drive her everywhere, back when I still drove." She exhaled. "Uncle Jan took my car keys away. He's afraid I'll drive, but I wouldn't get far before the police caught me."

The car keys were still on the hallway table, but whatever. Images of Phebe flitted across my mind. Oma shouldn't act like my sister was little more than crap.

Oma continued. "I told Lesley about the Goat Children. She believed me. No one ever believes me about the Goat Children, but you believe me, don't you? Everyone used to think I had a wild imagination, and now they just think I'm a crazy old woman. Ha!" She barked a laugh. "I'm not crazy."

No, Oma wasn't crazy. She had dementia.

"I told Muriel, too." Oma sighed. "Poor Muriel. She believed me, you know. I used to tell her if she kept taking things from my garage, the Goat Children would come after her."

We strolled away from the bakery. I had to keep Oma on the sidewalk by steering her, else she walked into the grass.

"I want to be a Goat Child again." Oma stumbled over a crack in the sidewalk. "I left them to marry your grandfather, but now I miss them. It was so much fun having that kind of power."

"What kind of power?" Even if Oma had dementia, at least she could find happiness in her stories.

"All sorts, but you never grow old. You remain the age you were when you joined them. They don't accept anyone younger than fourteen, or older than nineteen. I was there for so long, and I was always sixteen, never a day older or younger. Then I met your grandfather. I had never cared for a man as much as I loved him. I left them to be with him."

"Can you go back?" Someone had left a baseball bat on the sidewalk. I kicked it away so Oma wouldn't trip.

"Yes, they'll take you back, sometimes, but then you can never leave again, and you'll always be the age you were before. I'll be sixteen again, forever." Oma really should've published these stories as books.

"Why did you join in the first place?"

"My parents died of pneumonia. I would have had to go and live with my uncle in Holland, but then the Goat Children came to me. They asked me to join them."

"That must've been nice." No one ever mentioned Oma's parents. I didn't even know their names. A pang of regret stabbed my heart.

"It was. Isn't it weird how, back then, I would be amazed to get a peppermint stick from the store, but now I'm buying sweet cookies?"

I remembered those words when we reached the bakery, and looked around for an old-fashion peppermint stick stand. No such luck. Oma picked out a jelly bun and two half-moon cookies for her friend, and I paid since Oma couldn't see which bill was worth five dollars.

"How much longer before we reach Lesley's?" I asked once we left the bakery.

"What?"

"How much longer till we get to your friend's house?"

"What?" Oma scratched the mole on her cheek.

I shouted the question.

"There's no need to yell at me. Where's my little Keziah gone off to?" Oma's brows drew together, and her lips pressed into a thin line, whitening.

I tightened my arm around my grandmother. Tree roots grew under the slabs of cement, cracking it. *If Oma's toe caught in one of those cracks...*

The silence became unbearable, and I racked my brain for something to say. Cars zoomed by, yet we only met a woman walking a fluffy white dog.

"Hello," the woman said.

Oma had, of course, not heard her. I hadn't wanted to stress that Oma couldn't hear, so I only waved at the woman.

"What are you looking at?" I asked Oma as she stared across the street.

"Things that aren't right," she said.

*Okay then.* "Cool."

"That's when you know something is wrong. You have to memorize the right so you can see the bad."

I wanted to say Oma couldn't remember what "right" looked like on the street since she didn't go out much, but instead, I stepped on an orange leaf. It crunched beneath my Converse sneaker.

"It's a Goat Child thing," Oma added. "You wouldn't understand."

*No, I don't understand at all.* I stepped on another leaf, this one with a reddish shade.

"Here we are." Oma turned toward a walkway leading from the sidewalk to a squat yellow house with green shutters. What an awful color combination.

"Your friend lives here?" I had a sick feeling we were about to knock on a door and be greeted by a stranger who would have no idea who we sought, this friend of Oma's named Lesley.

Oma pulled away from me and marched up the walkway to the front stoop, so I ran after her. First, I'd had to hold her just to keep her from falling, and now she walked like an athlete.

The walkway was strewn with fallen leaves, the tree in the front yard turning colors earlier than most others in the neighborhood. The leaves hid the edge of the stoop, so Oma wasn't lifting her foot to step up.

I grabbed her arm. "Watch out for the step!"

"What are you talking about?"

"Here, see?" I brushed the leaves with the side of my foot and tapped the edge of the step with my toe.

"I can see that."

Oma missed the step and stumbled, grabbing the railing to keep from tumbling over. I kept my grip on her arm.

"The step's broken," Oma exclaimed. "Ring the doorbell."

I pressed the glowing doorbell. From inside the house, a faint chiming sounded. When the stranger opened the door, what should I say? *Hi, excuse us, but my grandmother seems to think her friend Lesley lives here.*

What if Lesley didn't even exist? She could be a friend from years ago, no longer alive.

The front door opened a crack, and an elderly woman peered at us. The pale eyes narrowed, and she opened the door wider. "Leontien?"

"Lesley?" Oma looked down at me to comment, "She certainly hasn't aged well!"

I winced at the rudest comment I'd heard all day.

"Leontien, is this your granddaughter? My, she's grown. What grade are you in now, honey?"

The wind blew a strand of hair into my mouth when I started to speak and I spit it out. "I'm in twelfth."

"What's her name again?" Lesley seemed to ask Oma, but she stared at me.

"I'm Keziah."

"That's pretty name," Lesley said. Wow, Lesley existed.

Oma smoothed her hat. "We've come calling. I brought you some cookies. Give her the cookies, Keziah. Oh, Lesley, you have to watch my girl like a hawk to make sure she does what she should. I said give her the cookies."

I already held out the bakery box, but Lesley didn't take them.

"Won't you come in?" Lesley stepped back, frowning at the doorframe. She held out her hand and pawed at the air as if expecting a screen door. There were hinges for it, but someone must've taken it in for the winter.

Oma stepped passed Lesley into the house. I followed with one hand still on my grandmother's arm. Lesley muttered at the missing screen and shut the inner door.

"My mother was here earlier." Lesley led us down the narrow hallway into the first room on the left. "She made me some iced tea. Would you two ladies like some?"

"Your *mother* was here earlier?" Lesley's mother had to be dead. Lesley looked to be at least eighty years old.

"Yes." When Lesley nodded, her short white curls bounced. "See, here's a picture of her. Here's my mother." The elderly woman pointed to a picture on top of a table near the doorway. Lesley looked the same; the only difference was a change of dress. A younger woman stood beside her on a pier, with a sailboat in the background.

"You mean daughter?" I asked. "She's your daughter?"

"Yes, my daughter." Lesley quirked her right eyebrow. "Who else would she be? She's found me a nice lady to come every day and just sit with me for company. If I need anything, I tell her, and it's all free. You should have Jan find someone like that for you," Lesley told Oma.

"Jan's mother isn't feeling well. It's her back."

"Oma, *you* are Uncle Jan's mother," I said.

"What?" Oma scratched her mole again.

"How about some iced tea?" Lesley asked. "My granddaughters love iced tea. They're both working at the *Gap*. Do you ever go there?" She peered at me, licking her wrinkled lips.

"I never go there," I said.

"Well," Oma flared her nostrils. "I'm glad I came. All you two do is talk without me. I feel like I don't belong here at all."

My heart plummeted into my stomach. "But Oma, I was just answering her questions!"

Oma huffed, rolling her shoulders as if ruffling her feathers, and glared at Lesley. "How's your cat?"

"Mr. Fluffy died." Lesley frowned as if she tried to think if Mr. Fluffy really was gone.

I opened my mouth to say I was sorry about the loss of the pet, but Oma still had a pout on her face, so it would be safer to keep quiet.

"Jan's mother got hurt," Oma said.

*Wife*, I corrected in my mind.

"How did that happen?" Lesley asked.

"She…fell, I think." Oma frowned.

My aunt had pulled a muscle in her back lifting a box, but I decided not to correct her.

"That's a shame." Lesley shifted in her seat. A lace doily slid off the armrest to land on the hardwood floor.

"Do you have a boyfriend?" Lesley waved her hand at me.

"Of course she doesn't," Oma snapped. "She's too young. She's a good girl."

I picked at my blue nail polish; an edge loosened and the chip drifted onto the floor. How long before Lesley served the iced tea?

\*\*\*\*

*I am eight years old. Since I have a cold, I am staying home from school. Dad is home, so I don't get to spend the day with Oma. When she watches me, we play games and I forget about being sick. Dad, however, keeps working on a new article while I watch TV.*

*"What would you like for lunch?" he asks.*

*"Garlic knots and dill pickles." My belly craves them.*

*"We don't have any. I'll make you some seaweed soup later." He returns to his office.*

*Oma calls. "How are you, honey?"*

*"Still stuffy." My nose runs, so I wipe it with a tissue. "I really want garlic knots and pickles, but there aren't any here."*

*She drives to the pizzeria for garlic knots and stops at the grocery store for pickles. After she brings them over, she sits with me in bed for the rest of the day. While I doze, she reads to me. I feel better, even if I still can't breathe through my nose.*

# Chapter 14

Iced tea haunted me. Ever since the visit to Lesley's, the beverage seemed to be everywhere. A huge sign hung in front of *Ann's*, advertising a special of iced tea and egg salad sandwiches. Every teacher at school seemed to carry around a cup of iced tea instead of the normal coffee thermoses. Even some of the students guzzled iced tea.

*Who has iced tea in autumn?* Puffy white flakes of the season's first snowfall drifted towards the ground, visible through the window of the school's computer lab. On the news, the weatherman assumed the children would trudge through snow on their trip from house to house next weekend during Halloween.

Every Halloween, I stayed home with my parents and Phebe. We watched black-and-white movies with bowls of popcorn. I could almost, but not quite, remember when we used to live in New Winchester, and I went trick-or-treating around the block. Mostly, I remembered snowflakes in the air and shaving cream sprayed across sidewalk squares.

Too bad Phebe couldn't come for Halloween. I'd asked Mama, promising to escort Phebe house to house with her bag for gathering candy.

"Absolutely not," Mama had said. Oma wouldn't want to watch Phebe while I was at school, and Mama couldn't get time off to accompany her upstate.

I tapped my lower lip with my green pen. Was I too old to go trick-or-treating? It would have to be alone, since I didn't have any friends, yet. Maybe I could hint to Matt. No, Matt was going to a party on Halloween. He'd already told me that at our lockers. I rubbed the crease forming between my eyebrows.

"Listen up," the computer teacher said. "We will be researching our family trees and creating PowerPoint presentations on them. Our school subscribes to some great search engines. Those are listed on the papers I passed out earlier."

The packet included systematic instructions on how to create the presentation, and the last page was a list of helpful sites, along with a doodle page to sketch my family tree.

"Excuse," a boy called.

"What is it, K'Paw?" the teacher asked.

"What if I don't know? I'm adopted."

"Don't worry, baby," his girlfriend cooed. "I'll help you with your current family. You know I *always* help you." She licked the edge of K'Paw's stubbly jaw when the teacher looked down at his desk. I stifled a gag.

"You have today dedicated for research, and next class, you'll start your PowerPoint. Then, the third class you present. If you need extra time, ask me for a pass to come in during lunch or study halls. Any questions?"

I gazed at my computer screen. The sign-in window was open, and in the dark blue background, my mirror image reflected. Brown hair hung limp around my face. I hadn't bothered to braid it last night, so the tresses lacked their usual waves. Two sparkles indicated where my glasses reflected the electronic glow.

The teacher clapped his hands. "Get to work."

I flipped to the last page of my school agenda, where I'd written my computer username and password. I typed them

129

into the system and shut my agenda as I waited for my information to load.

The girl next to me twirled her ponytail. She wore a white summer dress and kept pulling the hem over her bare thighs. How was she not freezing? Perfume oozed off her like a disease.

I folded back the first page of my assignment packet and pulled the cap off my pen, using my teeth. I spit the cap into my hand and scrawled my name on the correct family tree blank. The space branched into two areas. Beneath each blank space what family member's name belonged there was written in tiny font. Over where it said "mother," I wrote Mama's full name. Following that, I wrote Oma's maiden name, Leontien Kinbeer.

My information loaded, so I clicked on the Internet icon. The classmates chatted; some hadn't typed in their login information yet. I glanced at the teacher. He sat at his desk drinking iced tea from Dunkin' Donuts. A boy in the back of the room had his hand raised with a question, but the teacher hadn't looked up yet.

"I haven't gone tanning since last week," the girl in the summer dress complained to her friend.

"I went last night," her friend said.

I logged into the first search engine on the list. It utilized names to browse through old newspaper articles dating back to 1880. I used the school's provided password and login name, then typed Oma's maiden name into the search space. A timer came up, and I leaned back in my seat to wait.

The search finished, resulting in one match. I clicked on the link and an article came up. It was from 1930, about a woman named Lina Venus who had written a book about her ancestors.

I skimmed the article until my eyes landed on Oma's name. Back in 1850, Lina's grandmother had an uncle and aunt who had died from pneumonia, orphaning their only daughter. The daughter's name was Leontien Kinbeer.

That was Oma's name, only Oma hadn't been a child back in 1850. This girl was probably a relative, since the name couldn't be that common.

For the fun of it, I read on. Leontien had been set to move in with Lina's grandmother. Lina recounted how much her grandmother had looked forward to spending time with her American cousin.

Leontien had disappeared from her small town of Logan, New York. Authorities had no idea what had happened to her, and Lina's family had never learned the truth about the missing relative. Lina mentioned that, when she and her husband moved to America, she'd almost expected to meet Leontien, but she hadn't yet, and wouldn't know if she did, since no one knew what Leontien looked like.

Lina was probably dead now. The newspaper article portrayed her as a middle-aged woman back in the 1930's. Leontien would be gone now, too.

*Unless Leontien had been captured by the Goat Children.*

I laughed at my own silliness. The Goat Children were the imaginings of a woman who now had dementia and didn't understand reality versus fantasy. Oma might have heard about this other Leontien and used her in the book. After all, this Leontien's childhood was the one Oma had spoken of as her own. The loss of parents, the uncle in Holland, the disappearance before moving. Oma had taken another girl's story because she and that other girl shared the same name.

I tapped the stiletto heel of my boot against the tile floor. I exited that website and opened another. This one offered a service to members so they could build an electronic family tree, either public or private. I entered the school's offered password to browse the private genealogies and discovered one match for Leontien Kinbeer.

The family tree belonged to a man with the last name of Venus, and this Leontien Kinbeer was a distant cousin, the same girl Lina Venus had mentioned. Scanning the family tree, I spotted Lina as being the maker's grandmother.

I flipped over the packet and wrote down the names of the Leontien's parents.

This project was going to suck if I couldn't find the Leontien Kinbeer I needed. It would be fun to keep looking up this woman though, if only to find similarities.

\*\*\*\*

The snow still fell as I walked home from school, now a thin dusting – the flakes huge and fluffy. I caught one on my palm. The delicate crystalline shape melted against my flesh. I turned my hand over, flexing my fingers. The edges of my fingernails turned purple. I hadn't thought to wear mittens, and the fingerless gloves I wore in New York City were banned at the school because a gang used them to designate membership.

I slid my hands beneath my hair, cooling skin against heated scalp. I shivered at the delight, sighing as my scalp warmed my fingers. Some snowflakes clung to my hair where strands dangled over my face.

Squirrel and dog prints littered the sidewalk. One person had walked by wearing boots. I studied the star pattern left by the rubbery soles and stepped into one of them, removing my foot to study the contrast. My print was much smaller, with an oval behind belonging to my heel.

I walked backwards up the hill so I could watch my footprints form in the snow; fresh and crisp, untarnished yet by filth. Too soon, that filth would invade the pristine haven, staining it with darkness.

I took smaller steps since the man had moved with long strides. Cat prints joined in, but then the cat had moved off over a yard, abandoning the sidewalk.

Did Oma feel like that when she thought of her imagined world of the Goat Children? She'd adopted a teenage girl from the past to join her on the adventures. In fact, Oma had given that girl the adventures. What did the real Leontien think of as she stared down from Heaven?

I stepped off the sidewalk into the nearest yard. The man's footsteps had stopped. He hadn't walked off somewhere else. He hadn't turned around. He'd taken a step and disappeared.

*Impossible.*

I licked my chapped lips. Maybe some snow had fallen, hiding his tracks. I ran ahead to the driveway, but there were no footsteps there either, only the tracks of the dog I'd assumed the man had been walking.

I forced myself to laugh. What, had he started levitating?

A car drove by, tooting the horn. I jumped, landed on a hidden patch of ice beneath the snow, and spun sideways.

Cold wetness exploded around my face, biting my hands as I crashed into the ground. My messenger bag hit and flopped open, and a book slid out.

"Crap." I snatched the book from the snow to shake it. Flakes flew off. I stuffed it back into my bag. The car pulled into the next driveway. As I stood, brushing off my jeans, Michael opened the car door.

I expected him to wander down the street, asking if I needed help. It was his fault I'd fallen, after all, but Michael only stood next to his car with his hands in the pockets of his coat. I slung the strap of my bag over my shoulder and stepped out of the snow.

Snow soaked through my jeans. Oma had told me to wear winter boots, but I'd insisted I couldn't. I loved the way jeans looked with heels, and the knee boots were waterproof.

I snorted. So much for loving the way I looked.

"That was quite a fall," Michael drawled.

"Yeah, it hurt."

"How's your grandma doing?"

"Fine. Uncle Jan came over yesterday, saying mice always move in when the snow falls. He set up a mousetrap in the living room. I didn't believe him, but this morning, I found a huge rat squished in the trap. I called up Uncle Jan and made him promise to not just remove the rat, but purchase a humane trap in case there were any others." Remembering the gory sight, I shuddered anew.

"How's school?" Michael pulled a pack of cigarettes from his coat pocket.

"I didn't know you smoked." *You don't give a crap about my mouse story.*

"I quit." He spun a cigarette around his fingers before holding it to his lips, winking at me. "I just play with them a little. Bad habits are hard to break. Don't ever start smoking, kid."

"I won't." My heart skipped a beat as he licked the end. "I think it looks disgusting."

Michael chuckled. "So it does. I might be moving soon."

"Really?" I found it hard to swallow. He was odd, but when I thought of New Winchester, I pictured him as a part.

"Where are you going?" I kept my voice light, as if I didn't care.

"Places." He balanced the cigarette on his lips. "But really, my job is transferring. I might be moving to Alaska."

"What do you do for a living? I thought you worked at the library."

He flashed a grin, lifting the cigarette from his lips. "I'm a mercenary."

I leaned back on my heels. My panties were wet from the snow, clinging to my butt cheeks. "Ha ha, very funny. I'm serious. What do you do?"

"Fine then, don't believe me." Michael spun the cigarette through his fingers. "I still might be moving. I'll know in a month, maybe."

I turned away, to hide the anger at his proposed move. "Okay, but I have to get home now."

"You know," his voice drifted with the snowflakes, "if you ever want to just come over and hang out sometime, you can. I'm home when my car's here." He laughed. "I don't bring friends over, either."

"Okay." I increased my pace. Therefore, I wasn't his friend, since he never brought *friends* over.

Did he like me? At twenty-three, he was too old for me. Right?

What if Michael only wanted to get in my pants? I wanted to wait until I was married for sex, even if that seemed old-fashioned. Tiffany called it prudish.

I pulled open the screen door, propping it with my shoulder while I fitted the house key into the lock. I turned it, frowned, and turned the other way. It clicked.

The door had been unlocked.

I turned the key once more, unlocking it again. I pushed the door open and dropped my bag on the stairs as I stepped inside. "Oma, the door was unlocked!"

My heart stopped as a male voice said, "Company's here."

I grabbed a decorative snowman off the hall table and lifted it in front of me like a baseball bat for protection. I pictured Oma tied to a chair, gagged. The man might brandish a gun, but I would have to take a chance with that, no time to call 911.

The floor creaked beneath my feet, heels clicking against the wood. I swore under my breath, surrendering the chance for sneaking up on the intruder. I bolted into the living room swinging the snowman. "Get away from her!"

"Keziah," Oma gasped.

"Is this your granddaughter?" The man held his arms akimbo as he leaned against the fireplace.

Oma sat in the chair near him, glaring at me.

I tightened my hands around the snowman. The new mail carrier *was in the living room.*

"Get away from her," I repeated, softer this time.

The mailman looked from me to Oma.

"This was an interesting evening," he said. "I hope you take my words into account." He swung his gaze to me. "It was nice meeting you, my dear."

"What are you doing in the house?" I growled through clenched teeth.

He lifted his hands. "Am I in the house?"

Oma's eyebrows furrowed, as though she had no idea what was happening. The mailman was taking advantage of a senile old woman.

"I'm going to call the police." Still holding the snowman, I grabbed the portable phone off the table near the couch.

"My dear, put that down." Laughter remained in his voice. "There was a package your grandmother needed to sign for. I brought it in to make it easier for her. There has been no harm done."

"Where is this *package*?" I had a feeling it was illegal for mail carriers to bring packages into the house. Sweat broke out across my face.

"Why, right there." He swept his hand toward my mattress. I followed the movement with my gaze, and my jaw dropped open. A large box rested on the bed. That had *not* been there when I first came in. It was huge, able to fit a chair in there! I would've noticed it.

"Go ahead, read the label," he purred.

"Isn't that nice?" Oma asked.

I inched towards the bed. The label had our address, but the addressee was Rex Curatola—whoever he was—and the sender company was in Michigan.

"This isn't for us. This man doesn't live here."

"So he doesn't? That's what your grandmother was saying," the mailman said. "I will return it to the office and have everything straightened out."

He hefted the box as if it weighed no more than a feather. When his gaze met mine, they were dark and gray, so dark the pupils seemed to dissolve into the irises.

I gulped, backing towards the door.

"It was nice meeting you, Leontien," the mail carrier said too softly for Oma to hear. I ran to lock the door behind him. Once he got into his mail truck and drove away, I set down the snowman.

"I feel like I knew him a long time ago." Oma stroked the doorway with a blank look on her face. "He was an enemy, one of those against the Goat Children. He told me not to go back. There's going to be a war. There's always a war." Oma shook her head as she walked toward her bedroom. "I feel like I knew him before. Isn't that weird?"

I gnawed my lower lip. Maybe it was good for Oma to believe in her imagination.

Should I tell Mama about the mail carrier? No, I'd let it go unless it happened again. If Mama thought I couldn't take care of Oma, they would put Oma in a nursing home, and she wouldn't like it there. It was best this way.

\*\*\*\*

*I am nine years old. Oma takes me to the mall to get my ears pierced.*

*"She won't go through with it," Mama says, but I'll show her I will.*

"How come you don't have your ears pierced?" I ask Oma.

"Not too many girls got theirs done when I was little."

Oma helps me pick out a pair of studs in my birthstone. The woman who will use the piercing tool gives me a stuffed bear to hug, but I hold Oma's hand instead. My earlobes sting, yet I don't cry until after we're walking away from the pagoda.

Oma buys me a Sprite from the food court. We sit at one of the tables while I sip it. My head feels light, and I'm not sure if I can walk to the car without fainting.

"Pain is only in your mind." Oma strokes my shoulder. "Some people enjoy pain."

"I don't." The icy drink does make me feel clearer.

"My mother pierced her own ears," Oma says. "She used a sterilized needle and a cork."

"They didn't have a piercing gun?"

"Not back then."

If her mother could survive doing her own ears, then I can make it through this.

# Chapter 15

Oma pressed fifty dollars into my hand. "You have to have a Halloween costume. Be a princess." I might not be a princess, but I would love a costume to wear to school.

A thin layer of murky white covered the sidewalks as I walked to the mall. Bundled against the frosty wind, with cars rushing by, I stared at the houses and offices. Inside those houses were probably nuclear families: a mother, a father, and some kids. Then, there was me. I'd lost my nuclear family.

I shoved that thought aside. Oma needed me. Only that mattered.

At the mall, I visited *Hot Topic*. A black skirt and matching corset went well with the black lace Oma had at home, which I fastened around my neck with one of her cameos. Oma's elbow gloves finished off the outfit. I wasn't sure what I was, but I liked it. I was going to look awesome at school.

During math class, Meg, sitting behind me, tapped my shoulder. "Psst, hey."

"What?" I turned my head away from my worksheet.

"What are you supposed to be dressed up as?" Like always, Meg wore jeans and a Batman T-shirt.

"I'm a Goat Child," I said.

Meg lifted her eyebrow. "Cool. That's hot. I'm Batgirl. What's a Goat Child?"

I took a deep breath. "A mythical warrior woman who flies around in the sky on a Pegasus. She fights evil only she can see."

"That's different." Meg scratched her cheeks. "We're all going to a party tonight, over at my place on Munn. We might do some trick or treating, too. Why should kids get all the fun? You wanna come too?"

I licked my lips, tasting cherry lip-gloss. *Yes, yes, yes!* "I'd love to, but I don't think I can." Uncle Jan had brought over candy, and Oma expected me to pass it out to the children who came to the door. "I have to give out candy."

"Sure." Meg's frown said she didn't believe the excuse. "It'll be cool. Stop over if you change your mind."

*I can't change my mind.*

"Okay." I returned to my worksheet.

****

"This is so exciting," Oma rambled. "I'll sit on the bed, and I'll tell you when they come, then you can go to the door. Okay?"

"That's fine." I pulled back the curtain so Oma could see out. "You need new curtains," I said. The colors on the blue roses had faded, the hems ragged, and the material had rotted with age. I poked my finger through one of the holes, wiggling it to prove my point.

"Well." Oma snorted. "How nice of you to make me feel bad. You just can't give me one day, can you? You have to be the one in power."

"But, Oma, all I said was—"

"You just have to make me feel bad and old. Go away." A tear slid down my grandmother's cheek. "Just go away if you only want to make me feel bad."

"What do you think I said?" I groaned.

"Go away," Oma stretched her legs on the bed, shoes catching in the comforter.

I wanted to scream at Oma to stop talking. I wanted to tell her to make sense again. Instead, I stormed out of the room. It wouldn't help to yell at her. My grandmother couldn't help the way she was.

A sentence followed me into the hallway.

"Where has my little Kezy gone?"

**\*\*\*\***

The first trick-or-treaters knocked ten minutes before five o'clock in the evening; little boys dressed like pumpkins and carrots with huge smiles and rosy cheeks. Snow clung to their costumes.

"Aren't you adorable?" I propped open the door with my hip as I leaned out.

"Cold out," the mother called from the sidewalk.

I dropped a miniature candy bar into each of the baskets held out by two children.

"What do you say?" the mother asked when the boys turned away.

"Thank you," the small voices chimed.

I smiled. "You're welcome." I shut the door and set the bowl of candy back on the hall table.

"What are you doing?" Oma hovered in the doorway to the kitchen, nibbling on potato chips.

"Handing out candy." I wrote two tally marks on the notepad to designate the two trick-or-treaters. "What?"

"It's Halloween." I snapped the cap onto the pen. "Those were the trick-or-treaters."

"But no one knocked."

"Yeah, they did."

"You didn't tell me it was Halloween. I was going to sit in the bedroom and watch."

More knocks sounded at the front door; a group of five children this time, three mothers standing at the sidewalk chatting. The children wore glow-rings around their necks.

"Isn't that cute? You all match." I dropped a piece of candy into each of their plastic bags, colored to look like pumpkins.

"Happy Halloween." I drew the bowl of candy away from the children, but one of the boys lunged and seized a handful. He stuffed the candies into his bag as he ran off the porch.

"Hey! You can't just steal candy," I yelled.

The other children laughed, running after their friend. The parents remained intent on their private conversation. I glared at them before swinging my gaze up the street. Through the branches of the front magnolia tree, I spotted the next group of trick-or-treaters.

What a weird holiday. It held its background in evilness, yet people encouraged kids to love it. Those kids went to the houses of complete strangers begging for sweets.

Footprints in the snow remained on the front walkway and porch. I gave the new set of children their candy, careful to keep the bowl out of reach.

"Keziah," Oma shouted from the bedroom.

I almost dropped the candy as I ran in. "What's the matter? What is it?"

"I saw a squirrel." Oma pointed out the bedroom window. "He ran up the tree and into the roof."

"Huh?"

"The squirrel went into the roof. What's the matter? Are you deaf?" Oma's voice dripped with sarcasm.

"No." I hid my fists behind my back. "The squirrel can't get into the attic."

"It did. Go up and look."

"The squirrel probably just ran *across* the roof. They do that all the time. They can't get into the attic. There aren't any holes."

"Go look." Oma grabbed the flashlight she kept next to the bed. "Or I'll look."

Oma might fall over the junk up there and get hurt. I glanced out the window, but didn't see any approaching trick-or-treaters.

"Here, I'll go look." I held out my hand for the flashlight.

"Good. We'll have Jan make sure they can't get in anymore." Oma smirked.

I left the hall light on and checked through the door to make sure no one was on the way to the house. I hadn't noticed how warm it was downstairs until I ascended the stairs. Without any insulation upstairs, the temperature dropped about ten degrees. I lifted the hook on the door and pulled it open by the handle while pressing the button on the flashlight to turn on the bulb. The yellowish glow illuminated the gloomy attic. As I stepped inside, I wondered if I should be scared.

I wasn't, though. There couldn't be anyone up there, and the squirrels weren't getting in. I stepped forward, and the wood creaked beneath my slippers. I nudged a shoebox. I walked to the vanity and shone the flashlight at the mirror, seeing only me and the beam of light so bright it made me blink. I was about to look away when I noticed something else reflecting in the mirror: a wardrobe. Taller than me by a foot, it rose above the other contents of the attic.

Picking my way around old boxes and stacks of magazines, I wound toward the wardrobe and shone the flashlight on the brass clasp. I swept the beam downward and the glow rested on a scratch. I squinted, leaning over to study it. Someone had tried to scrawl a word, but the scratches were uneven and discernable. I moved the beam and saw the scratches everywhere across the wood.

I turned the clasp to open the door. Maybe it would be a werewolf about to lash out or an old wedding gown. Two garments hung on a metal rod, one black, the other orange. I separated them, shining the flashlight on an orange dress with a frilly collar and a black velveteen coat.

A cardboard box rested at the bottom of the wardrobe with green shoes on top. I took the shoes off and opened the cardboard box. A layer of gritty dust clung to my palm, and I wiped it on my jeans. The box contained spiral notebooks. I lifted out the top one, the paper old and yellowed.

Someone pounded on the front door and yelled, "Trick-or-treat."

I stumbled out of the attic, closing the door and latching it. Leaving the notebook on the stairs, I grabbed the candy bowl and opened the front door.

Five teenagers greeted me. The boys thrust pillowcases out, one of them grunting the classic "trick-or-treat," and the rest guffawing. Unless the gorilla masks counted, they lacked costumes.

"Can I give you a treat?" one of the boys asked when I passed out the candy.

I glared at him, which made them guffaw like hyenas again. They kept laughing as I slammed the door.

I retrieved the notebook and leaned against the wall. The cover felt dirty, had a bent corner, and smelled of cigarette smoke. I opened to the first page and read the heading. *1980, Chapter One.*

Age had faded the penciled words and yellowed the paper. I read aloud in a whisper:

> *The day was rainy, that day I was born, but I don't remember it. I was a baby, but my mother always told me about the rain. It came down like cats and dogs, and she always said that's why I love cats. We always had a cat growing up. That's what I remember most about those days.*
>
> *Then, I became one of them, the Gootchiluns.*

"Gootchiluns?" I repeated the word.

*Goat children!* Oma had said "gootchiluns," and I'd misheard.

I flipped through the other pages in the notebook. They were written similarly, broken into chapters. Oma *had* written down her story. She'd gone to so much effort, used so much imagination, that it was no wonder she believed it to be truth now. As I flipped back to the first page, someone knocked on the front door. Meg from class stood on the porch with five other people covered in silly string.

"Hey, Keziah." Meg grinned. "I didn't know you lived here. Small world."

A boy behind her sang the *Small World* song in a high voice.

"Hi, Meg." I peered at the other faces. Covered in Halloween make-up, no one except Meg looked familiar. She'd smeared fake blood over her face and neck, and her clothes were all in crimson.

"Come on and join us." Meg clapped. "It'll be a blast."

"But you have to wear orange," a boy dressed in turquoise said. "We don't have anyone in orange yet."

I pictured the orange dress upstairs in the wardrobe. "Um, I can't. I have to pass out candy."

"Let your parents do it," a girl in hunter green, with a lit cigarette pressed between her lips, said.

"My parents don't live here."

"You live alone?" The hunter green girl swayed and burped. "You got any beer? I could go for a beer right now, or tequila. You got any tequila?"

"No. I live with my grandmother." I wanted to add that she was drunk enough, but pointing out the obvious wouldn't help.

"That sucks," She meant living with my grandmother sucked, or the lack of beer and tequila.

"Hey look," a boy jumped over Oma's row of rosebushes lining the walkway and whipped a can of shaving cream from his coat. He shook it, and sprayed the white foam over the trunk of the magnolia tree.

"*Hey.*" I pushed open the screen door to shove past Meg. "Don't do that."

"It's Halloween." He finished his makeshift drawing of a penis.

My fuzzy slipper fell off as I climbed over the porch railing, snow soaking through my jeans, and grabbed his arm. "That's vandalism!"

"So?" he asked.

Matt, my locker neighbor. My steps backpedaled, snow-covered leaves crunching beneath my feet.

"Aren't we going to get any candy?" Matt shook his can again.

"N-n-no," I sputtered. "You can't spray shaving cream on people's trees."

"Happy Halloween," a girl screamed from the porch.

I turned to look and silly string sprayed into my face. Laughter scalded my ears and my face turned beet red.

"See you in school," Meg called as her gang strolled to the sidewalk.

The silly string, sticky and cold, stung my skin. Tears pricked my eyes. This was what Mama had warned me about, the teasing by other children.

No way was this *teasing*.

"Watch out," I muttered, "or the Goat Children will come after you."

\*\*\*\*

*I am six years old. It is Halloween night, and I am supposed to go trick-or-treating with a girl from school. Her mother is taking us.*

*The phone rings. Mama answers it, but the caller is the girl. "My mom's going out tonight, so I can't go with you."*

*I cry in the living room. Oma wipes my eyes and then fixes my green face paint. I am dressed as the Wicked Witch of the West.*

*"I'll take you," Oma says, since Mama is passing out candy and Dad is away.*

*I make Oma dress up as a gypsy, in lots of colorful scarves. We walk around the block. She stays on the sidewalk while I run up to the house to ring the doorbell or knock. At the end of the night, I have my pumpkin bag filled with goodies.*

*Oma and I watch a movie and sneak a few, since Mama only allows one candy per day.*

# Chapter 16

"Hello. Keziah?" The guidance counselor peered at me over coke-bottle glasses.

"How are things going?"

"Okay." I read *Mrs. Rosnay* off the name plaque.

"I checked your file and noticed you didn't join any sports or clubs. Can I ask why?"

I almost corrected the counselor by saying the correct word was *may*, not *can*. "I don't have time."

"Everyone has time."

"I take care of my grandmother. She needs me after school."

"And you need to make time for yourself. You're only young once." The counselor tapped a pen against her lower lip.

"I have a familial responsibility. I can't be away from her that long."

"I'm going to call your parents and discuss it with them," Mrs. Rosnay said. "In the meantime, I noticed you wrote on your college dreams paper you want to be an elementary teacher."

I nodded.

"There's a club we have called Teachers of our Future, or TOOF." Mrs. Rosnay laughed as if that was funny. "It meets during school hours and goes to the elementary wing to help out classes whenever there's a study hall. Here's the info."

I accepted the paper.

"You can speak to Mr. Krainski now, if you like. He's in charge of computer technicians. His office is just down the hall from here." Mrs. Rosnay stabbed her pen at me. "TOOF looks great on college resumes."

I had no idea how TOOF could look great on anything, but the concept of helping elementary classrooms sounded fun. Not wanting to go back to economics class, I sought out Mr. Krainski's technician office, the next room after the counseling office.

I rapped my knuckles on the open door. "Hello, Mr. Krainski?" The room consisted of a desk and bookshelves. Instead of books, they were covered in boxes with wires hanging out.

The black-haired man at the desk looked up. "Yeah?"

"Mrs. Rosnay sent me over. She wants me to join TOOF. I'm Keziah de Forest."

His weathered face broke out into a smile that reminded me of a seaman returned from a voyage.

"Excellent. Just let me know when your study halls are, and I'll talk to the elementary teachers. Any preference in grade?"

I shook my head. "No."

"Excellent. You'll be easy to place." His gaze roamed me from head to foot, frowning at my combat boots and lace corset. "You just have to make sure to always wear professional clothing whenever you go. Keep your hair short or tied back. Wear dresses or dress pants, nothing sleeveless. Wear blouses and jackets. Will this be a problem?"

"No." I could walk to the mall if the snow held off.

"No cussing. No talking back. Do whatever the teacher wants. Understand?"

"Yes, sir."

"Excellent." He smiled broader. "Usually we don't take newbies after September, but Mrs. Rosnay mentioned your case to me the other day, so I'll make an exception."

I wanted to ask what exactly my case was, but I kept my mouth shut.

"And," Mr. Krainski continued, "we meet every Monday, Wednesday, and Friday at lunch to discuss what's been going on in the classrooms."

My heart dropped into my stomach.

"We meet in the back room of the library," he said. "The librarians don't care as long as we clean up after ourselves, but future teachers are always tidy."

"Mr. Krainski, I can't meet at lunch. I have to go home and feed my grandmother."

He blinked. "What do you mean?"

"If don't go home at lunch, she won't eat." That sounded weird. "She has dementia," I blurted out.

He shook his head. "I'm sorry, Miss Keziah. I can't make an exception for you. We meet to discuss what's going on. That's the point of TOOF. We're a *group*. We have to act like one. Teachers need to work together. I'm sure you understand."

"Yes." I groaned. "I understand."

"Let me know if your situation changes." He shuffled the papers on his desk.

I left feeling numb.

\*\*\*\*

I sat in the back of global history class and rubbed my hand over my face, taking off my glasses to massage the corners of my eyes. A headache started to build pressure.

The desk next to mine creaked and a male voice said, "Hi."

I peered through my fingers at the blurry blob of a boy surrounded by pale gray walls.

"Hey," I muttered.

"You're Meg's friend."

"No." I put my glasses back on.

"Cool panties."

I squeaked, jerking upright in my chair, and yanked the edge of my turtleneck over the back of my jeans, glaring at him while I adjusted my corset vest. He drew back his lips to show uneven teeth. He had nice lips, though, perfectly sculpted, like the lips of a cherub.

"Sorry. I couldn't help myself." He had a nasally voice, but those lips made up for it. "That was mean of them to spray you like that, but they were drunk. You can't blame them for being drunk."

"Were you drunk?" His hair, or what was left since he had a buzz cut, was chocolaty brown.

"I don't drink beer. I'm allergic to wheat."

I wondered if that was a joke. "That sucks."

"I'm Domenick."

"Keziah." I hoped he wouldn't try to shake my hand, and he didn't disappoint.

"I've been really bored lately." He stretched out his arms and cracked his knuckles. "My parents are looking at new houses. They want to move over the summer."

"To where?" I hoped he would stop talking soon, but didn't want to act rude.

"Buffalo."

"Oh," I said.

"That's by Niagara Falls."

"I know where it is."

"Yeah, I figured you would. You got a boyfriend?"

I tore my eyes away from his lips again. "No."

"Got a girlfriend?"

"I don't like girls like that."

"I do." He waggled his eyebrows. "You wanna go to the mall sometime?"

"Um…"

"Like a date."

No one had ever asked me out on a date before. I opened and shut my mouth, then licked my lips. He was nice, and I wanted to say yes, but what would Oma say?

"I'm b-b-busy a lot," I stammered, "but I'd like to go sometime. I live with my grandmother. She's got dementia, so she needs me a lot."

"That's cool. I get it. Maybe over break for Thanksgiving?"

"My parents are coming up from the city, but yeah, sure. Um, how about I give you my cell number?" My heart raced. I could be like Tiffany, swamped with love.

I tore off a corner of my notebook page and scribbled down my name and number, and passed it to him. "Text me over the weekend. They don't come until Wednesday."

"Cool." He lifted one side of his mouth in a lopsided grin. "I'll make sure to text you."

Domenick waggled his eyebrows again, and I giggled before hiding behind my essay.

**\*\*\*\***

*I am ten years old. It is summer vacation, and we take a trip to an amusement park in Pennsylvania. Dad can't go, since he has work.*

*Mama keeps grinning. "I haven't been here in ages. I was a teenager then."*

*"She had to go on every ride twice," Oma tells me.*

*Mama laughs, so I laugh with her. I don't feel well, though. My stomach hurts. I tell myself I'll feel better after we get inside, but after five minutes, I feel worse.*

*"I think I'm sick."*

*Oma feels of my forehead. "Hmm, you do have a fever. We should leave."*

*"But we just got here," Mama says. "We already paid for your tickets, and they were expensive."*

*"You stay. I'll take Keziah back to the hotel. If she feels better, we'll find you. If not, I'll come pick you up at eight."*

*"Okay." Mama hugs me. "Feel better, honey."*

*The hotel room's air conditioning does make me feel better, but soon I have a sore throat and can't stop coughing.*

*Oma frowns. "Promise you won't leave this room."*

*"I promise," I say.*

*Oma walks across the street to a cafe and buys me a hot mint tea. I sip it and feel better, but for the rest of the trip, I stay in the room with Oma while Mama visits the tourist sites.*

# Chapter 17

"No." Oma laughed. "Don't be a loose woman. You can't go to the mall with Domenick."

My hands trembled. "Why can't I go?"

Oma laughed again. "I'm responsible for you, and you stay right here where I can see you. I know what you'd be doing out there."

"But, Oma!" The veins in my forehead throbbed. "That's not fair. I won't do anything bad, and you wanted me to go out before." There'd been that little boy on the sidewalk.

"You'll be doing *bad* things," Oma said. "You'll smoke, do drugs, drink, and be rude. You'll put on makeup and short skirts."

"I wear makeup every day."

"Are you trying to break my heart?" Oma turned away, but reached for the wall to steady herself. She drew a deep breath and continued to the bedroom with her face pinched, tears on her cheeks.

I stomped into the living room and threw myself on the bed. My cell phone slid off my pillow like a sign.

Mama answered on the third ring. "What's wrong, sweetheart?"

I sniffled. "How do you know something's wrong?"

"Is it Oma?" Mama's voice trembled. "Is she hurt?"

I rubbed my hot cheeks. "Oma's okay, I guess. This guy in class asked me to go to the mall with him on Saturday…"

"Keziah, that's great. What's his name?"

"Domenick. So then—"

"I know I don't have to ask if he's a nice boy. I trust you, Keziah."

"That's the thing. Oma doesn't! She said I can't go, and now she's in the bedroom crying."

Silence. Mama's breathing rasped.

"Mommy?"

"Oma doesn't want you to grow up. I wasn't allowed to date, either. I had to wait until I was out of college."

"Then you met Dad?"

Pause. "Yes, then I met your father. When he'd bring me flowers, Oma would throw them out. She wouldn't let him call, so he'd have to come to the door to talk to me. Oma had a difficult childhood."

"Huh?"

"I don't think she was ever given much attention, so this is how she makes up for it. Does that make sense?"

*No.* "Sure, I guess so. Yeah." My nose burned with tears. "But what about Domenick? It's not fair. Why can't I go out? I've never been on a date before."

"Keziah." Mama sighed. "I don't want you lying to me *ever*, but I know how Oma can be. Tell her you have to go to the library to study. Whatever you do, make sure he doesn't pick you up at Oma's. He has a car, right?"

"Um, I don't know. I can ask him."

"Whatever you do, make sure Oma doesn't see you leave with him. Now, you'll be good, won't you?"

"Of course," I promised.

"I'll see you at Thanksgiving."

"I love you guys." I hated lying, but I would lie to Oma about Saturday.

\*\*\*\*

157

Domenick picked me up at the library. Walking around the block to meet him seemed like I was really doing something bad.

As I read the back of a historical novel, a hand tapped my shoulder.

I jumped, glancing up to see Domenick. "Hello!" I set the novel back with a little too much force; a corner of the cover bent.

"So I was thinking we could go back to my house and play video games or watch a movie."

"I thought we were going to the mall." The automatic doors slid open as we exited the building.

"We can, but I was just at the mall, and I figured we could get to know each other better at my place."

*He wants to make out.* I licked my lips. "Are your parents home?"

"They're over at my aunt's. Nobody's home. If you really want to, we can go to the mall. Whatever you want to do is fine." The tops of his cheeks seemed to reddened. Adorable. Usually I was the one blushing.

The mall would be loud, so we couldn't talk, and I didn't want to poke at clothes. Guys didn't like clothes shopping.

"Okay, let's go to your house. That sounds fun." I tried to smile, except my lips felt tight. He didn't seem the type to push me into kissing if I said no.

Slush slickened the parking lot. My feet slid when I opened the door to his green jeep, and I hit the side of the car. Mud and salt from the road smeared across my coat.

*Great.* Was I going to get his car seat dirty? Peering through the window, I saw an empty bag from McDonald's on the floor. At least he wasn't spotless.

Keith Urban played through the stereo system. I hated country music. Tiffany had once said country singers only sang about love lost, their trucks, their tractors, and their dogs. This particular song was about a man losing his truck.

I wanted to compliment him on his jeep, but the seats were stained and mud streaked everything. "It's cool you've got a driver's license."

"Thanks." He slid his hands on the steering wheel to turn down a street. "I got it when I was sixteen. You don't have one, do you? People in the big city don't usually drive."

Domenick slid into silence as he concentrated on the road. Was I making him nervous? That thought sent a thrill through my blood, and I smiled.

He turned into a driveway. "Here we are."

"Is this still New Winchester?"

"The outskirts of it, but yeah." He parked the car in front of a two-stall garage. "Home sweet home, you know?"

Snow crunched under our feet as I followed Domenick to the front door. Potted plants, dead now, lined the walkway and light-up reindeer stood in the yard.

"Isn't it a little early for Christmas decorations?" I asked.

"Huh?" He fitted the key into the lock and turned it with a grunt.

I poked at one of the dead, brown plants with my toe. "The deer in the front yard. Isn't it a little early to have them out?"

The top of the withered plant broke off. I sucked breath through my teeth and jerked my foot away. Domenick had his back turned, so I hoped he hadn't seen.

"They're just decorations." He pushed open the door and stepped inside with a stiff bow. "Welcome to my humble domain, my lady."

The house smelled like cat pee and vanilla. The vanilla, emitting from a plug-in at the wall, failed to overpower the unpleasantness, only making it more intense. I almost gagged, covering my reaction by wiping my hand across my nose as if it itched. The sleeve of my coat slid over my mouth as I slid off my boots.

Domenick pulled off his ski jacket and threw it over the hallway radiator.

"Isn't that going to catch on fire?" I pointed at the radiator.

"Nah, it hasn't yet." He wandered into the next room: the kitchen. Dishes overflowed the sink. Papers and a laptop covered the table.

"You want something to eat? There's some pizza in the fridge."

"No, I'm good." I peeled off my black coat and set it over the back of a kitchen chair. "Um, do you have a cat?"

"We used to. My grandmother took him."

I waited for an elaboration, but none came. Had no one cleaned the cat pee? Oma's house might have dust bunnies and peeling paint, but it didn't smell.

He opened the refrigerator and took out a bottle of Gatorade. "Want one?"

"I'm not a big fan of Gatorade. I don't work out enough for all that sodium."

"He snapped his fingers. "You're hot and as skinny as a stick. You gotta be kidding. I bet you work out all the time."

I licked my lips; his eyes riveted on them and he lifted a brow.

I turned my head away. "Thanks."

"Let's go watch a movie in the basement." He unscrewed the lid and chewed on the edge of his plastic bottle.

Was the cellar going to stink, too?

"Come on, my lady." He motioned with his bottle.

I trailed him into the next room, a dining area. A crystal chandelier hung over the middle of the huge table. This room had a vanilla plug-in too, and scattered painting supplies.

"My brother paints." Domenick opened a door and switched on a light. "Right this way, mademoiselle."

Hippie orange carpeting covered the steps. They moaned like banshees as we descended into the depths. The air grew cooler with each step down.

"Welcome to my hide-out." Stuffing seeped out of the cushions of two couches; cat claw marks streaked the fabric. A large screen TV rested over an assortment of video game devices. The cellar also contained a card table surrounded by chairs, stacks of hardcover books, and colorful dice.

"*Dungeons and Dragons*. Ever play?" Domenick asked.

"Isn't that the game that makes people kill themselves?"

"No." He pulled DVD boxes off a bookshelf. "What movie do you want to watch?"

A movie meant sitting closer together, our shoulders touching. Spit dried in my mouth. Was I ready for my first make out session?

No, I didn't even know this guy.

"We could play video games," I said.

"You like 'em? Most girls don't." He took a long sip of the Gatorade.

"My sister and I are always racing each other at home."

"I have some racing games." He set the DVD stack on the floor. "How old is your sister?"

"Seven." I sat on the edge of the couch. and tugged the heart pompom on the back of my ankle sock for something to do with my hands.

"Is she staying here with your grandmother, too?" He knelt in front of the *PlayStation 3* to fiddle with wires.

"No. My grandmother…doesn't like her all that much."

"Really?" He looked up. "How come?"

I opened my mouth, but I wasn't sure what to say that wouldn't make Oma sound heartless. "My grandmother's weird."

"What do you mean?"

I paused. Where to start? I began by talking about the phone call from Uncle Jan saying Oma showed signs of suffering from dementia.

\*\*\*\*

*I am nine years old when a bookstore opens in New Winchester. Oma and I go for the Grand Opening. They give away free bookmarks, so I take one for Mama.*

*"Here's fifty dollars." Oma hands me the bill. "Get whatever you want."*

*We spend two hours in the children's section looking through books. I finally select a few, and one classic,* Around the World *by Jules Verne.*

*"This is for us to read when I spend the night."*

*"Excellent choice."*

*I take an extra bookmark and keep it in the classic.*

# Chapter 18

I didn't want to be home. I'd rather stay with Domenick, who listened, but instead I had to deal with Oma. At least I got to look forward to my parents and sister coming for Thanksgiving.

My stomach muscles felt tight, and the insides ached. I slid my hand beneath the hem of my shirt to press my cold palm against my hot belly. *Please don't throw up, Kez.*

"How long am I supposed to wait?" Oma called from the bedroom. "I've been sitting here for hours. I want to lie down. This is ridiculous!"

"Mommy called from the bus station. They should be here any minute." I dropped the sheer curtain at the front door to walk to the bedroom.

"I don't see why they have to come *here* for Thanksgiving," Oma muttered.

"We're going to Uncle Jan's for Thanksgiving," I corrected. "They're just staying here for a few days."

"Aren't you enough? I'm already stuck with you." Oma snorted.

I hoped deep down, my grandmother liked my presence.

I touched my stomach again. It took a lot to make me nervous, but my parents and Phebe coming to stay did it. What if they didn't like the way I took care of Oma?

Uncle Jan's car pulled into the driveway. "They're here!"

Oma huffed as I ran to the front door. I flipped the lock and yanked it open. Mindless of the slippers I wore, I catapulted off the porch. The thin soles stepped on ice, and I landed on my bottom, snow soaking through my pants.

"Are you okay?" Phebe's voice carried across the front yard.

I rocked to my knees and stood, brushing off my butt. Phebe raced up the sidewalk and across the front walkway, her face aglow. I caught my sister in my arms, her little legs wrapping around my waist as her little arms wound around my neck. Soft kisses rained over my face.

I staggered against the porch, snow slipping off the roof to fall over our heads and down the collar of my shirt. I laughed with Phebe.

Something caught my attention at the front door, and when I looked, I caught Oma glaring daggers at my little sister. I tightened my arms.

****

"None of you are sleeping in the bedroom upstairs," Oma said.

Other than that scathing announcement, she spoke next to nothing, but there were glares aplenty, multiple snorts, and huffs. The rest of the time was spent in silence.

My parents slept on my mattress in the living room. Phebe and I shared the couch.

It was amazing to be able to see them, not just hear their voices over the telephone. Oma took up so much of my thoughts that I hadn't realized how much I missed them. Dad told nonsensical jokes that sent everyone into hysterics— everyone except Oma. She refused to say a single word to him.

Mama rolled up her sleeves and got out the pail. She scrubbed the kitchen from floor to ceiling, and set to work on the bathroom. She scrubbed the entire downstairs, and all the while, Oma flapped her hands.

"You're just doing this to make me pay you. I won't pay you. You can't have my money. Stop pretending my house is dirty." She shut herself in the bedroom.

I spent my days sitting on the bed next to my grandmother watching television. Despite the snow, Phebe spent most of her time in the backyard.

Whenever Oma noticed Phebe, she spouted a rude remark. "Why does that *thing* have to run around? It could really use some self-control."

"She doesn't mean it," I promised Phebe, but my sister nodded without speaking.

Oma had said the same things since Phebe was born, way before she'd developed dementia.

Time dragged. I wanted to hang out with Domenick again, but I needed to spend as much time with my family as possible.

When Thanksgiving arrived, Oma refused to go to the restaurant.

"Please," Mama begged. "It won't be the same if you don't come out with us. Jan and everyone are going."

"Then how much fun is that going to be?" Oma squawked. "No one will talk to me. I'll be all alone."

"Everything doesn't have to revolve around you," Dad muttered.

"What?" Oma narrowed her eyes at him. "What did you say?" When he didn't repeat the words, she rounded on me. "What did that *man* say?"

"He wants you to go with us," I shouted.

"Please," Mama added. "You need to go. It's *Thanksgiving*. You used to love Thanksgiving."

Oma huffed, yet she allowed Mama to pick out clothes. My grandmother had stopped eating as much as usual. For lunch, she refused anything other than yogurt. The blue dress that had once fit her now hung off her body.

"You really need to start eating more." Mama tugged on the straps of the dress, yet the front still sagged, and the white turtleneck underneath bagged under Oma's arms.

"I eat a lot. I'm fat."

"Oma isn't fat." Phebe tugged at the Peter Pan collar of her velveteen dress. I hushed her in case our grandmother had a cruel comment about that.

Mama tried to get Oma into a pair of skin-tone pantyhose, but she refused. "They bunch. They ride down. I'm not wearing them."

"We're late." Dad tapped his watch over Oma's head, lifting his eyebrows at Mama.

In the end, Oma wore a pair of black sweatpants beneath the dress.

"She's old," Mama whispered. "People will understand. The elderly are always eccentric."

"Come on," I reached for Oma's hand. "Uncle Jan's going to be waiting for us at the restaurant."

"Where's my purse?"

"Here it is." Mama held it up. "I've got it. Come on, let's go. I'll lock up."

"Don't take my money." Oma clung to me as we meandered to her car.

Phebe bounced in the backseat.

"I'm going to fall." As Oma shuffled through the snow, it heaped and fell over the tops of her boots.

"Keziah, why can't you shovel?" Mama exclaimed. "Is it so hard to shovel? I always shoveled when I was your age."

I'd shoveled last night. This snow had fallen since then, but I knew Mama's frustration made her snippy. A squirrel ran over a magnolia branch above our heads, snow shaking free. Cold whiteness plopped onto our heads.

"You're trying to kill me!" Oma flapped her arms as I helped her into the front passenger seat.

"People are going to think we really are," Mama grumbled as we slid into the backseat.

I sat in the middle.

"You're elbowing me," Phebe complained.

"This is my car." Oma's face reddened.

No one answered.

"Did you ask if you could drive *my car*? No, you never ask. You're a *bumpkin*."

"What's a bumpkin?" Phebe questioned.

"So now you're going to talk quietly in the backseat so I can't hear?" Oma ranted. "Nice. Real nice."

"I was asking you, too," Phebe shouted.

I squeezed my sister's hand, shaking my head; no point in arguing with Oma.

"You're the sweetest family in the world," Oma said with sarcasm.

Mama fished a notebook and pen out of her purse, and passed them over to me. I flipped open to the first blank page and wrote the definition for bumpkin before handing the notebook to Phebe. We filled up three pages with messages by the time Dad pulled into the parking lot for the restaurant.

167

"Crowded, isn't it?" Mama said, but Oma didn't answer.

Dad dropped her off at the entrance. I waited with her, Oma sitting on a bench next to an Indian woman who tried to converse, except her deep accent prevented Oma from understanding.

"What?" Oma demanded.

The Indian woman looked away with pursed lips.

The restaurant specialized in Greek dishes, but every Thanksgiving they hosted a buffet. Uncle Jan's wife had insisted on the location.

A chandelier hung from the ceiling of the front foyer, reminding me of Domenick's urine-soaked house. He would move away if his parents has their way. Michael might move too, and I would still be with Oma, but friendless.

"You make me look like an invalid." Oma shuffled across the red carpet as I held her arm. "I can walk perfectly fine. Stop clinging to me like that."

"It's what the Goat Children would want me to do."

"Shush. Do you want people to overhear?" Oma yelled.

Dad gave our name to the hostess, and she escorted us through the spacious restaurant to a backroom where Uncle Jan's group waited.

"You're late," his wife snapped.

"We're sorry, Marta." Mama nodded towards Oma. "There were a few difficulties at home."

Aunt Marta rolled her eyes. "Difficulties could've been dealt with later. We don't have all day." Aunt Marta, ever a ray of sunshine.

"Here, Oma." I pulled out a seat. "You can sit here. I'll fill your plate for you." The air smelled of flowers and pita bread. I loved the restaurant already.

"Will you get me things I like?" Oma lifted her upper lip in what might have been a sneer. "Will they be things I can chew?"

"I know what you like." I helped Oma settle into the seat and set her purse beneath the chair.

Aunt Marta had already filled a plate, but Uncle Jan and their son, Jim, rose. Jim's long hair now sported a buzz cut, and he wore a fuzzy penguin sweater I guessed his mother had bought. It ruined his usual rocker look.

"So, what do you think of Mom?" Uncle Jan asked as we left the room for the buffet table.

My heartbeat increased; I wanted to hear what Mama answered.

Jim tapped my shoulder. "What's up, kid-o? Been to any wild parties here?"

"No." I glanced down when Phebe slid her hand through mine.

"Don't like parties?"

"I, um, haven't been invited." I imagined a bunch of teenagers getting drunk, high, and hooking up. Guys playing beer pong and girls making out with each other wasn't my idea of fun.

"No new friends? No good going to a new school?" Jim grinned.

I wondered if he found my antisocial attitude amusing. "Something like that."

"Nah, probably nothing around here compares to the city."

I wanted to say I wasn't into the party scene like he was. I didn't like getting so drunk I didn't know what my name was and had to spend the night at Tiffany's so my parents wouldn't find out. I also didn't like talking to complete strangers who all acted like idiots. Those reasons sounded dumb, though. Usually I didn't care what other people thought of me, but I didn't want my cool, older cousin to think I was a loser.

"Yeah. Everything around here just seems so tame." I winked and flashed a grin, hoping I looked mischievous. "There really is nothing like a party in the city."

"You never go to parties," Phebe said.

I rolled my eyes at Jim, and mouthed, "Sisters."

"Take the bus up to Syracuse sometime." Jim chuckled. "My new apartment is awesome. I'll show you a good time."

"Sounds like fun." My voice squeaked on "fun," and he laughed.

We arrived at the buffet table, so I picked up a plate. It was warm from the dishwasher, with a few beads of water still clinging. I handed it to Phebe.

"Sweetie, come up here, and I'll help you," Mama called.

"But I wanna be with Kez," Phebe whined.

"It's okay. I'll watch her." I picked up two plates, one for me and the other for Oma. It was a challenge to pick out tender foods Oma would eat and keep Phebe from spilling everything, all the while finding food I liked. Most of the dishes contained meat, and nothing was labeled vegetarian, like it was at my favorite buffet in the city. Phebe almost took a piece of souvlaki before I caught her hand. "That's lamb."

When we returned to the table, Jim now he sat beside Oma. She used her fork to pick at a piece of apple pie.

I set the plate I'd prepared in front of Oma and moved the pie away. "Here's your food. Where'd the pie come from?"

"I got it for her." Jim's teeth were bright when he grinned. "I remembered how much she loved apple pie." His gaze brushed past her to me. "When I was little, she used to watch me and my brothers before our parents came home from work. There'd always be an apple pie sitting around."

I couldn't remember Oma ever eating pie, but I nodded.

"I'm never allowed to eat dessert first." Phebe stabbed a hunk of feta cheese with her fork and popped it into her mouth.

"Don't eat, Phebe. We haven't said grace yet." I placed my hand over hers.

"Where's my pie?" Oma slapped me away when I tried to shred her lettuce with a knife. "Where'd you put it?"

"It's right there. You can have it after you eat."

"I don't want this." Oma shoved the plate away. It hit her water glass and knocked it over. Water and ice spilled over the white linen tablecloth.

"Shoot!" I bolted to my feet and snatched the basket of pita bread away from the spreading water. I grabbed my napkin, to mop up the mess.

"Where's my pie?" Oma shrieked.

"Can I help?" Phebe set her fork down to fold her hands in her lap.

"No, it's okay, honey. I'm getting it. Hand me your napkin." I righted the glass and dropped the ice back in. The cubes clicked together.

"I don't want this. It looks disgusting." Oma waved her hand over the plate I'd brought.

"You have to eat the food." Frustration tears welled in my eyes, and I left the napkins in a soppy mess near the glass, not sure what else to do with them.

"No, it's a holiday. She can just eat the pie first if she wants to." Jim patted Oma's shoulder. "Huh, Grandma? You can do whatever you want on holidays."

I'd always liked Jim, but now I wished one of my other cousins had made it to Thanksgiving – one of the cousins who wouldn't have given her pie.

"She isn't going to eat the pie *first*. She's *only* going to eat the pie," I wailed.

"You're creating a scene," Aunt Marta had ignored the commotion, eating despite the lack of saying grace. Now, she glared across the table at me. "Sit down and stop yelling."

I sat with a plop on the seat's brocade cushion. Phebe squeezed my arm.

"How are you, Grandma?" Jim asked.

I ground my teeth. *I* was the one who took care of Oma. Jim lived an hour away and only visited on holidays. He never called in between times. Yet, now, he acted as if he and Oma were close. *She is* my Oma, *not yours!*

"You're so nice." Oma smiled at Jim as he put the pie back in front of her. She swung her gaze to me. "Why can't you make anything pleasant?"

"So, Keziah." Aunt Marta paused to chew a piece of lamb. "How's school?"

"Fine." I let ice flow from my voice.

"How about you, Phebe?"

"I miss my sister." Phebe nuzzled my side with her nose.

"Right." Aunt Marta cut another sliver of lamb.

"Lamb is disgusting." The words bounded from my mouth. "Lambs are beautiful and precious. You have a dog. Would you eat your dog?"

Aunt Marta stiffened. "I almost forgot you were all *vegetarians*." She spat the last word as if we were cannibals.

"Oma started it." I wanted to add all Goat Children were vegetarians because I'd read that in one of Oma's notebooks, but that was Oma's secret world.

"Of course." Aunt Marta looked away.

Phebe sang a Cascada song, swinging her legs beneath the chair. Jim told Oma about his new job at a bank. I glared at my plate, wishing I had the wits and nerve to fling a scathing comment at Aunt Marta. Uncle Jan and my parents returned to the table with fake smiles.

"Keziah, don't let Oma eat the pie first," Mama said.

I winced. "Jim brought it and—"

"Let's say grace," Dad interrupted.

"About time." Aunt Marta kept eating.

"This is really fun. I like it when we all get together." Phebe smiled at me.

I kissed my sister's forehead. "I love you."

"Keziah." Uncle Jan's voice boomed, a laugh lost somewhere between his words. "Your mom said you went on a date."

"Her first date." Dad didn't sound as if he enjoyed the fact I was datable, so I avoided looking at him.

"Is he your boyfriend now?" Uncle Jan asked.

"No." Domenick and I had sent a few text messages since the outing, but he hadn't asked me out again. "Oma wouldn't like that."

"You wouldn't care, would you, Mom?" Uncle Jan asked.

Oma wrinkled her nose. "Were you talking to me? I thought I wasn't here."

"Come on, Mom. We're all in this together," Uncle Jan said.

I glared at my plate of food, my appetite gone.

****

That night on the couch, Phebe pressed against my back, snoring. The garbage truck rolled down the hill with its familiar growl of machinery. Streetlights shone through the front windows, playing in the hallway like pixies.

I moved the blanket off my legs, tucking my pillow against Phebe. My sister murmured, eyelids twitching, but she didn't rouse. I tiptoed across the room, past the mattress where my parents slept, and found my purse in the hallway. Clutching it to my chest, I sat on the last step of the stairs and took out my cell phone. I pressed the *on* button, hiding the vibration against my stomach.

The screen lit up bright blue. When it finished loading, I went into the messages folder and typed one to Domenick. *Want to go to the movies next week?*

Screw Oma. I could have a boyfriend if I wanted one.

He would have his phone off and be asleep, so I'd have to wait until morning for a reply.

"Keziah?" Phebe stood in the living room doorway.

I jumped. "Go back to sleep."

"What's the matter?" Phebe tiptoed across the hall to the stairs.

"Nothing. I just couldn't sleep."

"I miss you." Phebe crawled into my lap. I leaned against the wall with my arms around her. "When are you coming home?"

174

"Soon," I bit my lower lip. "I have to look after Oma. She needs me."

"Why doesn't Oma like me?" Phebe snuggled against me.

I should say Oma did, or blame the dementia.

"I don't know." I kissed Phebe's head. "I love you. Mommy and Daddy love you. That's all that matters, sweetie."

"I know. I love you, too."

The cell phone buzzed. I jerked and Phebe gasped.

My hand shook when I flipped it open to look at the message.

*Would your grandmother like that?*

I closed my cell phone and replaced it in my purse. If Domenick had really wanted to go to the movies, he wouldn't have countered with a question. He would've said yes. Tomorrow, I'd text back and say never mind.

"Was that your boyfriend?" Phebe's eyes appeared wide in the streetlight glow. "Are you guys getting married? Can I be your bridesmaid?"

"No." I shook my head. "He isn't my boyfriend. He's just a friend."

****

*I am eight years old. It is a snow day, so Oma walks with me to the library. We rent a children's craft book. Then, we walk to the craft store for supplies, and spend the next few weeks making every project.*

*My favorite is the rag doll. Oma sewed it for me out of an old sock.*

*"This will be Leontien," I say. "I named her after you."*

175

*We make her jewelry and dresses, and I give her yellow yarn hair. She sits on the piano to watch over us.*

# Chapter 19

"Do you ever wonder what it's like to know you're never going to see someone again?" Oma asked.

I stiffened before I finished closing the front door. When I flipped the lock, it felt like ice against my fingertips. "They'll be back."

"Of course," Oma said.

I lifted the corner of the curtain to peer through the door's window. Uncle Jan's car backed out of the driveway. Phebe pressed her face against the window and waved. I imagined my sister's eyes were tearful like mine.

"I knew I was never going to see my parents again." Oma sighed. "I was saying goodbye for good. They passed on, and when I joined the Goat Children, I had to say goodbye to others then. I had to know I was leaving everyone and never coming back."

Even when I walked away, Oma still stood at the door. She stared at it as if it was going to perform.

"You know," Oma said, "sometimes I wish I hadn't gone with the Goat Children."

Uncle Jan phoned that evening. "Do you need anything from the store?" My parents had gone shopping the day before, but I carried on the message to Oma anyway.

"You know I never know if I need anything," my grandmother snapped. Then, her gaze softened. "Okay, I'll go."

"What?" I almost dropped the phone. Oma never wanted to leave the house to go shopping.

"Yes. I want to go. Where's my coat?"

"I guess she really is going," I told Uncle Jan.

Oma opened the closet door to stare at the coats. "Which one is mine?"

"Where do you need to go?" Uncle Jan asked.

"Rite Aid. I can get some toilet paper," I said.

I helped her put on a coat, a brown one with spots all over the sleeves from a spilled ice cream cone. The ragged hat Oma wanted to wear was one she'd knitted years ago. Pieces hung like ribbons. They must've tickled, because she kept brushing her hand across her forehead, frowning.

When I handed her the winter boots, Oma stuck her left foot into the right boot, and vice versa. "These are too small."

"They're on the wrong feet."

"Stop trying to make me feel bad. You're a wicked girl."

The words sliced through my heart, catching my breath in my throat. I yanked them off and helped Oma put them on again.

She sat in the front seat of the car complaining it was too cold, so Uncle Jan turned up the heat. Then, she complained it was too hot, so he turned it off. It became too cold again, and the cycle continued until Uncle Jan pulled up in front of the Rite Aid in the shopping center. I popped out of the back seat and ran around the car to help Oma out.

"This way." I kept my hand on Oma's arm, guiding her toward the store.

A man walked toward us on the shopping center sidewalk, pushing a cart from *Hannaford's* grocery store. The wheels squeaked through wintry slush. *Creak moan, creak moan.*

"What a nice looking lady." Oma pointed at the man.

He glanced over his shoulder, as if seeking the lady, and frowned.

"Oma, that's a man."

"What? No, that's a woman." Oma pointed at him again.

The man sent me a half-smile and pushed his cart down the sidewalk. I led my grandmother to Rite Aid's entrance, the electric door whooshing open.

Inside, Katy Perry blared over the radio. A little boy played with a *Lisa Frank* notebook. A girl tried to get it back, screaming at the top of her lungs. A man finished paying the cashier, ignoring the kids. I wondered if they were with him.

"Did you want to look around or just get the toilet paper?" It felt weird to be in a store with Oma, rather than shopping alone.

"Toitey paper." Oma chuckled. A couple at the film counter looked at us.

I repeated my question.

Oma yanked her arm away. "Of course I want to walk around! Don't hold onto me like I'm some kind of an invalid. Let me hold onto you. I don't want people to think I can't walk."

"But, Oma—"

She marched into a fixture of movies. The red cardboard buckled and DVDs scattered across the floor, the thuds and plinks echoing throughout the store, drowning out Katy's song. I screamed, darting to Oma. There wasn't that much money in Oma's purse. What if the DVDs broke and we had to pay for them?

Oma tried to continue walking, as though she were oblivious to the fact there were DVDs underfoot.

"Oma, stop!" I yanked her around by the arm.

"What are you doing? Let go of me."

"You're going to step on them!"

"Step on what?"

"The *movies*."

"What movies?"

"The ones you just knocked over."

Oma tried to pull away again. "What are you talking about? Why do you always want to make me sound like I don't know what I'm doing?"

"You just knocked over the DVDs." I pointed at the ground. Oma squinted, and rubbed the corner of her eye.

"It's too bright in here. I can't see. Where are my sunglasses?"

"What's going on?" the clerk from the film counter asked. "Is there a problem?"

"What do you want?" Oma asked. "Keziah, where are my sunglasses? I can't find them."

"They're right here in your purse." I pulled them out and opened them for Oma to put on. "I'm sorry, but my grandmother knocked over the movies and—"

"What?" Oma asked. "I can't hear you."

"It's okay," the clerk picked at his ear as if intent on purging wax rather than look at us. "I'll clean it up for you."

"Come on, Oma. This way." I tugged my grandmother down the first aisle.

"Do you think I enjoy being dragged around the store?" Her glasses must not have gone on right, because Oma took them off and put them back on. "Is that candy?"

"Yes." I bit back a groan. "We've got candy at home."

"Get me a marshmallow bunny."

"I can't. They don't have any. It's not Easter." Not to mention the gelatin ingredient made them not vegetarian.

"Get me a candy bar. Milk chocolate. Get one for yourself, too, and one for Jan and your mother."

"Mama's back in the city."

"One for Jan, then."

I chose a dark chocolate bar for me and two milk chocolates before reaching for Oma again. She grabbed my arm, instead, smacking her purse into a shelf of cereal boxes. They scattered across the floor.

"Why did you just knock them over?" Oma stared at me with wide eyes. "You need to be more careful. You have to start *thinking*."

"No, I didn't do it."

"You're so embarrassing." Oma marched down the aisle, and almost collided with a man.

He reached out to steady her and she stepped away, nostrils flaring.

"Keziah, come here! This man tried to touch me."

The man only smiled down at Oma.

"You scared the life out of me," Oma exclaimed.

"Excuse us." I steered Oma away.

His voice followed us down the next aisle. "Where's your ring, my dear?"

I had no idea if he spoke to us, so I didn't answer.

Five people waited to be checked out. I drew Oma to the end of the line.

"We're leaving now, so can you wait here while I grab the toilet paper?" I asked.

"What's this?" Oma held up the candy bars.

"The candy bars you wanted."

"I only want one."

"You said to get one for Uncle Jan and—"

"I'm not buying all these." Oma thrust the two milk chocolate bars at me. "Take them back unless you want to buy them. I only want one."

I wanted to throw the candies in her face. "But you hate dark chocolate."

"What?"

"The one you're still holding is dark chocolate." I bit out the words.

The woman ahead of us turned to look. Into her phone, she said, "It's hard to hear with all these disturbances."

I groaned. "Okay, I'll go put these back." Oma didn't need a new bar, and I could eat the dark chocolate one later.

"Well," Oma growled, "if you really want one, I can guess I can buy you one, too."

I put the two milk chocolate bars back in their aisle and found the toilet paper next to shampoos and across from condoms. I wondered if it was embarrassing to buy condoms. I really wanted to buy a pack and tell the clerk I was going to have *a lot* of fun later.

When I got back to the checkout line, a woman had gotten behind Oma. She smiled at my grandmother, but in a "you're not all there and I feel sorry for you" way.

"The weather's nice," she said to Oma, "especially for the start of December."

"I speak…uh…" Oma frowned.

"I'm back." I stood next to Oma, then smiled at the stranger. "Hi."

The woman pointed at Oma. "She speaks Uh."

I blinked. "What?" *Someone else with dementia. Lovely.*

"English," Oma said. "I speak English!"

"No, you said you speak Um." The stranger giggled.

"She couldn't hear you," I explained. "She thought you were speaking a foreign language." It had happened one other time. A boy scout had come to the house collecting cans for the hungry.

"I speak English," Oma repeated.

"Speaks Um." The stranger still giggled.

I bit my lip to keep from joining in. No, I shouldn't find it funny.

"I just asked her how she's feeling in this great weather," the stranger said.

I raised my voice to Oma. "She wants to know how you feel." I didn't see how the snow and cold was great, but maybe the woman was a winter fanatic.

"I feel with my hands." Oma huffed. "Not that it's any of her business."

I led Oma from the store into the parking lot.

Once we got in the car, Uncle Jan asked, "How was the trip?"

"Fine." I folded my arms, leaning back in the seat.

"The air's muggy," Oma complained.

My mind jumped back to the man who'd asked about the ring. Maybe Oma had stolen a magical ring from him, an enemy of the Goat Children, long ago.

****

*I am seven years old. Oma, Mama, and I take our summer vacation in Niagara Falls, on the Canadian side. We visit the butterfly conservatory and frequent the tourist traps. My favorite part is taking a trip behind the falls, feeling the rush of water as it bathes my face.*

*We are leaning against the railing, overlooking the Horseshoe Falls.*

*"I would love to fly." I point at the rising mist. "I would fly down and soar up, just at the last second. Do you think I'll ever be able to?"*

*Mama shakes her head. "No. That would be dangerous."*

*"Maybe someday you will." Oma's eyes twinkle.*

# Chapter 20

On Monday, I met Domenick during the change between first class and second. My purse hit him in the gut, and he staggered. I feared I'd pegged him in the groin and imagined that he was going to crumple to the floor in howling agony.

"Oh, my gosh! I am so sorry. I can't believe I just did that." I'd just taken out the guy I liked.

"It's okay." He coughed. "What's the rush, speedy?"

I was embarrassed to say I'd drank one cup of apple juice too many for breakfast and had to run to the bathroom before the next bell rang, so I mumbled, hoping he wouldn't press the matter.

"How was your Thanksgiving?" He stepped over against the lockers.

*Dinner was awful. Oma ruined it, and Jim helped with that, and I miss my family.*

*When is he going to mention our botched relationship?*

"It was nice."

He had a cut under his left eye, the wound swollen and purple. I dragged my gaze away before he could ask why I was staring. I fixated on his dark irises.

He grinned. "That's good. How's your grandma?"

"She's doing well. Um, thanks for asking." Maybe the cut had come from a snowboarding accident. I imagined him owning a snowboard with a dragon image.

"We had a really nice time. My uncle came up from Florida." Domenick picked thorugh his pocked and pulled out an automatic pencil.

I should've asked how his time had been. Again, my gaze fell on his cut. He must have noticed this time, because he lifted his hand to finger it.

"Sorry." I stared at the mud on the tile floor. I wanted to say something comforting like, "It doesn't look *that* bad."

"I dropped one of the china plates."

"What?" A quarter rolled across the tiles; it hit the wall and stilled.

"Every year, at the holidays, my mom always gets out the hand-painted china. My parents are like obsessed with it. You know how it is with heirlooms."

Oma always wanted to bring heirlooms down from the attic and put them outside with "for sale" signs. She called them cheap junk she was sick of seeing, even though they stayed packed upstairs.

"Yeah."

"I broke one of the plates." He pointed to the cut. "So, you know, I deserved it."

"Wow." My eyes bugged. "One of the shards cut your cheek? That's awful! It's a good thing it missed your eye."

"No, not one of the shards." Domenick cupped my shoulder to draw me close. He lowered his mouth and whispered in my ear, making my heart race. "My dad hit me." He nudged me away. "Okay, see you around sometime, Keziah."

"Wait!" I grabbed his sleeve. "Are you serious? He *hit* you?"

"Shh." Domenick narrowed his eyes. "You know how teachers get when you talk about that kind of shit. Come on, Kez, don't make a big deal. I already told you it's my fault."

"You broke a plate on accident. That doesn't give him a right to...you know."

"Aw, come on." His smile didn't touch his eyes. "Haven't you ever been hit before?" He swatted my butt. "You never got one of those?"

"Never," I breathed. Domenick's father had hit him hard enough to cut his cheek.

He shifted his stance. "You won't tell anybody, will you?"

"No." The word swelled in my throat. "I won't tell."

He patted my shoulder. "I knew I could count on you." Instead of his retreating back as he walked down the hallway, I imagined him sprawled on the couch in his basement sipping Gatorade, intent on my words, the consternation in his eyes and his somber words of sympathy over Oma.

I refused to picture him beaten.

It clung anyway, the way his face had looked so haunted. He'd wanted someone to know. I'd told him my innermost thoughts, so he'd told me his. Maybe in some perverted way, he felt we were even on a scale somewhere.

*Should* I tell a teacher?

Everyone seemed to watch as I set my books down at my desk. They all knew. The secret was written across my face in bold, Sharpie marker. I tugged my unbound hair until it covered my head like Cousin It. A beep sounded over the loudspeaker, followed by some static, and then the principal's voice.

In a loud, calm, clear tone, he announced, "We are going into lockdown mode. Everyone in the hallways needs to enter the nearest classroom."

What did that mean? My class groaned.

A boy shouted, "We're all gonna die."

The mathematics teacher rushed to the doorway to beckon students inside.

"Come on." A girl grabbed my sleeve. "We have to line up against the wall. We had some of these drills last year."

"I don't think it's a practice round," a boy said. "They wouldn't do that in the middle of switching classes."

"They're practicing for a *real* emergency."

Great, the school pretended while I suffered through real emergencies, namely Oma and Domenick. When did I get to go into lockdown mode?

I followed them to the wall beside the door. What did "lockdown mode" even mean? Fire drills I understood. There'd been five of those in the autumn.

The students snickered and whispered as they sat down, their backs against the wall beneath the chalkboard. I bent my head to keep from smacking it on the chalk holder. Mr. McGraw, the mathematics teacher, shut the door and reached into the bottom drawer of his desk to remove a manila folder. He took out a rectangle of blue construction paper and taped it to the inside of the classroom window before joining the students along the wall. He made a few of them move over so he could sit beside the door, the manila folder clutched to his chest.

I ran the heel of my boot back and forth across the tile floor, savoring the slow squeak.

"Hey." The girl next to me leaned over. "You're probably used to this shit, aren't you? You're from the city? You must see, like, *ten* shootings a day."

"Yeah," I mumbled. "Maybe fifteen or more." I scraped my boot over a crack, digging it deep so the heel caught.

"Wow. That must be scary." The girl giggled.

"I'm kidding." Shiny spots dotted the tiles near the bulletin board. They looked like glue.

"Class, please," Mr. McGraw barked. "We need complete silence. This is an emergency drill."

The classroom phone rang. When Mr. McGraw answered it, more students chattered. His face whitened as he spoke, the words inaudible over the students. Mr. McGraw's cheeks turned red, the color spreading to his ears, and then his hands shook. When he hung up, he had to cough twice before speaking.

*This can't be good.*

"Everyone needs to stand up and get in line in a neat, orderly fashion." The words sounded repeated, robotic.

Someone laughed. No one moved. He had to repeat it before a couple girls obeyed. I followed.

"This is not a drill," Mr. McGraw announced. "We need to evacuate the school as soon as possible. You need to get in line."

*Whoa.* I tucked my hands into the pockets of my jacket. How exciting, a sudden half-day.

"We're all gonna die," someone yelled sarcastically. A few students snickered.

"We're not going to die, but we do need to get in line *immediately*," Mr. McGraw said.

"But it's snowing out and we don't have our coats," a girl whined, which set other students firing out agreement.

What could the emergency be? Maybe a gas leak. Did schools have gas leaks? I'd never heard of one, but that didn't mean it wasn't possible. Maybe we would get the rest of the week off.

Mass exodus spilled out from the school. I spotted Domenick in the hallway, but he didn't look in my direction.

Outside the school, instead of lining up for buses, we were led down the street. No one looked put out by this, just excited, and a little scared. I elbowed my way through the crowd to Mr. McGraw.

"Excuse me. Mr. McGraw?"

"Hush, get in line. Now isn't the time." Snowflakes clung to his graying hair.

"But, Mr. McGraw, where are we going?"

"To Saint Stephen's Church."

"Why aren't we going home?"

"Because this is an emergency evacuation." Mr. McGraw increased his speed. "The high school goes to Saint Stephen's. The junior high goes down the street to the Methodist. The elementary goes to the Baptist church."

I fell back in line, not sure how to argue with that. I *had* to argue with it, though, because "emergency evacuation" sounded like a long complication. We probably wouldn't leave the church any time soon, and it was almost lunchtime. I had to get home by lunch to feed Oma. She wouldn't eat if I didn't make it.

Why couldn't I just walk home? It was right up the street. I wasn't even Catholic.

When we got in Saint Stephen's, a teacher I didn't recognize announced, "Everyone, please go sit in the chapel." I hovered in the back while everyone crowded onto the benches, then I ran over to the principal.

"Excuse me, but I have to go home," I said.

"Young lady, sit down." He didn't look at me.

"But I have to feed my grandmother."

"This is not the time. *Sit down.*" He walked back out of the chapel.

I stomped my foot. The teachers in the doorway ignored me.

"Hey, Keziah." Meg's voice drifted to my ears. "Over here, girl."

I didn't feel like talking, but I walked over to her anyway. The chapel smelled like incense. My nose watered, and I wiped it on the back of my sleeve since I didn't have a tissue.

"Wasn't it cold out?" Meg asked. The chapel, although large, rang with voices, so she had to shout.

I shrugged. *I have to get home for Oma.*

"What's the matter with you?" One of Meg's friends popped a stick of gum into his mouth. "Why does your foot keep tapping like that? It's wicked annoying."

"So I heard," Meg exclaimed, "it's a bomb threat! Can you imagine? They found something that looks like a bomb in the dumpster and then a note came in. Dude, we're gonna be here a while."

"But we can't," I blurted. "I have to get home."

"Chill," the gum-chewer said. "We'll get home eventually. You know, if the bomb doesn't blow us up here, too. You know what all the teachers are doing, right? They're calling home. They've all got those folders with our info."

Oma would think I was in danger, or worse, dead.

"I have to use the bathroom." I darted for the doorway.

The gum-chewer called after me, "Yeah, don't pee your panties. That'd be nasty."

The school psychologist hovered near the doorway with a walkie-talkie.

"Excuse me. I have to use the bathroom," I said to her.

The psychologist pointed down the hallway. "Hurry up. There might be a line."

My heart sank. I'd hoped it would be possible to dart out of the church and run home, but the principal spoke to two police officers in the foyer.

I wandered into the bathroom. since the psychologist watched me. Five girls waited around the filled stalls. Two more hovered near a frosted window. They had propped it open and were smoking cigarettes.

I ran my hands through hot water and rubbed them over my face, careful not to get my glasses wet. On television, splashing water always helped calm a person down.

It just made my face sticky. I wiped my hands on a paper towel and left. Right outside the bathroom, a young man pushed a mop. He nodded to me with a toothy grin.

"Howdy, miss. Enjoying all the excitement?"

"Not really. I have to get home for my grandmother." The story slipped out, about how I had to feed her, but now I wouldn't be home for lunch. She might eat something bad— like laundry detergent. Oma sobbed whenever I was late coming home from school. She also cried when I came home on time, but only if she forgot what time school let out.

When I finished talking, I panted. The janitor smiled.

"It's tough," he said. "My grandmother had Alzheimer's. She lived with us for years, and I still miss her every day. Your grandmother is lucky to have you."

"Thanks." I wiped my nose on my sleeve again. Was it allergies or had I driven myself to hysterics?

"But," he continued, "you must always remember everything in life is an adventure as great as in any classic. Take *Treasure Island* for example. Little boys who miss their father shouldn't be the only ones to go off after a treasure map. Don't you agree?"

"I never read that book."

"All of us can find treasure maps. We can all hunt for gold at the ends of rainbows. I have as much of a right to have an adventure as you do. Just think, we're all having an adventure right now just by breathing! Life is an adventure." He paused to dunk his mop. "You know what I always picture as a big adventure? Going to another world. It's a world up above ours, lived in the clouds, but unseen by everyone, even the pilots flying by in planes! Even if we don't know they're there, they're protecting us. Someone's got to do it, huh?" He squinted at me.

I stepped back. My mouth was dry, so I gulped. Oma had described the world of the Goat Children just like that. They were unseen, even by planes, yet they were there, protecting the Earth. They lived in the clouds.

I'd read one of the notebooks last night. In it, Oma had described her time with the Goat Children as a constant adventure.

*I never knew what adventure meant before. Now, I'll never forget.*

I tipped my head to study the janitor. *Impossible.*

"Yes." It came out as a squeak, so I had to cough. "Right. An adventure." I edged around him, hurrying into the chapel. I sat with Meg's group and listened to them talk. No one tried to include me; good. My mind rotated around the Goat Children.

I was going insane, just like Oma.

****

When I got home after the bomb scare, water soaked the kitchen floor. The tiles glistened with moisture, and when I crouched to look closer, I noticed a film along the surface. Oma had the lid to the washing machine lifted, and when I peered inside, I saw a few pairs of underwear wadded in the corner.

My grandfather, once upon a time, had known to install the dryer in the cellar, out of the way, but the washing machine resided in the kitchen.

"Oma, I'm home. Where are you?"

Silence. *Charming.*

"Oma!" I dropped my pack in the hallway, seeking the bedroom. Oma lay in bed with her arms folded across her chest, lips pursed, and eyes spitting fire.

"Oma, I'm home. Why didn't you answer me?"

"Were you talking to *me*?" Oma snapped.

I straightened my back, steeling for the battle. "I'm so sorry about lunch. I'm sorry I'm late, too, but didn't the school call? They said they would. They were supposed to. They probably called Uncle Jan since he's the contact. There was a bomb threat, so we had to go to the Catholic Church, but everything is settled now. It was just a scare or a prank. It wasn't a real bomb, just made out to look that way."

Oma glared out the window. "Are you done now?"

"What are you talking about?"

"I'm waiting for you to confess."

"Confess to what? I just told you where I was."

Oma snorted. "You know what I mean. Don't play your little games."

"I have no idea what you're talking about."

"You put something in my dinner."

"Um, what?"

"I had a stomach ache all night, and I couldn't sleep, and my stomach still hurts. You poisoned my food!"

"Why would I poison you?"

"Why would you?" Oma countered.

"Oma, be reasonable. I don't even have any poison."

"Where *do* you keep it?"

"I'm not discussing this." I ached to slam the bedroom door. Instead, I stormed into the living room. Oma would forget. She always did. She forgot everything.

Except for that.

Oma had found an old box of laxatives in the far back of the kitchen cupboard. She'd eaten the whole box and had "accidents." I fought back nausea as I cleaned up the mess after school, the empty box on the counter and dirtied sheets in the washing machine.

Oma swore I'd tried to poison her. She refused to eat anything I prepared. Aunt Marta threw a fit because it meant Uncle Jan had to visit Oma on his lunch break to make sure she ate, and he had to feed her at dinner.

"We must put her in a home," Aunt Marta insisted.

At night, I laid awake, plagued with nightmares about putting Oma in a nursing home. She wouldn't be able to handle it. That step seemed so cold and unfeeling.

I blamed the bomb scare for the whole issue. If I'd come home at lunch, Oma wouldn't have eaten the laxatives.

Yes, it was the bomb scare's fault.

I also blamed the janitor, just in case he was a Goat Child enemy.

\*\*\*\*

*I am eight years old. It is Christmas, but I have a cold. Uncle Jan and Aunt Marta are visiting. Mama baked a spice cake. They're eating dessert and drinking some red wine Uncle Jan brought.*

*I sit on my bed, playing with a new dollhouse. It is shaped like a castle, and the figures wear crowns. Oma combs the princess doll's hair.*

*"You can go out with them." I feel bad she has to stay with me.*

*"I would rather be here with you." She leans close. "Adults are so boring."*

*I laugh and hope I'll be better soon, since Oma says that laughter is the best medicine.*

# Chapter 21

The social studies teacher partnered Meg with me for the December project. At least it was Meg, since I knew her, even if we weren't friends. I picked the assignment from an old-fashioned top hat the teacher carried around the room.

"What did we get?" Meg slid her hands into the pockets of her jean shorts. Ever since it had started snowing, Meg wore shorts and striped knee socks every day. Logic!

I unfolded the yellow paper to read the black ink. "Cemeteries."

Meg whistled. "There is nothing hotter than cemeteries in the dead of winter. Get it? *Dead* of winter?"

I forced myself to laugh, even though her comment was more morbid than humorous. "Yeah, very witty."

The December project involved receiving an assignment place and then writing about how that place fares in the winter. We needed to include pictures, facts, fiction and nonfiction stories, as well as personal reflections.

"We've got three weeks before it's all due." Meg pointed to the date written on the top of the project description form. "You wanna procrastinate until the last minute or do it this weekend?"

"This weekend," I said.

Meg chuckled. "You don't have to bite my head off over it."

I wondered if she joked. Her lips quirked, but they always looked happy.

"Um, sorry."

Meg lifted her chin, tucking a black tress behind her ear. "I was kidding."

It's a great feeling, awkwardness. "So, um, the cemetery... this weekend?"

"You know where the place is?"

"Yeah, Mama and I went over the summer."

"You need a ride? You don't have a car yet?"

"No car."

"I'll pick you up. I know where you live. Noon a good time for you, or do you want to make it for midnight?" Meg wiggled her eyebrows.

I closed my eyes and imagined moonlight reflected off pristine snow, tombstones watching like little soldiers, guarding over the dead. Wind howled, then clouds passed over the moon, and the gravestones turned black.

My eyelids flew open. "Noon is fine."

"I was kidding, you know, about going at midnight." Meg's piercing eyes didn't look as if she joked.

**** 

Walking home from school, I rehearsed what I was going to tell Oma about Saturday. She probably wouldn't find the New Winchester Cemetery a good place for a weekend romp, so I would have to say something good, but also convincing, without actually lying.

"So, Oma," I said aloud to a maple tree. I stepped over its root as it grew over the sidewalk. "Meg and I have to do a project on Saturday for school." No, Oma would think Meg was a codename for a boy. Even if I could convince Oma that Meg really was a girl, she would say something like, "You'd rather spend time with your *friend* than with me?"

Oma had said that when I'd asked to stay after school to help set up for an art show.

Something twinkled from the ice encrusted alongside the sidewalk. I caught my hair back in a fist to keep it out of my eyes, and bent at the knees. I poked at the twinkle with my silver-lacquered fingernail. The brightness blinded, boring into my retinas. The twinkle lay trapped within ice coated with snow.

I picked at the ice even when it tore a hole in my glove. I stopped only when my finger bled. Beads of blood formed on my skin.

"What the…" Never apt to fixate on things before, but as I felt compelled to have whatever it was that so twinkled. I used my boot, digging in my heel. The best use for kitty heels had finally been discovered. Using the point as an ice pick, I chipped away until the ice cracked. Crouching, I pulled off my gloves and used my fingernails to maneuver it free.

The twinkle belonged to a silver ring. A small charm shaped like a woman with a unicorn's horn protruding from her forehead attached to the circular band. In her hands, she clasped a blue stone.

When I tipped the ring, tiny silver flecks winked at me from the blueness. When I turned it sideways, the flecks turned black.

The ring didn't feel cold, even though it had been in ice for quite some time if the thickness of that ice stood as indication.

"It must not be real silver." I slipped it on my middle finger. It was a little loose, so I moved it to my pointer. The ring still wobbled, but it didn't fall off. I pulled my gloves back on, fingering the bulge in the wool. My heart swelled with pride for having saved the ring.

The jewel whispered into my mind, *I was lonely.*

Wow, Oma had me so worked up that now I heard voices. I couldn't let her get to me like that. I still had a life. *Right?*

****

Uncle Jan had his car parked in the driveway. I groaned. That was never a good sign when he was there right after school. Walking up the snowy cement to the porch, a squirrel darted across the road and up the magnolia tree. The branches swayed, moaning, and snow drifted to the ground.

The house smelled like burnt toast, and I made a mental note to hide the toaster and unplug the microwave. Oma might forget about it, or set it too high.

"I'm home." My bag hit the floor with a thud that rattled the winter decorations on the table.

"Hi, Keziah!" Uncle Jan's booming voice filled the house. "We're in the bedroom. Mom, Keziah's home."

In the bedroom, Uncle Jan hung a prism sphere on a clear cord from the curtain rod. Oma lay flat on her back in bed, the pillow fallen on the floor unnoticed. A seam had torn sometime that day in the comforter, and Oma had attempted to fix it with a bobby pin.

"Hi, Oma." I dropped onto the bed beside my grandmother.

Oma pursed her lips, nodding.

"Ta da." Uncle Jan clapped his hands like a child. The prism twirled on the cord, sunlight bouncing through to reflect as rainbows across the white walls.

"Look. Rainbows," Oma exclaimed. "It's good luck. They're happy with us."

"I saw it at the gas station and thought she might like it," Uncle Jan said.

Oma touched a rainbow on the blanket. A pain jumped through my veins when I realized Oma didn't know where they came from.

"After lunch," he whispered, "she called me up to say someone had broken into her house and moved the furniture around."

"What?" My breath caught in my throat.

Oma scowled at a rainbow.

"She forgot. She thought the kitchen table was moved." He shook his head.

Oma always knew where her things were—at least the things she used every day, like the kitchen table. Little things, such as extra bars of soap, I always had to retrieve.

"Are you talking about me?" Oma demanded. "It's rude, you know. If you want to go whisper, do it in the other room." Her voice trembled. "You're just trying to make me feel bad."

"We're discussing the prism." Uncle Jan chuckled. Oma stared at him without blinking, so he pointed at the prism. "We're talking about the rainbows."

"Right." Oma folded her arms and glared out the window from the bed. I followed her gaze to see the squirrel leap onto the birdfeeder. The bottom half popped off and seed sprayed into the air.

"Dumb squirrel," Uncle Jan roared. "Look at what he just did. I bought that seed and he wasted it, dumb thing." He bolted away from the window, and bumped the front door on his way out.

I laughed as Uncle Jan ran across the yard after the squirrel. It ran up the magnolia tree and he shook his fist. "Stop breaking my birdfeeder. That's the fifth time this month you've knocked it apart."

"Look what I found." I peeled off my gloves and showed Oma the ring, wiggling my fingers so it twinkled. Oma squinted, then pawed around the bedside table for her glasses.

I leaned over my grandmother to pick them up. "Here they are." I helped Oma open them.

When I twisted my wrist, more lights caught in the gemstone.

Oma sucked in her breath, grabbing my wrist so hard I gasped. Her long fingernails bit through my skin.

"Stop it. You're hurting me. Ow! *Oma.*" Fear tingled through my nerves.

"Where did you get that?" Oma shook my wrist, fire in her eyes.

My heart leapt into my throat. "I…I f-found it. On the way home from school. It was stuck in some ice on the sidewalk."

"It's from *them*. It's from the Goat Children!" She reeled back, her eyes wide.

"Oma, *I* found it. It's not from the Goat Children. They aren't even real."

"This is what they do," Oma hissed. "This is a zerain jewel. Only the Goat Children have it, and only those they choose to join them can see all the colors. They leave the jewel somewhere you'll find it. My jewel was on a bracelet."

"Oma." I peeled my grandmother's fingers off my wrist. "It's just a ring. There's nothing else to it."

202

"The Goat Children *are* real, and now they'll approach you. They want you because I was one of them. They like choosing from bloodlines." Oma's face turned ashen. "Don't go with them. Say no!"

"But, Oma—"

"Don't go with them. I need you. You can't leave me."

"Okay, I'll say no! I won't go with them. I'll stay here with you." It wasn't a good time to bring up Saturday. I extricated myself off the bed. Outside, Uncle Jan yelped when he pinched his finger while trying to reattach the bottom of the birdfeeder.

****

Meg's black Mercedes drove through the cemetery entrance. A massive wrought-iron archway welcomed us into the sacred depths, a sudden chill creeping up my spine with icy claws. On either side of the archway brick towers rose and windows reflected the sunlight.

Meg must've seen the direction of my gaze, because she said, "Those used to be the offices. Now, the office is way over there by the old church. You'll be able to see it in a second."

I didn't want to mention I already knew in case she felt proud, so I didn't answer.

She turned the car along the road. "See, over there." Rounding the corner of the hill, Meg took one hand off the steering wheel to point at a church and a small brick building. A maintenance truck rested in front, covered in snow.

"Are you sure we're supposed to be here in the winter?" I shivered again, recalling the time I'd come with Mama and planted flowers for strangers.

"People go to cemeteries year round. Actually, though, they don't open if there's been a blizzard, or *a lot* of snow, so it's kind of hit or miss. This part of the road is paved, so they plow it, but they don't do anything with the other paths leading over the hills. Those are just dirt roads, so we'll have to walk if you want to go all the way to the top."

I peered out the window at the passing whiteness. The stone tops of graves peeked through the snow. Crosses guarded the occupants. Angels pled for forgiveness.

Meg pulled her car into a roomy area of cement, and extinguished the engine. "This is as far as it's plowed, so come on, it's time to hike. At the very top of the cemetery, there's this really old mausoleum, and if you climb on top of it, you can see the whole city."

I followed Meg from the car. When she slammed the door, the sound echoed across the graves, and I shivered again.

"This place isn't giving you the chills, is it?" Meg snickered.

"No." I slid my gloved hands into my coat pockets.

Meg crunched through the snow to my side of the car. "Do you ever think about dying?"

"No!"

"I do. Sometimes." Meg shrugged. "My family's buried over here. My mom said that, someday, I'll be buried here, too. It's a family tradition. Your parents never talk about stuff like that?"

The "no," froze on my tongue. I shook my head.

"Come on, this way." Meg stepped off the plowed area. "We'll go to the top. You haven't lived until you've seen a view like this one."

"We have to work on our project." My breath plumed in the cold air. A snowflake landed on my cheek, melting into a tear.

"We will. I've got my cell phone, so we'll have pictures, and you've got the notebook, right?"

I nodded, feeling the mini spiral notebook in my pocket.

"See, we're all set. Bam, let's go."

My thighs ached after five minutes of trekking through the unplowed snow. Neither of us spoke. I concentrated on setting one foot in front of the other. Meg must have been frozen in her knee socks and shorts, yet she never complained.

The graves watched us with silent, condemning glares. We were alive, and they were dead. If there was less snow, I could have read the names. How old were they when they perished? Were any of them related to me?

"You're shivering again." Meg's voice traveled to my ears. "You're either really cold or really freaked. Which is it?"

I blew a breath, pretending to smoke a cigarette. "Honey, cemeteries don't freak me out. I'm as cold as ice."

"Yeah, you've totally never smoked a cig in your life. That's not how you hold one."

"You smoke?"

"A long time ago. I quit."

*A long time ago* made it sound like decades. Poor Meg. She was too young to have smoked *a long time ago.*

I wrapped my arms around myself. My breath came thicker now, and my nose felt ready to break. The hairs inside had frozen together, making it feel like someone had stuffed

205

tissue paper up my sinuses. I cupped my hands over my ears, but I couldn't feel them.

"Let's take the pictures and leave." My cheeks were so cold they felt hot.

"Scaredy cat," Meg sang. "Scaredy cat, scaredy cat!"

"I'm cold." I licked my lips, tasting the coarse, chapped skin.

"We're almost there." Meg bounced.

We were *almost there* when we arrived fifteen minutes later. By then, I sneezed. The snow on the hill was deep around the mausoleum, so it didn't take much for Meg to grab the edge of the roof and swing up. When she held out her hand for me, I was too tired and frozen to care about danger. I laced my fingers through hers, grabbed a corner of the roof with my other hand, and jumped.

I felt the roughness through my jeans, the material was soaked all the way through to my leggings underneath. I sneezed when I stood, wobbling as my legs adjusted to the slope. Snot clung to my nostrils, and without a tissue, I wiped it off on my coat sleeve. It left a shiny, pale streak across the black fabric. *Ew.*

Meg spread her arms wide, stepping in a circle. "Isn't the view freakin' amazing?"

The cemetery lay before us, guarded by the wrought-iron gate, and the buildings lay past that. Tall offices towered over houses. Streetlights glimmered through enveloping whiteness, and it gave the city a feeling of majesty and magic. Everything was clean, verging on perfect. My lips parted in awe.

"See?" Meg grinned. "Now, let's take those pictures, huh? Unless of course, you want to jump or something."

I stepped to the edge of the roof, savoring the sound of icy snow crunching beneath my boots. With my toes hanging over the edge, I stared down. If I jumped, I would land in snow. I was already soaked. What would it hurt?

*No,* a nagging voice in the back of my head whispered. *You don't want to jump...yet.*

"I'll pass." I stepped away.

****

*I am ten years old and want to sign up for a gymnastics class over the summer. Other girls at school are taking it. Mama can't drive me, though, because she is teaching summer school, and Dad will be away in Albania for most of the summer, writing an article.*

*Oma takes me instead. She watches from the bleachers with a few parents, and when I do really well, she cheers. I like gymnastics well enough, but the balance beam scares me. I am afraid I will fall.*

*"If you think you won't fall, you'll be steadier during the moves," Oma assures me.*

*Her advice helps a little, but I still wobble.*

*After every class, Oma takes me to Wendy's. We each get a Frosty and eat them in the car while we watch people walk by. We guess what their stories are.*

# Chapter 22

When the sunlight struck my face the next morning, I couldn't get up. My head throbbed, the veins inside feeling ten-times too big. My sinuses ached, and when I tried to breathe, hot stickiness slid down the back of my throat. I rolled over, gagging, and my stomach churned, tightening.

"Jeez."

The longer I lay in bed, the more my body ached.

"Why aren't you up?" Oma demanded.

"I'm sick." Mucus in my throat made it hard to talk.

Oma's cheeks reddened. "Get out of my house before I come down with it, too."

Oma called Mama and repeated her statement. After a second, she passed me the phone.

"I'm sick. I can't get up." Tears burned my eyes.

"Stay in bed." Mama paused. "Stay away from Oma, too. Don't get her sick."

What about me? Didn't I matter? I was the ill one, not Oma.

"I can't get sick," Oma ranted. "I'm old. I'll die. You're trying to hurt me!"

I buried my face into the pillow, but the tears still came. What had happened to the good old days when Oma took care of me?

"Where has the old Keziah gone?" Oma stomped away.

"She grew up," I muttered at my grandmother's back, "and now she's sick, and you don't even care."

When Uncle Jan came at noon to feed Oma, he brought medicine and juice. I fell asleep with my lips parted so I could breathe. My last conscious thought involved whether a spider would crawl into my mouth.

Oma kicked the side of my mattress. I groaned, pulling the blankets tighter to my chin.

Oma kicked the mattress again. "Get up."

"What?" I propped myself up on my elbows. Snot dripped out of my right nostril, so I wiped it on a tissue.

"Where are they?"

"What?" My dry throat hurt so bad my voice croaked. I repeated it three times before Oma heard.

"You know what." Her voice was as frigid as the graveyard had felt.

"I have no idea what you're talking about!"

"Where are my teeth?"

"Your teeth?" I snuffled.

"They're gone," Oma yelled. "Where did you put them? Why do you have to be so mean to me?"

I smothered my groan into the pillow as Oma stood over the makeshift bed shaking with sobs, tears dripping down her cheeks.

"I didn't touch your teeth." *Ew. Just...ew.*

"They're gone. You put them somewhere."

"Why would I touch your teeth?" I couldn't believe we had such a conversation.

"You hid them," Oma snarled. "You mean, wicked girl. You hid my teeth."

"I didn't hide your teeth!" The shout made my throat hurt more, and I coughed as my lungs contorted in a spasm.

Tears drenched Oma's cheeks as she left the living room. "Where are they? Why do you keep doing this to me?"

"It'll pass," I muttered as the bedroom door slammed. "Oma will forget."

What *had* Oma done with her teeth? She must've put them somewhere, or maybe she forgot where she kept them. In the bedroom, maybe Oma would remember.

When I squinted, I saw the glare of the red lights in the alarm clock. I wouldn't have to call the school pretending to be Oma, or Mama, for another hour.

The furnace kicked on and the house shook under its ancient force. I felt for the tissue box and found it caught in the blankets. I blew my nose, pondering what would happen if the furnace exploded. It lay right beneath the living room. I would blow to smithereens. Somehow, when sick, that didn't seem so bad.

As sleep began to reclaim my senses, the bedroom door opened. Oma stormed back into the living room to kick the mattress yet again. How could she have energy for that?

"Why do you do this to me? Why do you hate me? What have I ever done to you?"

I stifled the groan as I sat up. Snot ran down my face into my mouth, so I slapped a tissue over my nose. "Oma, I didn't do anything. When did you have them last?"

"Last night, as you perfectly well know."

"Did you look under the sink? You always keep them under the sink." I coughed into my elbow.

"You hid them on me this morning."

"I never even got up in the night. Oma, I'm sick!" I found another tissue for my nose.

"How old are you?"

"What?"

"Are you ten?" Sarcasm dripped off Oma's voice.

"No, I'm seventeen."

"Exactly. You're too old to be playing these wicked tricks on me. Where are they?" Oma's voice rose with hysterics.

"They're under the sink. I never touched them." I shoved the blankets aside, managing to sit up before the room spun. I staggered, reaching for anything, and my hand contacted the chair. It tipped, but steadied. My stomach rose into my throat and I gulped. *Please no vomit.*

"Why are you so wicked?"

Despite the whirling in her ears, I made it to the bathroom. Oma followed, hovering like a cloud. Her narrowed eyes bore daggers into my back. I snapped open the cupboard beneath the sink. The magnets on the corners of the doors squeaked.

Nope, no the plastic cup in which Oma kept her dentures. I dropped to my knees, pausing a moment with my eyes squeezed shut until the throbbing in my forehead lessened. When I opened my eyes again, I pawed through the contents: cotton balls, pads, a bottle of rubbing alcohol, and a box of Q-tips.

"No teeth." My heart raced.

"Where are they?" Oma's hands shook as she tried to rub her wet eyes with a wadded tissue.

"Do you want me to call Uncle Jan?" I grabbed the doorframe to keep my balance.

"No, don't bring him into your mess," Oma yelled.

When I dragged myself back into bed, I pulled the covers over my head. Safe within the cocoon of warm cloth, I dialed Uncle Jan's number on my cell phone.

"Hello?" Uncle Jan answered on the fifth ring.

"Hey, it's me," I whispered. "Can you come over? Oma's being weird. She must've put her teeth somewhere, but now she doesn't remember. She's crying. She blames me."

Silence.

"Can you please come over?" A sob burned within my throat. Why did Oma always think the worst of me? I was her *granddaughter*. I was living with her so she wouldn't be put away.

Uncle Jan laughed. "I'm sure she'll find them."

"Please, can't you come over? If you're here, she won't be so mad at me."

"Everything will be fine. Look, I'm going out with the guys to Burger King later on. I'll stop by afterwards to see how things are, but I'm sure she'll have them by then, okay?"

"*No.*" Tears stung my eyes. "Please. You don't get it. She's screaming at me and crying. She thinks *I hid them.*"

"No, she doesn't think that."

"You don't know what it's like here!"

"It's hard when they're on their last leg."

I cringed. No one should describe Oma like that. She couldn't help the anger and frustration. It was the dementia's fault.

"Please, can't you help find them and calm her down?"

"I will. I'll be by later." He disconnected the call.

I stared at the phone. He really didn't think it important. I cried despite the pain that lashed through my skull and the sticky bile in my throat.

Uncle Jan stopped by three hours later, sipping a cup of coffee from Burger King. Oma was still hysterical, but after searching the house, he found the dentures wrapped in a tissue. Oma had shut them in her dresser drawer among cosmetics older than I was.

Uncle Jan stayed to feed her. After she'd eaten and he'd left, Oma asked me, "Do you want to help clean out the bedroom desk?"

I ground my teeth, wondering how I could act as if nothing was wrong, but I followed Oma to the desk in case a refusal reminded her of earlier.

I sat on the edge of the bed rubbing my temple while Oma dumped the desk drawers onto the bed. Sponge rollers spilled across the comforter. Broken combs plinked against each other. Pencils fell onto the floor.

While Oma picked through tangled necklaces, I poked at a stack of crumpled notepaper. The top paper featured Oma's childish scrawl.

*"Keziah hid my teeth"*, it read, and included the date. I stiffened. My grandmother knew she would forget, so she'd made herself a note.

While Oma fiddled with old watches, I stuffed the paper into my sock to throw away later.

\*\*\*\*

*I am four years old. Mama sees a flier in the teacher's lounge for a new ballet school.*

*"This will be great exercise. You'll love it." She signs me up.*

*The classes for children my age happen during her work hours, so Oma takes me. The studio is an hour away, in another town. I have to wear a pink tutu, tights, and slippers.*

*The tights hurt my legs, and the shoes pinch my toes. The tutu is scratchy.*

*I hate the instructor. She yells at me when I don't get the motions correct, but it's hard because I'm double jointed.*

*"I want to quit," I whine after class.*

*Oma helps me into my jacket. "Your mother really wants you to learn this, and she already paid."*

*On the way home, we stop at the library. Oma finds a book of ballet moves. Every day while Mama works, Oma and I practice the moves until I get better. The instructor doesn't yell as much, but I still don't like it.*

*"I don't want to take another class," I tell Mama after the end recital.*

*"But you were so good. You learned so much." Mama thanks the instructor for "working magic" and making me more graceful.*

*Oma and I wink at each other.*

# Chapter 23

For a week after losing her teeth, Oma acted as if nothing had occurred; she must have forgotten. Sometimes, I would awaken in the middle of the night, wondering if she would soon forget about me.

Then, my thoughts drifted back to the anger in Oma's eyes. How could my grandmother believe I was capable of wicked deeds?

"I've got something I want to show you," Oma said, and popped a cracker into her mouth. A few crumbs landed on her chin.

A blue jewelry box rested on the foot of the bed, dust smearing onto the comforter. The cover was decorated in "gold" embossing, but parts of the curlicues had peeled off. Red paint streaked the edge.

Oma sat beside it and ran her hand over the top, a glazed look flitting across her face.

"This is my jewelry." She leaned over as if it was a secret.

I wanted to point out she kept it in plain sight on the floor near the dresser, but I refrained. If she wanted it to be a conspiracy, it hurt nothing.

"Do I get to look at it?" I grinned.

"Yes!" The happiness slid off her face, and for a second she looked confused, as if unsure where she was. Then, she smiled again, and popped the brass clasp on the front of the rectangular box. The lid snapped open an inch on hinges in need of oiling. Oma had to force the lid up the rest of the way.

She ran her hand over the contents in the top tray. "Pick up something and look at it." Oma leaned back. "Unless you don't want to play. Then, you can just go back into your room and *pout*."

"No, I will." I picked up a piece of paper from the box; a receipt for getting a ring resized.

"What is it?" Oma held out her hand.

I handed it over. "A receipt."

Oma squinted at the faded print. "There's nothing on this." She set it on the bedside table.

"Let's throw it out then."

"It's mine. I'll throw it out when I'm ready to throw it out."

"Okay." I dragged out the word as I picked up the next item, a pink cameo. The point on the clasp pricked my fingertip.

"That belonged to your great-grandmother."

"Your mom?" I wondered if Oma even recognized the cameo.

"No, your grandfather's mom. All the old jewelry in here is from her. She gave it to your mom, but you know your mom. She'll never want it, so you can have it."

"Really?" I picked up a pair of emerald earrings. A woman in my family had once treasured those. Maybe my great-grandmother had worn them to a tea.

"Isn't there any jewelry from your mom?" I turned a brass locket over to read the back, but the cursive engraving was too elaborate.

"I lost everything when I joined the Goat Children." She picked up a silver bracelet. "This is my charm bracelet. I started collecting on my fortieth birthday. See this one? It's my favorite."

A miniature outhouse hung from the link bracelet on a small silver loop was.

"There's a tiny latch. Can you find it? Open it up," Oma said

I took the bracelet from her and used my fingernail to swing the latch over. The outhouse door opened to show a man sitting inside. The charm was unique, sure, but disgusting.

"Cool." I hoped I sounded sincere. Since Oma watched, I flipped through the other charms. A tiny silver ship's wheel had a date, *1987*, on the back. The rhinestone star and silver dove also had dates, both from 1989. The silver puppy and silver paintbrush didn't have dates.

"You can have it." Oma waved her hand.

I unclasped the bracelet and dangled it over my wrist. "I'll give it to Phebe." My sister had a kid's charm bracelet and always wore it. The adult version would brighten that little face into a ray of sunshine. I smiled.

"No," Oma shrieked. "No, it is *not* for her. If you're just going to give it to her, then give it back. I gave it to *you*."

"Okay, fine!" I closed my fist around the charm bracelet. "I won't give it to her. I won't even *show* her."

How long before the pain of lying faded altogether? I gazed into the mirror over the bedroom desk and didn't recognize the girl looking back. Her brown hair looked darker, tied in a thick braid down her back. In the city, I'd only worn make-up when hanging out with Tiffany, but now it became another way to stand apart from everyone at school.

"And there's this one." Oma held a gold necklace, the thin chain wrapped around her middle finger so the charm dangled.

"Pretty." I bumped my palm against the heart-shaped charm consisting of a brown stone set in a gold back.

"This one," Oma held up a bracelet, "is from the Goat Children."

I sucked breath through my teeth. The bracelet was silver with tiny gemstones. The gemstones were the same color as the stone in my ring. I closed my hand into a fist.

"This is the stone of the Goat Children," Oma continued. "They gave me this before they asked me to join. If I had refused, they would have taken it back. Ever since I joined, I wore it, up until I left. I never put it on again."

Oma set the bracelet back into the box and reached for a strand of pearls.

"Let me go get the jewelry cleaner," I said. "We'll make all of these shine again."

As I spent the next hour sitting on the bedroom floor using a rag made from an old nightgown to rub polish over silver, Oma stared out the window muttering memories.

"My mother and I used to share half a sandwich," Oma said.

"What kind of sandwich?" I wished I could turn the TV on; it was frustrating to listen to Oma's stories and not know what was true.

"Cheese. Chicken." Oma sighed. "I used to eat meat back then. I didn't stop until I joined the Goat Children. I told you that before, didn't I?"

"Yes." I rubbed harder at the silver brooch.

"I'm sorry," Oma whispered.

My head jerked up.

"I always forget things." Oma's voice broke on a sob. "I don't know why. What's wrong with me?"

"Oma." I chewed my lower lip.

"I don't mean to be like this." Oma sniffled. "If there was something wrong with me, you'd tell me, wouldn't you?"

I hesitated. Mama didn't want Oma to know about the dementia.

"She'll forget as soon as you tell her," Mama said. "What's the point in upsetting her? She won't know what dementia means."

"I'd tell you," I lied. "I'll always be here for you, Oma. You know that." I set down my supplies to crawl onto the bed beside her.

Oma slid her arm around my back, tugging me close for a quick hug. "I'm tired. I'm going to take a nap now."

"Okay, I'll put everything away." I retreated to the living room and took out the Goat Children notebooks from my stack of novels.

I flipped back through the ones I'd already read. One of them had mentioned the bracelet, but I hadn't paid much attention. The gemstone on my ring twinkled in the sunlight streaming through the window.

*Ah, here.* I held the notebook closer to my face as if it would give the words more power.

> *My first hint as to their existence came in the form of a bracelet. I found it wrapped in a paper on the step of the backdoor. In fact, I almost stepped on it when I was leaving. My parents were ill, then, and I had to fetch groceries from the market.*
>
> *There was no name on the paper, but it was sealed with a ribbon, wrapped like a gift. I*

*took it inside and opened it, shocked to find such a beautiful bracelet. We were not poor, but we did not have money, either. The only jewelry my parents owned was their wedding bands.*

*I wondered if I should find the owner, but I didn't know how to do that. I didn't want someone laying a false claim. I then considered selling it. We needed the money, especially for medicine. In the end, I tucked it into my pocket and decided to wait until my mother was well. I would show her and see what she said. For all I knew, it could have been meant for her.*

*My mother and father were wise. They would deal with it properly, and in the meantime, an inner rationale told me to keep the bracelet close. I thought it was because I was keeping it safe, but rather, it turned out that it was my destiny.*

I studied the ring on my finger. The swarm of colors reminded me of exploding fireworks. I yanked the ring off with a gasp and threw it at the couch. The gemstone flashed as it struck the cushions.

*Silly, silly me. It's just a ring.*

In the bedroom, Oma screamed, and I flew off the mattress. My feet could have had wings as I rushed to her.

My grandmother blinked her bloodshot green eyes.

"Oma, are you okay?" My heart felt as if it wanted to thrust from my chest.

I stared at my grandmother's face and felt like crying. The skin that had once been smooth and supple was wrinkled and flecked with dark freckles and warts.

"They're coming," Her lips looked thin and dry, but she didn't lick them. "The Goat Children come for me. They want me to go back to them."

"It was just a dream…"

"No." Oma grabbed my arm, but her grip wasn't strong enough to hurt. "They want me to go back. What if I do?"

I rubbed my grandmother's arm. Oma settled back against the pillow, but her gaze burned.

"What if I give in?" Oma whispered. "What if I go back?"

"Then you'll be happy?"

"If I go back, I won't be able to leave again. I can only leave once." Oma closed her eyes. "I will be young again. I will be the same age I was when I first joined. That's how it works." Tears pooled in Oma's eyes.

"What will be, will be," I said.

Oma nodded.

I pictured the ring.

****

*I am eleven years old. In the summer, I will move, but for now, I have a week left of school.*

*"We will be writing stories about what we hope will happen over the summer," my teacher says. "Make it a fictional story, like something you would read in a book."*

*I write about my family moving to New York City. We hate it, so we move back. Oma hugs me and says, "I knew you wouldn't leave me alone here."*

*On the last day of school, I bring the story home. When I show Oma, she reads it and then sets it down. "You write well."*

*I wish she would praise it more. Maybe it isn't any good.*

*Later, during dinner, Mama puts down her fork and taps the table with her fingers. "I spoke to Oma today."*

*"How was she?" Dad asks.*

*"She is concerned. Keziah showed her a story she wrote about how she doesn't want to move."*

*I stop feeding Phebe. "I had to write it for school." My parents are glaring, so I'm afraid the story really is awful. "You guys didn't get to read it yet."*

*"You know we have to move, right?" Dad speaks into his glass of tomato juice.*

*"I know. It was just a story." I don't understand what's so horrible about it.*

*"Don't talk to Oma about moving anymore," Mama says.*

*I run upstairs to my bedroom and tear up the story. I want to be a good writer, but that project has made everyone upset. Next time I want to tell a story, I will talk into Oma's tape recorder again and make her write it.*

# Chapter 24

"There're people outside," Oma said.

"What?" I looked up from my homework, a six-page essay on how poverty affected Richard Wright in his autobiography, *Black Boy*.

"They're watching me." Oma wrung her hands. The oversized sweater she wore hung off her body. "They want to come in."

"Wait, what are you talking about?"

"There are people outside my window," Oma said.

I pictured Michael clipping the bushes around his stoop. "What are they doing?"

"Watching me."

Groaning, I stood and stretched. "I'm sure they aren't, but I'll go look, okay? Where exactly are they?"

"Out in front."

I parted the ragged bedroom curtain. The streetlight glowed in the dusk, brighter than the lights in the windows across the street. Nothing moved outside, neither animal nor human.

"There's no one there."

"Yes, they're watching." Oma's voice rose.

"Shut the curtains."

A tear slid down Oma's wrinkled cheek. "They'll be back, and you don't care. You hired them to scare me so you can take my money and my house."

*Oma, don't go off on one of these tangents.* "That doesn't make sense. Why would I do that?"

"I don't know. You're not my little Keziah anymore."

"Ah!" Each time my grandmother said that, it stabbed deeper. The words nagged and haunted me, yet Oma always forget she'd said them and moved on.

That night, a sound roused me from sleep. I shifted on my mattress, tugging the blanket closer to my chin. The noise came again: a footstep in the hallway. I opened my eyes, adjusting to the darkness. In the glow of the bathroom light down the hallway, Oma walked toward the kitchen.

I nestled into my pillows. At least tonight, Oma knew how to get herself a glass of water. Sometimes, she would wake me up to ask, "Where'd you put the fridge?"

The doorknob to the cellar rattled, then the door creaked open.

"Oma, what are you doing?" I called. The door creaked louder. "Oma?"

After a few quick footsteps, Oma appeared in the doorway to the living room. She held her finger to her lips. "They'll hear you,"

"Who?" I crossed the living room to my grandmother.

"They're in the cellar!"

"Oma, no one's in the cellar. The house is all locked up."

"They came in through the special door," Oma said.

"What special door?"

"The one in the cellar," Oma exclaimed. "They're all down there, and they're dancing."

"They're dancing," I repeated.

"I'll show you." Oma waved for me to follow her into the kitchen. Once there, she pointed down the gaping cellar door. "See?"

"I can't see anything. It's dark." I reached for the light switch.

"*Stop*. If you turn on the light, they'll know we're onto them. They're hiding right now."

"That is ridiculous." I flipped on the light switches. Both the cellar and kitchen burst into life.

"Don't," Oma yelped.

"There's no one there. Come on, I'll show you." I stepped onto the first cellar stair. My grandmother hung back, tears shining in her eyes.

"What if they attack us?"

"If they were just dancing, they seem friendly enough," I muttered. Louder, I said, "Then I'll get a baseball bat. I'll protect us."

Worn out orange carpeting covered the narrow cellar stairs. I gripped her hand lest she trip. Oma clung to the railing with her other hand, each step small and shuffling.

At the bottom, I waved my hand around the cement room. Rust kept the windows shut. Shelves contained glass bottles of nails and piles of old cookbooks. Other than a broken birdbath, table saw, and dryer, the cellar was empty.

"See, Oma, no people."

"They ran out the door."

"Then wouldn't we have seen them on our way down?"

Oma pointed at the cement wall. "They went out that door."

I picked my way across birdbath pieces to tap the wall. "There isn't a door here. There isn't *any* door in the cellar."

Oma's lips quivered, muscles twitching in her chin. "Why do you lie to me? There's the door. Lock it."

"There's never been a door down here, ever."

"Why can't you see it? You're doing this to me. You want my house." Tears drenching her face, she shuffled toward the stairs. "When the people don't come back, I'll know you were behind it."

"There are no people." My voice bounced off the cold cement.

**** 

Come morning, Oma insisted the people had left the cellar and sat in the living room.

"I'm in the living room." I braided my hair for school. "I was all alone last night." Realizing how defensive that sounded, as if I'd slept with a boy or had lured strange people in to dance, I clamped my lips shut.

"I saw them," Oma whispered. "The man had a comb. He said he'd be coming. They were Goat Children."

"Oma, are the Goat Children good or bad? Why would a Goat Child be after you?"

"They want me back." Oma grabbed my arm. "They're here. They're watching me."

I disengaged myself. "There's no one here. I have to go get ready for school." Sleep nagged the corners of my mind, fogging my eyes. After Oma's episode in the cellar, I'd been afraid to fall back to sleep in case my grandmother crept around the house more. In the dark, Oma might trip.

"You're not leaving me here with them watching."

"Hey, Oma. Let's put out some peanut butter, and you can watch the squirrels eat it. You love doing that."

I swung open the refrigerator door to retrieve the jar of organic peanut butter. After unscrewing the lid, I grabbed a knife from the dish rack and stirred the oil into the thick substance. From the loaf of bread, I took the heel and smeared peanut butter over it.

"Here, Oma." I placed it in my grandmother's hand. Since Oma didn't move, I propelled her from the kitchen to the front door. Oma still didn't move, so I unlocked the front door and opened it.

"Toss the bread out for the squirrels," I said.

The bread flopped, peanut butter side down, on the front porch. The birds and squirrels would clean that up.

As I rubbed lotion over my dry forehead, Oma hovered behind me. In the bathroom mirror, I saw her narrowed eyes.

"Why are my hands sticky?" Oma held them up, palms facing me. "What did you give me? You're trying to poison me."

"It's probably from the peanut butter."

"What peanut butter?"

"The peanut butter we just put out for the squirrels." I ground my teeth.

"You're trying to hurt me," Oma screeched. "Why are my hands sticky? Why are you doing this to me?"

Fear blossomed in my heart. Oma was always so angry, so distrustful. Rage flared to the surface.

"I'm going to school," I snarled.

****

*I am nine years old. It is the first time that I can remember my parents fighting in the living room. I sit on my bedroom floor with my knees tucked to my chest, and I rock with my headphones in my ears, but I can still hear them.*

*"Stop it," Mama screams. "None of that is important."*

227

*"I don't care what my brother says, or what you say. I'm going to tell her," Dad threatens. I wonder what Uncle Tom has done, but I am afraid to ask, in case they yell at me.*

*Hearing perky songs by Britney Spears makes me feel sick, so I yank the headphones out and toss the iPod onto my bed.*

*"What good will that do? We're a family!" Mama's voice crackles.*

*My uncle has done something horrible, and Mama doesn't want me to find out. Why is my father pushing?*

*"It's her life," Dad says.*

*Mama runs up the stairs and opens my bedroom door. Her eyes are red, swollen, and her lips tremble. I start to cry with her. She grabs my arm and pulls me up. Her grip hurts, but she's so upset that I don't want to complain.*

*"There are things you don't need to know about your father." Mama rushes me out the front door.*

*"You can't take her," Dad calls.*

*I'm too scared to look back at him. He must have done something awful to make Mama act this way.*

*When we get to Oma's house, Mama lays in the bedroom. I sit next to her, rubbing her shoulder and petting her hair, but she doesn't look at me.*

*"Come watch television with me," Oma says, but I don't want to leave Mama.*

*"Why did I have to do that?" With her face still buried in Oma's pillow, Mama strokes my hand. "You're too old now. You wouldn't understand why I did it."*

*"I don't care." I mean it, too.*

*Mama could have robbed a bank, and I would still love her.*

*My father comes the next morning with donuts: a peace offering. I eat in the kitchen with Oma, while my parents converse on the front porch. Mama comes in and hugs me.*

*"When you finish, we're going home." She smiles.*

*It doesn't matter what they don't tell me, as long as Mama is happy.*

# Chapter 25

"Hey!"

I almost slipped on the driveway as the shovel caught under a hunk of ice. I brushed back my braid to glance next door. Michael waved. Despite the snow falling around us in flakes like cotton balls, he only wore an unzipped leather jacket over what appeared to be an undershirt. He tucked his bare hands into the back pockets of his jeans.

"Hello." I yanked the shovel free as he strolled up the sidewalk.

"Another two weeks and it's yo-ho-ho Christmas." Michael flashed a toothy grin.

"Pretty sure the 'yo-ho-ho' time is the pirate holiday." I couldn't help but grin back. "What's up?"

Michael shrugged. "Visiting the folks for a week. Christmas and New Year's, that whole shebang."

I leaned against the shovel. "That doesn't sound so joyous. Don't you like them?"

"I'm the youngest in the family. They never let me forget that, if you know what I mean." He winked.

"Right." I had no idea what he meant. My back hurt from shoveling, so I rolled my shoulders.

"Here, let me do that." He held out his hand for the shovel. "Pretty little ladies shouldn't be breaking their backs over snow."

I handed it over and stepped back. "Wow. Gee, thanks."

"'Gee, thanks'?" he mocked. "What, are we on the *Brady Bunch* now?"

*Oops.* "Um…"

He winked again, but I didn't feel as if he'd meant it as a kind joke. "Are your folks coming up or are you going to see them?"

"My mom's coming for New Year's."

"Not the rest of them?"

I bit my lip. "My grandma doesn't like Dad or Phebe all that much."

He stared at the shovel. "I'm sorry. How come?"

I shrugged, and then bent for a handful of snow. I sculpted it into a ball. *Good packing snow.* "I dunno. Oma can be really antisocial sometimes."

"She never says hi to me."

*She never says hi to me, either.* "She doesn't go out much at all."

"Right."

He shoveled a wide path across the pavement, getting down to the blacktop. When I shoveled, a layer of slush remained.

"I like all the decorations you put up in the windows. Very festive."

"Thanks." I stared at the house. "There's a bit more in the garage. My grandpa used to work with wood a lot, but now nobody will hang those pieces up."

"Do you miss him?"

"I didn't really know him. I wish I had."

"I'm sorry." He paused to lean against the trunk of Oma's car. "I'll hang decorations up for you."

I blinked at him. "For real?"

"Sure. I don't mind ladders, hammers, or nails. I'll do it right after this."

"Cool!" I jumped across the snow and flung my arms around his waist in a hug. "Oma will be so grateful. She probably misses having them hung up."

Realizing I still had my arms around him, I pulled back. My cheeks flamed, and for a second, my mind dwelled on the fact I'd felt his abs through the thin jacket and shirt. He laughed, making my cheeks burn hotter.

"You really don't mind?" I asked.

"Not at all. What are neighbors for, if not to help?"

\*\*\*\*

I borrowed a holiday book from the school library to read to Oma on Christmas Eve. When I started to read the stories, Oma couldn't hear, so I gave up and read them to myself. Uncle Jan stopped by on his way to church to pick us up, but Oma stayed home. I sat on the pew beside my aunt and pretended Phebe was there. I would hold my sister close, helping her read the words from the Bible and Hymnal by using my finger to follow along.

I struck a match and lit the bayberry candles when I got back home. It was Oma's tradition that bayberry candles burn to the socket every Christmas Eve for good luck.

In their brass holders, the sleek candles appeared majestic. The tiny flames danced across the wicks. When I went to bed, I moved them off the piano into the bathtub so they wouldn't catch anything on fire.

In the morning, there weren't any presents from Santa under the tree, nothing except the fuzzy white cloth. Mama would bring everything with her when she came for New Year's.

I helped Oma get her breakfast ready, and I gave Oma her present. Uncle Jan had taken me to the mall the week before, and I'd bought a glass bluebird. Oma used to collect them, and she kept all ten on a shelf in the bedroom. When Oma opened the present, though, she stared and didn't say thanks.

Oma always gave out money for Christmas. Mama and I got one-hundred dollars. Phebe always got fifty. Dad received twenty. This year, Oma made no offer of money.

Uncle Jan visited after breakfast to give out gifts, and then he went with his wife to visit her family in Syracuse. I changed into the pajama set he'd given me, even though it wasn't bedtime, and baked eggplant parmigana for dinner.

I ground up some in the mini-chop for Oma. "Uncle Jan brought it."

"It's chewy," Oma complained.

Mama called the day before she was supposed to visit. "Keziah, I am so sorry, but your sister's sick. It's the flu, and I don't think I should leave her. She said to go, but you know I can't. You know how Phebe is when she's sick."

*Poor Phebe!* She always looked so weak when she was sick, lost in a pile of blankets and used tissues.

"I get it," I whispered. "I want you to stay with Phebe. Tell her to get well soon and make sure she calls me when she feels like it. I love you, Mommy." I closed my eyes.

"I love you, Kez."

I sat beside Oma in bed, both of us propped up with pillows, watching the ball drop. We sipped red wine at Oma's insistence. My ears buzzed after the second glass, and the room spun.

Five minutes left until midnight. I swirled the red wine around the cup and wondered if it would be okay to dump it.

"Too bad Phebe couldn't go this year." I pictured my little sister pouting at home while squeezing her stuffed pig.

"It's not appropriate to take children to those kinds of functions." Oma snorted.

"Dad takes care of her."

Oma snorted again.

"Oma." I twisted around to gaze into my grandmother's face. "Why don't you like Phebe?"

Oma stared at the television.

"Oma, please. Tell me why. You want me to tell you everything, but you never tell me anything."

Oma took a sip of her wine. The silence was so long I figured I wouldn't get an answer, but then my grandmother spoke.

"I don't like *him*."

"Dad's never done anything to you!" He never yelled, not even when Phebe or I did something naughty.

"He took your mom away."

"From you?" I groaned. "Oma, they're married! That's what happens when kids grow up. They get married."

"Not from me," Oma snapped. "He took her away from your father."

I sucked my lower lip into my mouth. *Oma has dementia. She doesn't know what she's talking about.* "He *is* my father."

"He's *not*." Oma slammed the plastic cup onto the bedside table. Wine sloshed over the rim, soaking a notepad. "Its high time you found out. I always told her she would have to tell you someday. One look at your birth certificate will tell you the truth."

"Oma." My voice cracked, heart pounding. "Dad isn't my father?"

"Of course not, but you wouldn't remember. I don't know how old you were, maybe two, when they got married."

I tried to picture the wedding pictures I'd seen at home. I couldn't recall seeing anyone in the pictures holding a baby.

Oma didn't know what she was talking about.

"He is my father." Tears burned my eyes.

"No, it's that other man. John."

"Who's John?" I squeaked. *Impossible.*

"John...No, not John. That other man. I can't remember his name."

"Who is *John*?"

"Your uncle, whatever his name is. He's your father."

Not John, then. *Tom.* "Uncle Tom is my real dad? That's not true!" I rolled to my knees. "Oma, you had a dream. You dreamt it."

"Of course I didn't dream it. Your mom met that man, Tom, or whatever his name is, and they fell in love. I told her not to get married too soon, but she went and did it anyway. She had you, and then *that man* came back from somewhere. He was off in some other country writing, or something, and then she met him. She left your father for his own brother." Oma snorted.

"But Uncle Tom wants nothing to do with me! If he was my dad—"

"He never wanted a kid. I don't know if he even wanted to get married. Your mother pushed him into it. All he cared about was becoming a priest."

"Reverend," I corrected numbly.

Uncle Tom rarely called us. He never sent anything to Mama or the man I called Dad. He never wrote to Phebe, either, just me.

"Doesn't Uncle Tom like me?" Phebe had asked once.

My heart had broken for my sister. Oma shunned Phebe, and the little girl accepted it with bravado, but to have an uncle ignore you, too…

"He's never met you, sweetie," Mama had explained. "He only met Keziah, and that was once. He and your father were never close."

*Your father.* Phebe wasn't my sister. She was my *half-*sister.

"Is Phebe Uncle Tom's daughter, too?" I asked, but my heart already knew.

"Of course not. Look at what they did to that poor man, your mother and *him*. That girl, too. Poor Tom, he was so nice. Always so nice. He called me sometimes, after your mother left him. He never held a grudge. I'll never know what pain that little girl brought to him."

"Oma," I said, "I don't believe you." *I can't believe you.*

"Go upstairs, then." Oma shrugged. "You asked me to tell you, so I did, but don't you dare tell anyone I said it."

"What's upstairs?" My hand shook around the cup, and I gulped the wine before it could spill. The drink burned my throat and sinuses.

"A copy of your birth certificate. It's somewhere in the desk upstairs. Go look if you want to." Oma shrugged again. Another musical guest came onto the television.

I set the cup next to Oma's and ran upstairs before my grandmother changed her mind about allowing me upstairs.

My bare feet echoed off the stairs. When I turned on the light, the click of the switch echoed like a boom. The desk beneath the window hulked in the shadows like a giant. My legs wobbled as I picked my way across discarded boxes and worn-out shoes. When I opened the top drawer, my hands felt like someone else's.

*This is a dream, and I'm going to wake up soon.*

I picked over bingo dotters and address labels so old they'd lost their stickiness. There were papers, but they were receipts and letters from people I didn't know.

Three more drawers to go.

In the next drawer down, I found more letters, also some old Christmas cards and check stubs.

Two more drawers to go.

I opened the next to find manila folders. I opened them, dropping them on the floor as I went along, and there it was. The folder in my lap contained certificates. The first was a death certificate for my grandfather. Next were his birth certificate, Mama's, and mine.

I sat down on the floor, staring at the writing. I'd been born at New Winchester hospital. I read the date, nodding. Yup, that was my summer birthday. Mama's name was written out fully, and then my father's.

Thomas Geller de Forest.

I squeezed my eyes shut. Uncle Tom really was my father.

Downstairs, Oma turned up the television, and the house rang with the countdown to the ball drop. Far away in the city, my parents and Phebe would watch it too.

No, not my parents. My mother and my uncle. He was my uncle, not my father.

I wondered if Oma had turned up the television on purpose.

I didn't feel like going back downstairs. I rolled onto my side. The wooden floor was cold and hard. I tucked my arm under my head and let the tears come. The copy of my birth certificate floated next to me.

\*\*\*\*

*I am six years old. A boy at school is absent for a week. When he returns, he wears a yellow T-shirt that reads* "Florida".

*"My grandpa died," he says. "My grandma was so sad, she died too.* The next day. *" He emphasizes his last sentence by widening his eyes.*

*I never knew people died from grief before that morning.*

*My grandfather is dead. Will Oma die now, too?*

*I go to Mama's classroom after school to cry. She hugs me.*

*"Oma is fine. Don't worry."*

*I can't get the thoughts out of my head, so later, Mama walks me to Oma's house.*

*"I don't want you to die," I wail.*

*"I'm too strong for that." Oma kisses my forehead. "I was very sad when your grandfather died, but I have you. You're my special one."*

*"You'll stay with me?"*

*"Always."*

# Chapter 26

I played the conversation I wanted to have with Mama in my mind, but each time, it didn't sound right. It came across as whiny or immature, so I didn't say anything. Oma never brought it up again, and I assumed my grandmother had forgotten about telling me.

"How was your Christmas?" Meg asked after we returned to school.

*I found out my uncle is really my dad.* "Fine," I barked.

"Right." Meg drawled out the word before backing away.

"You okay?" Domenick asked when I failed a Spanish test.

*My family has lied to me for all of my life.* "I'm fine."

"But you never fail anything."

It irked me that Domenick could know me so well. "I don't get all hundreds!"

"But you don't fail."

He walked away, and I stuck my tongue at his back, not caring I'd been rude.

I finally felt calmer when Michael helped me take down the decorations. Instead of his usual shaggy hair, he'd gone with a buzz cut.

"My mom hates really short hair," he handed me a wooden candy cane. "After one day of having her treat me like a little kid, I went and got it cut. Do you like it?"

I set the candy cane down. "It looks cool, but I like long hair."

"Into the rugged, bad-boy look, huh?"

I laughed, accepting another candy cane. "Sure, we'll go with that."

"Want to see my tattoo, then?" He wriggled his eyebrows.

My laugh wasn't so much over that as the idea sparkling in my mind.

Mama and I shared the same hair shade of light brown. My "dad" and Phebe both had dark brown hair. My real dad, Tom, had black hair.

"What will it be?" The buxom hairdresser asked when I entered the boutique next to *Ann's*.

"Short." My lips trembled, but I smiled. "Black. Short and very black."

When she started snipping my silky tresses, I almost cried, but I bit back the tears. Somehow, the emotional pain of detachment felt amazing.

Two hours later, I walked out of the small boutique with shoulder-length black hair. I'd never known how heavy hair felt before, but the absence was palpable.

"Hey, Oma," I walked into the house with the hood of my coat hiding my head.

"Well," Oma snarled from the bedroom, "are you going to share how your day was, or just ignore me today?"

"It was okay. I needed help on Spanish." My nerves tingled. "I'm going to go take a shower and try a new hairstyle, okay?"

Oma ran her fingers over her oily hair. It hung in limp strings around her face. "You never wash *my* hair."

"Do you want me to wash your hair?" Whenever I asked, Oma refused, saying she was too tired.

"No, I'm too tired. My toenails need cutting, too."

"Um, what?" I dropped my shoulder bag and flexed my arm.

"Just look!" Oma pulled off her loafers and socks. What lay beneath sent me reeling.

The *things* couldn't even be called toenails. They were thick and yellow, with grayish fuzz around the cuticles, and at least two inches long. The ends curved sideways and under, forced that way by constant wear of shoes. Whitish lumps of skin grew around Oma's joints like mushrooms.

I gagged. "When was the last time you cut your toenails?"

"I can't remember," Oma snapped. "I can't bend over anymore. I'm *old*."

"You want *me* to cut that?"

"I'm not!"

I backed to the doorway, the back of my hand pressed to my mouth to keep out the sour stench. "Can I take you to a foot doctor?"

"Doctors make up illnesses."

"I'm going to do my hair." I couldn't do anything about the feet without gagging more. "I'll...do all that...later."

*How am I supposed to cut those toenails?*

I still didn't know after my shower, but I got out the nail clippers and a file. Holding my breath, I tried to snip a corner of the littlest toenail, but it was too thick.

"I'm going to have to take you to a podiatrist," I said through the scarf wrapped over my mouth.

"A pedifialatist?" Oma mutilated the word. "Anything's better than a foot doctor."

I didn't bother to say a *podiatrist* was a foot doctor.

Oma pointed at my hair. "Did you just do that to yourself? You look ugly. You'd better hope it grows out soon."

I winced as the words cut deep. So what if it made my skin look sallow and my eyes glossy?

Later that night, I wrote my blood father a letter to ask why he didn't contacted me more. I was his *daughter*, and the more I wrote, the angrier I became. How could he abandon me like that?

By the end of the four-page letter, there were at least two-hundred exclamation points and a dozen underlines. I tucked the floral stationary into a matching envelope and sealed it, but I didn't remember Uncle Tom's address, so I only wrote his name on the outside, along with my address as the sender, and hid it in the desk to mail later.

****

For English, I had to write an essay about something I wanted. I chewed on the end of my pen while staring at the assignment sheet, the voices of my classmates winding around my mind. What *did* I want?

"Gustavo?" The teacher called on a boy in the back row. His friends snickered as he coughed, standing up from his desk.

"I want," he boomed, "a girl with giant jug tits and a—"

"That's enough," the teacher interrupted. "I should have known you'd say something like that. When will I learn?" She waved him back into his seat when he used his hands to form an image of that perfect girl.

"What *I* want," the teacher exemplified, "is world peace. All of these so-called leaders of the 'free' world need to unite. Instead of having hundreds of individual countries, we should all be one, big country. The country of Earth…"

She continued talking, but I droned out the high-pitched voice.

World peace would be nice, but what I really wanted was for everyone to live together—Mama, my dad/uncle, Phebe, and Oma. We could live in New York City or New Winchester. It didn't matter, just as long as we were together.

I sighed. It could never happen. Oma would never forgive my dad/uncle for marrying Mama when she'd been wedded to his brother, and Phebe was a constant reminder of that shame, as Oma saw it.

I tapped the corner of the notebook paper with the pen, smearing a faint trail of indigo ink across the crisp whiteness. I couldn't write about that because I couldn't tell anyone about who my blood-father was. People would look at me funny. Even if they had skeletons hiding in the closet, it was easier to target other people than sympathize.

"Rachel?" the teacher called on a new student.

"I want a new pair of pumps." Rachel lifted her foot to point at the shiny pink shoes she wore. "I saw a really cool pair in *Macy's*."

"What a dumb blonde," a boy whispered in the back of the room.

"They're wicked expensive, though," Rachel continued, "so Mom said I can pay for them instead of my car insurance next month. So," she finished with a grin, "I'm going to write about the world of fashion."

"Okay." The teacher crinkled her nose, maybe put off by Rachel's selfish want as compared to the world peace theory. "Any other ideas? Angelo?"

"I want more practice time," Angelo replied. "You gotta love dirt bike racing."

"So you do. Meg?"

"I want to get my art into an online magazine." Meg already wrote in her notebook.

"That's nice." The teacher smiled. "What about you, Ricky?"

"I don't know yet," Ricky said.

"Get to thinking. Time is precious." The teacher's gaze flitted over the class. Her hand rested on the Smart Board, but she hadn't written ideas down, yet. She honed in on her next victim. "Ah. Keziah. We never hear from you. What are your ideas?"

I tucked a wayward strand of short hair behind my ear. "I want my grandmother to remember."

"You want your grandmother to…remember." The teacher rolled the sentence around her tongue. "That's an interesting concept, but you need to elaborate. What do you want her to remember?"

"I want her to remember all the times she used to dress me up and walk me down to see Mom for lunch." I closed my eyes, recalling the pictures I'd found from those moments "I want her to remember where she puts her glasses, so she doesn't think I always hide them on her. I want her to remember she already ate lunch, so she doesn't eat two yogurts a day. I want her to remember what a balanced meal is, so she isn't just eating yogurt."

I set the pen on my desk to stare into the teacher's eyes, daring her to stop the tirade. "I want her to remember Phebe is just an innocent little kid. I want her to remember she paid Uncle Jan for the milk and stop giving him all those tens. I want her to remember how to use the remote control for the television."

Angelo snickered.

"I want her to *remember*."

"That…is an interesting topic to write about." The teacher rubbed her nose before she swung her gaze over her students. "Any other ideas? I need hands raised high and tall, people!"

I wrote my name on the top of the paper. Across from it, I wrote the date, and in huge print, I titled the paper *Oma*.

\*\*\*\*

Meg darted in front of me in the hallway. "That was really powerful stuff you were saying about your grandma. I didn't know it was that bad."

"Thanks." I shut my locker. Metal clattered against metal. "It's not really all that bad. I love Oma."

"You know what you need?" Meg rested her shoulder against the locker beside mine. "You need a break."

"If you say so." I shrugged. Why wouldn't Meg go away? I didn't *get* a break.

"Excuse me, Megs." Matt emerged from the crush of hallway walkers. "I need to get my stuff."

"Sure thing." Meg tugged on my sleeve. "Hey, Keziah, we're all hanging out on Friday night. We're going to do the whole dinner and a movie thing. We'd love for you to join us."

"We?" Matt repeated as he opened his locker. "I'm going too?"

"No. It's a girl's night. Okay, Kez, *I'd* love for you to go, too."

"I can't. Oma wouldn't like it."

245

"She's your *grandmother*. Grandmas love it when their grandkids have fun. It's all part of the grandparents spoiling you syndrome."

*You have yet to see how Oma treats Phebe. That would dispel your syndrome.* "Oma isn't quite like that."

"Keziah, please." Meg tightened her grip. "At least promise me you'll ask your grandmother if you can go?"

"Okay." Anything to make Meg go away. I would ask, but I would also do one better. I would tape-record the conversation to play back for Meg later. After Meg got a whiff of the tears and screams, the *why-do-you-hate-me-so-much*, she'd never ask me to hang out again. I could be left alone with my misery.

**** 

When I told her about the offer, Oma smiled. "That's so nice. I love it when you have friends."

I blinked. *Oma will change her mind before Friday.*

When Friday came around, Oma went through her dresser and took out a sleeveless beige shirt with pink curlicues. "Here, why don't you wear this? I've never worn it, but you'll look decent in it. There's not much that looks nice on you since you ruined your hair."

I accepted the shirt, but I didn't wear it. I'd expected Oma to change her mind about allowing me to go out, so when Meg pulled her car into the driveway, I realized I didn't even want to go out. Oma preferring I stay home had been a truth, but it had also become an excuse. Without that, I was stuck going and having to socialize. I hadn't had to do that in a long while.

*Awesome.*

I groaned as I picked up my purse. Oma stood in the doorway waving, a huge smile on her face.

"Have fun, Keziah! My, you have such nice friends." Oma winked. "They remind me of the Goat Children."

"Sure." I hesitated with my hand on the screen door, then rushed back to give Oma an embrace. "Bye. I'll be home soon." I didn't want to release her frail body. If only my hug could make her strong again.

"And I'll be here if the Goat Children haven't whisked me away." Oma laughed.

The sound echoed in my ears as I stepped through the snow on the porch to the driveway.

Meg drove and Olivia sat next to her in the passenger's seat, a girl from economics. Marianna, another girl from school, sat in the backseat. I opened the back door and slid into the only empty spot.

"Hey," Meg sang. "See, I told you your grandmother would be okay about you going out."

"She seems cool." Olivia chewed a hangnail.

"My grandparents in Mexico—" Marianna began, but Meg cut her off.

"Cool it, Anna. You can sprout your Mexico stuff all the time at school, but we all know your parents are from Louisiana."

"And," Olivia contributed, "your real name *is* Louisiana. Marianna's your middle name."

"Please." Marianna rolled her eyes. "So you say."

"Your name is Louisiana Marianna?" I tried to smother the giggle, but it escaped anyway.

"Smith," Marianna added. "My last name is Smith. So you see why I don't go around bragging about being named Louisiana Smith."

Meg laughed as she backed out of the driveway. Maybe the evening wouldn't be so horrible.

****

*I am nine years old today. Oma takes me on a shopping spree. I get to buy anything I want, but I know not to ask for too much.*

*"Oma doesn't have a lot of money," Mama reminds me before I leave home.*

*I request new pants, a new shirt, and a porcelain doll from the toy store. It reminds me of the one in my favorite movie.*

*Oma gets us matching, lime green, fingerless gloves. We wear them every day.*

# Chapter 27

"Let's eat at Applebee's," Olivia suggested.

"I've never been to one," I said.

Olivia smacked my arm. "That does it. We're eating there."

"You're in for a big treat," Meg gushed as she parked the car. "It's one of my favorite restaurants. You're going to love eating here."

The glow of the restaurant lights cascaded over the seats. The hostess sat us with a beaming smile. Looking at the menu, though, proved there were few vegetarian options. I ordered a veggie appetizer.

"I can't believe you're a vegetarian," Olivia said. "I could never live without a good steak."

"I need my burgers," Marianna said.

She and Olivia slapped hands.

"Don't you have any pets?" I swirled the straw through my lemonade.

"I have two dogs," Olivia said, as Marinna answered, "I have ten cats."

"Jinx. We said it at the same time." Olivia laughed.

"And she really does have ten cats." Meg blew bubbles into her diet Coke.

"Don't you realize pets are animals, too? Would you eat your pet?" I pressed. "Can't you imagine what it must be like to be meant for slaughter? What gives us the right to mass murder living things?"

"But animals eat other animals," Olivia argued.

"Only as much as they can eat. Pounds of meat go bad every day."

"Only pounds?" Marianna gasped and rolled her eyes.

I winced.

"Enough of these downer talks." Meg tapped her fingernails over the tabletop. "Let's see if we can get the waiter to serve us some alcohol."

"No, thanks." I took a long sip of my lemonade. Friends were cool, but not ones who didn't understand my life choices. I put up with enough crap from Oma.

When the meals arrived, I ate in silence, listening to Marianna gush about her boyfriend.

"Manuel is so sexy with his shirt off!"

*At least we'll be quiet in the movie.*

After the car doors had slammed shut, Olivia kicked the windshield from her seat. I jumped, but Marianna and Meg kept talking about Manuel.

"Let's go to the park instead," Olivia suggested.

Meg chuckled. "You mean our old haunt?"

"Awesome!" Marianna clapped her hands. "Keziah, you're in for it."

My stomach churned. *Uh oh.* I didn't want to go to an old haunt at a park. "It's winter. Isn't the park closed?"

"Technically, yeah." Meg nodded. "They plow one of the parking lots, though. I guess that's so park management can still keep an eye on things."

"Won't we get into trouble?"

"That's what's so much fun about it," Olivia said.

"Shh," Meg hissed at her friend. "We won't get in trouble. People do it all the time. They go cross-country skiing and snowshoeing. We'll just go hang out at the playground. It's really peaceful. You'll love it."

I might start to enjoy myself. They weren't *that* bad.

Yes, I was going to make the best of things.

****

A wooden fence surrounded the New Winchester Park, only the tops visible above the buildup of snow. Meg turned into the main driveway, the pavement dusted in white. She drove past the empty baseball field and a wooden pavilion with snow-covered picnic tables inside. Beyond the maintenance building and soccer field, Meg pulled into a parking space and turned off the car.

"We're here," Olivia sang. "Welcome to our hideout."

I peered out the window at the white wonderland playground. Car doors slammed and I realized everyone except me had gotten out. I pulled on the handle and swung my door open, dropping my feet into snow that crunched, deep enough to reach my ankles.

Meg popped the trunk and Olivia pulled out two beers. She tossed one to Marianna, but her friend dropped it. Laughing, Marianna picked it up and blew snow off the lid.

"Want one?" Olivia asked Meg.

Meg glanced at me before shaking her head. "Nah, I'm driving."

"How about you?" Olivia asked me.

"No, thanks."

Meg led the way through to the playground. I swore under my breath as snow deep enough to reach our knees soaked through my cargo pants. Marianna used her bare hand to brush off a swing and sat down, wiping her palm across her coat.

Olivia and Meg did the same, sitting to face me. Marianna popped the lid on her beer and drew a long gulp, smacking her lips.

I took my black gloves out of my coat pocket to brush off the last swing seat. I shook them off, snowflakes flying, and stuffed them back in. When I sat, water soaked through to my panties, nipping my skin. I placed my hands on the metal chains, but pulled back at their icy feel. How could the others grip like that?

"I wish I was a kid again," Olivia sipped her beer, her pinky finger lifted.

"I don't." Meg pushed off from the ground, pumping her legs. "I love driving too much."

"How about you, Keziah?" Olivia took another sip.

*If I were a kid again, I'd think my family was perfect. I wouldn't know about who my real dad is.* "Sometimes."

"That's not a good answer," Marianna said. "I like being a grown-up. Kids can't have sex."

"They aren't *supposed to* have sex," Meg corrected. "My little cousin told me the other day about doing it with some boy in her class, and she's in fifth grade."

I pictured Phebe. *If my sister started having sex...* I shuddered.

"Hey, you cold or something?" Meg asked. "You're shivering."

"I'm fine." I rose from the swing. "I have to call my grandma and check on her. I'll be right back."

"Have fun," Meg called.

Marianna poured beer into the snow. "What do you think frozen beer tastes like?"

252

"Dumbass, beer doesn't freeze. It's like soda." Olivia giggled.

"It does so." Marianna dropped onto her hands and knees like a dog to lick the beer snow.

I slammed the car door, sealing myself into what remained of the heat. I fished my cell phone out of my purse and dialed Oma's number. I only half wondered if beer really did freeze.

On the eighth ring, my grandmother answered. "What?"

"It's me, Keziah—"

"So you deign yourself to call me now?" Oma began to cry. "Where are you? I turn around and you're gone. You just leave without saying goodbye now. Who are you? What have you done with my little Keziah?"

"You saw me leave with Meg!"

"Stop your lies. I don't care anymore about you. Just go away and never come back!" *Click.*

"Oma? Oma!" I swore, ending the call. I dialed my condo in the city.

Mama answered on the first ring. "Keziah! Thank goodness, where are you?"

I looked out the window at Marianna licking snow. "I'm at the movies with a girl from school."

"You know you can't leave your grandmother at night."

*What?*

"She's worried sick about you. She's been calling us every five minutes to come down and get you," Mama continued. "If she knew how to call the police, she would have!"

"I told her where I was going, and she was cool with it."

"Keziah, you *know* how your grandmother is. It's your job to be there. You wanted to stay with her. You have to take responsibility for her."

"But that's not fair! I need a life and—"

"I wish I could be there for Oma, but I can't." Mama's voice broke. "Do you want her to be scared and alone?"

"I'll go home now." I hung up before Mama could say anything else and I stormed back to the group. "I have to go home."

"Are you nervous about the beer?" Marianna asked.

"I...no, it's my grandmother." I didn't have to explain to them.

"It's cool," Meg said. "Family comes before friends."

I wanted to say they weren't really my friends, but I bit back the retort.

"I hope you had fun," Meg said when she pulled into Oma's driveway. "We'll do this again sometime."

"I can't," I muttered. "I can't leave my grandmother alone."

"That's weird."

Meg might have said more, but I slammed the car door. They weren't great people and I was in trouble for trying to have fun.

I must have been the life of the party on the way back to Oma's; I never said a word, my arms folded across my chest. What was there to say? *Sorry my grandmother has dementia?*

I stormed across the front porch, not caring how deep the snow was. The top layer had crusted over with ice, breaking against my thighs. I yanked open the screen door and reached into my purse for my key. The porch light wasn't on, so I had to squint and angle my purse until the streetlight reached it.

"Great." I must have left my key on the table. I'd done that a time or two.

I banged on the door, and Oma turned on the hall light. After marching across the floor and parting the door curtain, her eyes blazed fire and she walked away. The light switched off.

I pounded on the door harder. "Oma, it's me. Let me in already."

Silence. I swore as I pulled my cell phone out and called Mama.

"Keziah—" Mama began.

"Oma won't let me in!"

"Where's your key?"

"I don't know. I forgot it in the house." I tried to squint through the curtain at the hall table, but the sheer fabric obscured my vision.

Mama moaned. "What's wrong with you? Where's your head at?"

I squeezed my eyes shut, blocking out her voice.

"Please, can't you just call Oma and ask her to let me in?" Tears burned my eyes.

Mama sighed. "Yes, I'll call her."

We hung up and a moment later, the house phone rang. I couldn't hear what was said, and I couldn't see Oma. My cell phone buzzed.

"Hello?" The caller ID said it was Mama.

"Why couldn't you have remembered your key? I'm going to have to call Uncle Jan. He has a key. He'll come over and let you in. Keziah, why do you have to make things so difficult—"

I snapped my cell phone shut and leaned against the door, my forehead pressed against the frosted glass. Tears scalded my cheeks. Why did Oma do this to me? It wasn't fair. My whole life couldn't surround Oma and dementia. *If Oma was normal, she wouldn't care if I went out with my friends.*

The phone rang inside the house. I pressed my ear against the glass, straining to listen.

"Yes," came my grandmother's garbled response. "She's here. No, you don't have to call the police. She's right here. Yes. Bye, Jan."

I banged my fist against the door. Uncle Jan had called instead of coming over. He wouldn't come over now that Oma had told him everything was fine.

I sat down on the porch steps even though the snow was cold. My pants were already soaked, what did a little more wetness matter?

I dialed Uncle Jan's house line, but his line gave me the busy signal. I considered throwing my phone at the magnolia tree, but that wouldn't do any good.

"Keziah?"

I blinked away tears to peer down the yard. Michael stood in his driveway with a bag of trash. I grabbed the railing to stand up, heedless of the icy snow biting my hand. As I walked down the sidewalk, it felt as if I floated. This wasn't real. Oma hadn't locked me out in the cold.

Michael met me at the driveway. "What's wrong, honey? You been crying?" He brushed the pad of his thumb across my cheek, obscuring the tears.

He was so warm. I squeezed my eyes shut against a fresh onslaught of tears, and then words tumbled out of my mouth.

"I didn't want to, but Meg said I should, so I went out to eat her and her friends. The food was awful, and then we were supposed to see a movie, but instead they wanted to go to their hideout thing. Now Oma's mad because I guess she forgot where I was, or I wasn't supposed to leave the house, or something. So now she's locked me out. My mom's mad at me, and Uncle Jan doesn't care." Breath rushed out.

"Aw, don't cry, babe." He cupped my frozen face in the palms of his hands.

They were such big hands, so warm. I leaned into his grasp with a moan.

"I don't know what to do."

"Come on over to my place to warm up. You can call your uncle, okay? He seems like a nice guy."

"He is nice, he just...he just doesn't care." *I'm surrounded by borderline neglectful adults.*

"We'll get him to care, then. Come on." Michael stepped away from me.

I stood in the driveway watching him glide over the snow, a specter dressed in black.

"You coming?" He stood on the stone stoop, the screen door propped against his back. His hand rested on the doorknob.

I hesitated before I nodded.

\*\*\*\*

*I am twelve years old. We are at my cousin's wedding in Virginia, and the temperature is ninety degrees.*

*I stand beside a pond filled with goldfish. Phebe is in her stroller next to me, and I help her learn to count by pointing out the fish.*

*"One," I say. "Two. Three." The goldfish keep swimming, so the total will be inaccurate, but Phebe is too young to care.*

*She claps her hands, giggling.*

*Oma stands with my cousin, his wife, his parents, her parents, and her grandparents.*

*"Get closer," the photographer says. They do, and he snaps a picture. "Only two more. We want to make this perfect."*

*Someday, that will be my husband and me. Oma will stand beside us and beam like that, happy for me. I will move on to a new life with her at my side.*

# Chapter 28

The hallway smelled like dust balls. The hideous green carpet and faded yellow walls did nothing to help the appeal. When I walked past Michael, he shut the door and threw the single bolt.

A shiver coursed through my spine, but I shook away the sensation. He was being nice and making sure no one broke in and hurt me, nothing creepy. The narrow stairs creaked beneath our feet with mournful wails. A diamond-shaped window provided the only light. I switched my attention forward and blushed as my gaze landed on his butt. It was a nice butt, I decided, watching it shift beneath his tight jeans, the back pockets accentuating its firmness. He opened the sliding glass door at the top.

"That's a weird door. It looks like something from a patio." My voice echoed through the empty stairway.

Michael shrugged, shutting it behind me, like the door downstairs. He ran his hand over my arm before stepping into his living room. The wooden floors had no rugs. There was a large maroon couch and a table with a lamp. Across from the couch, a large-screen television sat on a stand.

"You don't have much," Crap, that sounded rude.

Michael shrugged, touching my arm again. "I don't need much. Come into the kitchen and I'll get you a drink."

There was a table with four chairs, and other than the counters and refrigerator, nothing. I pulled out one of the chairs and sat down, setting my purse on the tabletop.

Michael opened the refrigerator and grabbed two beer bottles. "You like Bud Light?"

"No, I m-mean..." I stammered, "I don't drink b-b-beer."

He laughed. "Chill out, babe. I was just offering. When I was your age, I'd have killed for a beer. How about a soda instead, or green tea?"

I wanted to decline, but my mouth felt dry. "I'll have the green tea. Please." He handed me a can. "Thank you. I … I never had it in a can before."

"Huh." He swung a chair around and dropped into it, leaning against the high back. He popped the lid off his beer and took a swig, then wiped his mouth on the back of his hand. "You still cold? You got your coat on."

I pulled the zipper down with numb fingers and flexed my hand. The skin began to warm. I slid my arms out of the sleeves and spread it over the back of my chair.

Michael set his beer on the table and reached for my can. I watched his long fingers slide through the cap, snapping it open. They were man fingers—far thicker than mine, with stout nails.

"Thanks." I would have loved cocoa or hot tea, but he'd offered the can, and it seemed wrong to decline it now—especially after he'd opened it. I took a sip. It tasted tangy and delicious. I took a longer sip.

*I should call Uncle Jan.* Instead, I watched Michael drink his beer. The muscles in his throat tensed and relaxed as he swallowed. His small Adam's apple bounced.

He set down his beer. "You want to see my library?"

"You have a library in here?"

"Yeah. I collect classics. My grandpa got me into the hobby. Most of my stuff is at my mom's, but I've got a lot here, anyway." He stood up, and twirled the chair on one of its legs before pushing it into the table.

I stood and realized my boots were dripping snow all over the floor. So were his, but I blushed.

"We should, um, take off our shoes, I guess."

"Sure, but the floor's in pretty bad shape already." He kicked off his sneakers, then drank from his beer while I unlaced my boots and removed them. I set them behind my chair, adding to the puddle dripping off my coat. I grabbed my iced tea and followed him to a small hallway with three doors.

"Bedroom." He tapped the first door and moved to the second. "Bathroom, and this one," he turned the knob, "is my library. Voila!"

Beneath the window rested a cluttered desk, complete with a computer and telephone. There was a table with an electric keyboard, and the final wall contained a bookcase. Books piled one atop the other, overflowed corkboard shelves.

I stepped over a pair of plaid boxers, averting my gaze although my cheeks flamed. Most of the books looked like first additions. I sipped the tea while I read the titles on the bindings.

"I get them at book sales." His breath heated my cheek. I hadn't realized he was that close.

"Cool."

"My favorite is that one." He tapped a blue book. "The complete works of Jane Austen. People usually look at me weird about that. I guess only girls are supposed to read her literature."

"I think it's pretty sexy you read it." The words slipped out. *Sexy?* Why on Earth had I said that?

He chuckled, and his hand pressed against the small of my back. Then, he stepped away. Breath caught in my throat, and I coughed before taking another drink.

"Your pants are all wet," he said.

"Yeah. I…fell in the snow."

"You can't go around like that." He turned me around to face him. "I've got an old pair of pajama pants with a drawstring. Why don't you go change into them?"

"No, I couldn't."

He held up one hand while he set his beer on a shelf. "Hey, I don't mean anything by it. After you change, you can call your uncle. In the meantime, you really should change into something dry. You don't want to catch pneumonia."

"You can't catch pneumonia from having wet pants." *I shouldn't be here.*

"Keziah, please." He set both hands on my shoulders. "It would make me happy if you changed into something dry so you don't get sick. Trust me, your family will understand under these circumstances."

I opened my mouth to protest again, but then I thought about if I'd been back in New York City. If Michael were one of Tiffany's friends, I would have no problem changing into his clothes until my mom came. In fact, it had happened once. Tiffany and I had visited one of her friends when the sky decided to downpour. The friend had lent me a dress.

Of course, Michael was male, and Tiffany's friend was female, but overall it was the same thing. I shivered, aching for something warm and dry.

"Okay. Thanks." The can crinkled, and I realized I'd tightened my hand into a fist. I relaxed it and took another drink.

"This way, Kezy." Michael exaggerated a bow, leading me from his "library" to the bedroom.

The room was dark from the thick blanket spread over the window. There wasn't a bed, only an air mattress. The closet door stood open, clothing spilling out to spread across the floor. He picked through the items until he came across a pair of red pants.

"The drawstring can go really tight, so they should fit you." He pressed them into my hand. "I'll wait outside while you change."

He left the door open a crack; light from the kitchen spilled into the bedroom. I set the can on the floor and fumbled with the button on my jeans. The zipper was loud in the stillness of the room that smelled of Old Spice.

I pulled the pants down, along with my soggy panties, and stepped into the pajamas, the jersey fabric soft and worn. I tugged the drawstring, and tugged again. The fabric stuck, not wanting to tighten. I swore.

The door creaked and Michael drew a breath. I froze. He stood in the doorway with a dazed expression on his face, almost as if he'd seen something beautiful.

"I...um...it won't..." My voice trailed off and my hands shook.

Michael pushed the door open the rest of the way. The floorboards creaked as he stepped toward me, framed in the glow of the kitchen light. He stopped when he was so close I could have reached out to touch him.

"I should call my uncle," I whispered, but my lips didn't want to move right.

As if in slow motion, I watched his hand ascend toward my face. He cupped my cheek, and I squeezed my eyes shut, breath snaring behind my teeth. This was a dream. I wasn't the type of girl who got into compromising situations.

"Michael," I squeaked. "No."

"Yes." He used his hand to tip my face up, and his lips pressed against mine.

They were dry, rough, and then they were wet, moving against mine. He smelled of deodorant and shampoo. His other hand touched my back, sliding to my bottom, and he drew me against him. Something firm and large pressed against my stomach through his jeans.

I had to pull away before things went too far.

His lips parted against mine, and his tongue slid into my mouth. The scent of saliva filled my nostrils. I clung to the drawstrings until my hands hurt, but I couldn't bring myself to push him away.

I wanted to feel anything except anger. I ached to be needed, wanted, worthy.

His lips moved against mine, light kisses falling upon the corners of my mouth. He sucked on my lower lip, nipping it, and chuckled when I gasped.

"Keziah," His lips moved over my jaw, spreading down to my neck. He licked my collarbone before biting my shoulder through my shirt.

His hands left my body, and he fumbled with the button on his jeans. I stood frozen in place, eyes widening as he dropped his pants. They pooled around his ankles, and his black boxers joined them. I squeezed my eyes shut. *No, no, no!*

He pushed my shirt up to my shoulders and slid his palms across my breasts.

"We can't fool around right now." I forced myself to step away, and I stared at the doorway, unable to look at him.

"Keziah," he moaned.

My name sounded like magic on his lips. *His lips...* I really wanted to taste them again. Longing pooled in my belly, rippling through my limbs until my nerves jumped. My legs trembled.

He released me to pull off his shirt, then his undershirt. Muscles defined across his arms and torso. My hands had a will of their own as they traced his abdomen to count each dip in his six-pack abs.

This was unreal.

"You don't want me," I whispered. "I'm just a little girl."

"I want to make love to you."

"Michael," I rasped. "Michael, wait, listen to me, please. I'm...I'm a *virgin*."

He sucked on my lips harder. "That's okay, I'll be gentle. I've had virgins before. You don't have to worry."

The blatant way he stated he'd been with other women made me step back again. I wanted to ask him how old he was the first time he'd had sex, but the words dried on my tongue.

"Don't worry, I don't have any STDs. I've checked." His hands slid over my arms to cup my elbows, drawing me nearer. "Let me take away all the pain. I can help you forget."

*Pain. Forget.* I allowed him to kiss me, but my mind whirled in other directions. My mother's voice nagged my conscience: *"Do only what I'd want you to do."*

I leaned against Michael. *Yes, please, make me forget. Make me feel normal.*

*Make me feel loved.*

He dropped to his haunches on his inflatable mattress bed and yanking me down. I stumbled, landing on my bottom. The mattress shifted, th material thicker than I'd expected. Michael knelt beside me, gripping my shoulders to push me onto my back.

I turned my head away, gasping. "Michael, wait! I've always wanted to…to wait…until…until I got…married." The words blurted forth, enflaming my cheeks. I wanted my wedding night to be more than a new chapter in my life's story, a stepping-stone. Something to share with the man of my dreams.

*My parents— No*, I cringed, not my parents. My mother and *uncle*. They never discussed sex with me. It was one of those unwritten rules, like not running around naked or eating poison.

"Shh." Michael pressed his finger over my lips.

Maybe he thought about marriage too. Maybe there was something about me that gripped his attention. He might think of me as the one for him.

"I'm sorry." I wiggled away from him. "I want to wait until we've at least been on a few dates."

"Aw, babe, you know we can't date. It would be too weird. I'm done with college and you're still in high school."

He didn't think of me as *the one*. I stood up to grab my sopping jeans.

"Keziah—"

"No."

\*\*\*\*

*I am fourteen years old. A boy moves into the apartment below ours. His name is Chris, he is fifteen, and he goes to public high school. I take Phebe down to the lobby with me every afternoon to people watch, but I really want to wait for Chris to come home. He always says hi. Once, the three of us bought doughnuts from a vendor, even though Phebe and I aren't supposed to leave the building before our parents come home.*

*After a month, I gather my courage. "Will you go out with me?"*

*My parents and I have never discussed dating, but Chris lives near us, so I'm sure it will be okay.*

*He rubs his short red hair. "I'm sorry, Kez, but I can't. It would be too weird."*

*My face stings as though he slapped me. "How would that be weird?" My voice rises too shrilly, and the concierge glances at us.*

*"Because you already live here with me." Chris wanders to the elevator, leaving me alone with Phebe.*

*When Mama comes home, I meet her at the door. "Chris doesn't want to be my friend anymore."*

*"That's too bad." She puts her coat on its hook.*

*I wonder if she remembers who Chris is.*

*"Can I call Oma and talk to her?" I'm not allowed to call long-distance without Mama or Dad.*

*"Oh, honey, Oma doesn't care about things like that." Mama fills the teakettle with water from the faucet. "You'll make other friends."*

*"But we've been here for years, and I only know Tiffany and Chris." I hate the tears that threaten my eyes. "Chris hates me now."*

*"Oma already dislikes New York City. Don't give her more to hate." Mama puts the kettle on the stove. "Would you like peppermint tea or chamomile?"*

*"Neither," I grumble. Maybe Mama is right. Oma does hate the city, so she probably wouldn't want to discuss Chris. I don't call her.*

# Chapter 29

As I opened the door, Michael folded his hand over mine on the knob. "Keziah? Really, if she doesn't let you in, or your uncle doesn't do anything, or whatever, you can come back. I don't want you outdoors."

*I'd sleep under a car before I came back here.* "Okay." I jogged down the stairs and out into the night. Once the snow struck my red cheeks, I allowed the tears to flow. I couldn't call Uncle Jan. I couldn't face him after what had happened with Michael.

I couldn't face Oma, either, but I'd noticed something through Michael's kitchen window to solve the issue.

I ran around Oma's garage to the gate. Snow and ice covered the chain-link fence, but I grabbed the top and hoisted myself over, using my feet for purchase. The metal bit into my skin; I gritted my teeth and dropped into the snow on the other side. I fought my way to Oma's apple tree.

The branches rested on the roof of the enclosed back porch. I had never been athletic, had never tried to climb a tree, but I jumped to grip the lowest branch. Holding on, I walked my feet up the trunk of the tree, swung them over, and sat up. I grabbed the next branch and swung onto that one. If I fell, I would land in snow knee-high.

The branches higher up the tree were thinner, breakable. I crawled across a branch still relatively thick. I slid my legs along, holding my breath. The edge of the roof drew near, covered in snow, but I grabbed the edge, launching myself off the branch.

The snow slipped down my collar to nip my skin. I scrambled and clawed, fighting my way up the slope of the roof, all so white and pure.

I felt dirty and horrid after making out with Michael. At least the cold took my mind away from that shame.

When I got to the top of the sloping roof, I paused. That dormer window led to the attic, but the other window opened into the bedroom Mama and I had shared when we stayed over.

The lock on that window was broken, and it didn't meet the windowsill right, so Mama had stuffed a rag into the bottom. My hands shook as I opened my purse. I pulled out a pen and shoved it under the window, working it against the sill. It dented the wood, but the window moved a little. Good, it wasn't frozen shut.

The window lifted enough for me to fit my fingers into the crack. I stood, bracing my feet against the roof, and lifted the window higher. I pushed the rag away and tossed my purse in, then lay down on my stomach to squeeze inside. The sill pressed into my belly and ribs, but I curled my fingers into claws, grabbing the desk inside. My legs kicked without effect into the snow, so I used my arms.

My elbow struck the desk, and my shoulder bumped the lamp. I fell over, my hip striking the floor.

The full moon reflected off the snow to brighten the room, but I turned on the lamp anyway. The fake orange glow illuminated the boxes Oma left on the floor. At least they weren't in front of the window. That would have really hurt if I'd landed on them.

I closed the window and scowled, kicking a box. Snores came from downstairs.

"Good for you." *Why doesn't she care about me?* I couldn't even ask Oma that question because my grandmother wouldn't know. She didn't make sense.

I peeled off my wet clothes and threw them in a corner. In the dresser drawers, I found Oma's old clothes. I pulled on a pair of gray sweatpants and a black sweatshirt with a picture of a cat.

"You and your stupid Goat Children." I pulled back the blankets on the upstairs bed and huddled into them, turned my face to the pillow, and wept.

I didn't cry from the pain in my heart or the tingles as my fingers returned to life.

I wept because the Oma, who had once been my loving grandmother, was gone forever.

\*\*\*\*

In the morning, Oma was her usual self, relying on me to get her dentures brushed and breakfast laid out. I gave her clothes to wear, and like always, she didn't acted grateful.

At school, Meg asked, "Is everything okay at home?"

"Oma was really mad." I unwrapped a stick of mint gum, Meg's peace offering.

"But everything is okay?"

"Yeah, everything's fine." There wasn't any other way to answer that question.

"Cool, so next Thursday—"

"I can't," I interrupted. "I have to watch Oma. I can't go out."

"Whoa, chill." Meg held up her hand. "I was just asking."

271

"I can't go out."

"You don't have to be mean about it." Meg rolled her eyes before walking away.

The gum no longer looked appealing. After class, I threw it in the garbage.

\*\*\*\*

I saw Michael, but his open friendliness had faded. He didn't smile like before. After the fifth cold meeting, I called Tiffany. I needed my real friend more than ever.

"Keziah! I thought you fell off the face of the Earth," Tiffany yelled. The background sounded like a club.

"Are you busy?" A Paramore song blared in the background.

A shadow fell over the doorway. Oma stood there with fire blazing on her face, hands on her hips.

"No, it's cool," Tiffany said.

"What are you doing? Don't talk on my phone," Oma shouted. "That's my phone!"

"Oma, it's my cell phone."

"You can't talk on my phone," she shrieked.

"Tiffany, I can't talk," I sighed. "I'll be online later, so I'll talk to you there."

"Sure, like usual." Tiffany hung up without saying goodbye.

"There, happy?" I threw my cell phone at the bed.

"What's wrong with you?" Oma's face wrinkled into a sob.

I didn't call Tiffany again. I waited until Mama or Phebe called me, and even then, I didn't want to talk. All I could think about was how my mother didn't care enough to tell me about my real father.

Whenever I got on the computer, Oma complained I was ignoring her. Tiffany never got on much, anyway, and when she did, she acted cold.

"Fine, I'll be friendless." I finished my homework on the computer as fast as I could, and then read, since Oma didn't want to do anything except stare at the wall.

I finished reading the Goat Children notebooks. Oma stopped writing when she married my grandfather. She had loved him, and if not for him, she would have never left the Goat Children.

I never heard Oma mention my grandfather much, so I brought him up. My grandmother shrugged.

"He's gone now. I can return to the Goat Children, if they'll have me."

"You want to go back now?"

"I'll be young again. I'll be able to hear without having the sound up so loud."

"I can take you to get a hearing aid."

"There's nothing wrong with my hearing," Oma exclaimed.

Another day, Oma said, "If I returned to the Goat Children, I'd be able to see again. I hate not being able to see well."

I looked up from my criminology textbook. "I can take you to the eye doctor if you want."

"I don't need to go to the doctor. There's nothing wrong with my sight!"

As winter progressed, the days grew worse for Oma. After I went to school, she forgot her normal routine of eating breakfast, washing, and dressing. Oma would call Uncle Jan, and usually got my aunt instead. Rather than going over to comfort Oma, my aunt called me at school.

"I don't know what to do for her," my aunt said on my voicemail. "Get home, Keziah. I don't want her calling me anymore. If you can't handle her, then she needs to go into a nursing home."

The next time Oma called my aunt, she called my mother. "You need to rethink this living situation. She's crying to me over the phone, and I can't do anything to help her."

"I'm four hours away," my mother ranted to me. "Why can't *she* just go over? She's five minutes away, for crying out loud! What do you think, Keziah?" Mama's voice softened. "Do you think Oma would hate a nursing home that much?"

"Yes! We won't let anyone put her in one of those places. I'm here. It wasn't anything dire. Oma's fine."

"Maybe it's time we moved back to New Winchester." Mama's voice wavered.

"No, Mama. You can't. You work in the city, and...Dad..." I choked on the word. He wasn't my dad. He was my *uncle*. I still didn't know how to bring up that knowledge, but I knew it wouldn't work if they moved back.

I didn't dare mention going back to the city after high school ended.

\*\*\*\*

At the end of February, the high school hosted a college fair. Seniors traveled from their last classes to the gym, where the fair began before stretching into the main foyer and orchestra room. Most of the colleges represented were in New

York State. I picked up fliers for Utica, Hamilton, and Hartwick colleges to make the teachers happy. Before coming to New Winchester, I had planned to get my Bachelor's degree, but now that was out of the question.

Money didn't matter. My dad—*uncle*—had a college fund set away in my name, and he made enough at his job for any differences in price.

I had to stay within Oma's radius.

I zeroed in on New Winchester College on the outskirts of the town, in the ritzy section of mansions and gated communities.

The young man representing the college handed me a brochure. "The best part is that's it's part of SUNY."

"Suny?" I accepted the glossy paper.

"State University of New York," he explained.

I didn't know how that mattered. "I'm looking for a teaching degree."

"What kind of teaching?" He picked up a booklet off his table and flipped through the pages.

"Elementary education."

He nodded and chewed on his lower lip. He was cute in a boyish way, with brown curls falling over his high forehead and glasses slipping down his small nose, but he had to be older than me since he attended college.

"I really love the campus," he said. "The professors are great. Dr. Sparks is around here somewhere. She can talk to you when she comes back, if you want. Ah, here it is." He handed the booklet to me, his finger pointing to a paragraph on one of the pages. "This is part of the education department."

"Thanks." I didn't care about the professors, campus, or even the classes. As long as they had a degree and were within living distance to Oma, the college was golden. I would have to take the bus, but that wouldn't be so bad.

"Hey, Keziah," Domenick called from behind.

I forced myself to smile as I turned away from the booth. "Hi."

He waved a brochure in the air, grinning. "Where do you want to go? I'm thinking about Geneseo. My cousin went there and loved it."

"I'll probably go to New Winchester."

"Aw, really? You don't want to spread your wings and get away from this dump?"

*I can't.* I shrugged.

"This is like spreading your wings, huh? Do you miss the Big Apple?"

I smiled at his slang. "A little. Especially my family. I've never been away from them this long before."

"Yeah, that's what's going to be really rough for me when I go away. My parents are moving anyway, so it won't be like I have a choice. Keziah, you know what Saturday is?"

"You mean the date?" We stepped off to the bleachers as people walked by.

"It's my birthday." His grin revealed his teeth. "I'm turning eighteen. Officially, I'll be an adult. Hey, when's your birthday?"

"July."

He whistled. "You'll be eighteen soon too, huh? So anyway, every year for my birthday, my grandpa throws this big birthday bash at his place. He lives on Lake Winchester."

"Cool."

"Can you come? It's in the evening. Since it's still snowy this year, we won't go out on the boat or anything."

"I can't."

"No—"

"I have a grandmother, remember?" I didn't care if the ice in my voice froze him.

"Bring her too."

"What?" As a joke, that wasn't funny at all.

"Yeah, bring her along." He nodded. "That was what I was gonna say, but you never gave me the chance. My family will all be there, so there won't be drugs or anything. I mentioned it to my grandpa, and he said he thinks it's nice you're there for her."

"I can't bring *my grandmother* to your birthday party."

"Sure you can. It'll be awesome."

"My grandmother has *dementia*. She's not a normal old person. She doesn't sit home baking chocolate chip cookies or knitting fuzzy sweaters. She cries because she can't remember how old she is, and then she says she's like a hundred because she lived with Goat Children for a while!"

"Keziah, come on. It'll be cool. At least give it a try."

There was no point in arguing with him. "She won't go. She'll say no."

"At least ask her." Domenick held up his hand, curled it into a fist, and stuck out his little finger. "Pinkie promise?"

*Yeah, as if we're five years old.* I slid my little finger through his. We hooked and shook. "Yeah, yeah. Pinkie promise."

I wanted to tell him about what happened when I'd gone out with Meg, and what had occurred with Michael afterwards, but Domenick walked away.

"Keziah de Forest?"

I glanced over my shoulder at an approaching teacher. The woman held a folder in her arms, wrinkled papers poking out of the purple plastic. She wore tight black plants and a purple sweater with kites on the sleeves. I tried to place her name, but failed. I'd never had her class and recognized her only by sight.

"Can I help you?" I scratched the back of my head.

"I hope so. I'm Mrs. Naylor, from journalism. I run the school paper." The teacher fumbled with her folder before pulling out a crumpled paper. "Is this yours?"

I turned the page over to spot my name under the title. "I wrote this for economics. It's a poem about how expensive vegan foods are." I frowned. "How'd you get it?"

"Your teacher gave it to me." Mrs. Naylor's glossed lips broke into a smile. "I hope you don't mind, but he was really proud of it, and suggested I publish it."

My jaw dropped. "But it's just a poem about *economics*."

Her fake French nails tapped the folder. "I realize our paper isn't always *controversial*. We've never had a specific vegan article, and that's not even why I like your poem. Your words are raw. You wrote from your heart, and you made me think. When you make a reader stop and really consider what you wrote about, it's a sign of a good author."

I snapped my mouth shut. "Thank you. No one has ever called me a good author before."

Mrs. Naylor removed a blank sheet of lined writing paper and plucked a pen from her pocket. "Can you write down your contact info for me?"

I stared at the paper and blinked. In my mind, I saw Oma listening to the exciting news. *I might have my poem published in the newspaper!* Oma might smile and nod, but she'd probably say, "What?" By the time I finished explaining, Oma would be lost and snippy, or move on to something else.

"Sure." I crouched to use the floor as a writing table.

"It's always tough being a new student. I grew up in Boston, and moved to Rochester when I was in junior high. If you ever want to talk, I'm here."

I finished writing my name, address, email, and cell phone number, and handed the materials back. "I'm kind of used to it here, now."

"Really, though." Mrs. Naylor patted my shoulder. "This is one of the best high schools in the state, which makes all the teachers here very competitive. I know they can be hard sometimes, or seem uncaring, but we're really all here to help you succeed. Hope you don't mind, but I took the liberty of looking up your schedule."

"You looked up my schedule?" That sounded a bit creepy.

"You have a study hall Monday mornings, and I have a break. I thought maybe we could meet up and chat?" Mrs. Naylor shifted her stance. "I can help you with your writing or homework. They told me about your grandmother. I can't imagine how hard that is, but your teachers said you never complain. They called you strong. If I were you, I'd want an adult to bounce ideas off, someone I can just talk with and feel comfortable letting everything out. So, do you want to meet up?"

I tipped my head, considering what solid adult figure I had in my life. Before, I would have said my parents, but they'd lied to me about Uncle Tom. Oma would want to help, but she couldn't. Uncle Jan lived in his own world, and Michael had betrayed my trust.

"Why don't we try that?" I shook her hand. "I'd like someone to talk to."

\*\*\*\*

*I am seven years old. My instructor is teaching us Spanish words, because we have a new student from Mexico.*

*"Are you illegal?" a girl asks him.*

*I don't understand what she means.*

*"I've never been to jail," He speaks English with only a faint accent, but Mrs. Rankin, our teacher, wants us to make him feel comfortable.*

*I take my list of Spanish vocabulary to Oma's house.*

*"Have you ever learned Spanish?" I ask.*

*"No, but I love learning." She laughs. "What's the first word?"*

*"Hola. It's spelled with an H, but that letter's silent."*

*"Hola," she repeats. "What does it mean?"*

*"Hello." I move on to the next word, and we practice until both of us have them memorized.*

# Chapter 30

Uncle Jan pulled up in front of the house, except I wasn't sure if it could be called a house. Three stories sprawled over grounds surrounded by a large brick fence. Lights from the mansion spilled over the grass.

Uncle Jan whistled. "Wouldn't you love to live in a place like this?"

*If we all moved here to New Winchester, we could live in a house like this.* My dad—*uncle*—made enough money, but he and my mom would never go for such a gaudy home.

"Where are we?" Oma asked from the passenger seat.

"Domenick's grandfather lives here. You wanna go home?" I still couldn't get over the fact Oma had agreed to attend the party.

"She's glad to be included," Mama had said. "Just don't let her near anyone who's sick."

Domenick's family would wonder who I was, and everyone was going to ask why I'd brought my grandmother. I was going to have to spend the evening sitting next to Oma in a corner somewhere, and everyone was going to know Oma was insane.

People were going to talk to us, but Oma wouldn't be able to hear, so she would pout or cry, then I would take her home.

*I can't believe I'm doing this.* I opened the backdoor and stepped out, stretching from the tight confines of my uncle's car. Uncle Jan still marveled over the house as I walked around to help Oma.

"I can't get out," Oma exclaimed. "You should have taken more stops. I've been riding too long! My legs won't work."

"It's only been ten minutes." I grabbed my grandmother's arm, lifting her out of the seat. She leaned against me without trying to stand on her own.

"Who are we here to see?" Oma asked as Uncle Jan drove away.

"Domenick. It's his birthday." I'd gotten him a gift card to the bookstore, his present in my purse.

"Who?"

"Domenick."

"Peter?"

"No, Domenick!" My shout roused the attention of people smoking in the yard.

They looked over, and whispered. A girl giggled.

"I can't hear you," Oma snorted.

I led Oma inside via the front door, huge with stained glass panels. The foyer boasted a crystal chandelier. A maid garbed in a navy blue dress appeared to take our coats.

"What is this?" Oma shouted. "What does this woman want?"

"She just wants to take your coat."

"I'm cold! I'm not giving my coat to just anyone."

After taking my coat, the maid said, "Ma'am, you can wear yours if you want. I'll get it from you when you're warmer."

"Thank you," I whispered, but the woman walked away. Maybe she had an elderly relative of her own at home.

"Let's go find Domenick." I tugged Oma through the foyer into the next room.

People mingled around tables covered in food. Some of the people I knew from school—not names, but the faces looked familiar. Others were adults; they must be part of Domenick's family. The house was immaculate despite the crowd, and everything looked top of the line. Antiques rested on mahogany tables. The walls were dark colors, and the wainscoting was creamy white. The floors were hardwood instead of carpeted. Velvet and lace adorned the windows.

I led Oma to a tapestry sofa against the living room wall. My grandmother hadn't said anything, but her lips pressed into a firm line as if they'd been painted on. She narrowed her eyes and a flush blotched her cheeks.

"Pouty face," I muttered under my breath as I helped Oma sit.

My grandmother's hand shook. "You're trying to push me onto the floor."

"I just want you to sit, okay? I have to go give Domenick his card."

"I don't see why I had to come," Oma coughed into her hand and fished a tissue from her sleeve to spit phlegm into it. "He's *your* friend, and you don't need male friends. You're much too young for any of *that*."

"As soon as I find him, we can go. I'll call Uncle Jan." Hopefulness seeped into my voice.

"It's your party. You always do exactly as you please."

I bit back a groan. "Look, stay here, okay? I'll be right back. Don't…wander off anywhere."

"Like I'm an invalid?"

"No, if you were an invalid, you wouldn't be able to wander."

"What?" The comeback flew over Oma's head and she blinked.

"Never mind. I'll—"

"They're here."

"What?"

"The Goat Children." Oma pointed behind me. "They've come for me."

I looked over my shoulder through a space in the crowd. My gaze fell on a potted ficus. "That's a plant."

"No, they're here," Oma said. "I told you they'd come for me."

Domenick's guests glanced our way, and a woman whispered behind her hand. Her male compadre laughed.

"Look, I'll be right back, and then I'll call Uncle Jan." I slipped into the crowd before my grandmother could say anything else.

I had dressed up for the occasion, but it made me out of place in Oma's long blue velveteen skirt and pink shirt. Stylish vintage had seemed the right choice for a ritzy birthday party, but it no longer seemed stylish. The men and women in Domenick's family dressed the same— nice pants and nice shirts. My classmates wore jeans and name brand shirts. *Old Navy* reprimanded my outdated ensemble.

People stared at me as I brushed past them. "Excuse me."

A boy from my English class said, "Hey, look, it's Jessica."

Another boy from the same class corrected him. "Nah, I think her name's Keziah or something."

*Keziah or something.... I don't belong here.*

I spotted Olivia making a call on her cell phone near an open bathroom door.

"Hey, Olivia?"

"Hey." Olivia looked up, nodded, and went back to her phone.

"Do you know where Domenick is?"

"He's in the kitchen. There was some issue with his birthday cake."

"Okay, thanks." I turned away, but Olivia's voice broke through my rush.

"You know, I didn't expect to see you here. You aren't exactly sociable."

I paused. "I have a lot going on. I don't have time to be sociable."

"Bullshit."

"What?" I jumped. "You have no idea what I'm going through with my grandmother."

"My grandmother has Alzheimer's," Olivia interrupted. "I know exactly what you're going through. She lives with us for now, but we have no idea how long that is going to last. Every day I wait to see if she's going to look at me and not remember who I am."

I licked my lips. Olivia had never mentioned her grandmother before. The girl had her gaze on the cell phone, so I couldn't read her expression. "I'm … I'm so sorry. I … I didn't know."

"Yeah, I don't like to tell people. I feel like they're going to look at me and wonder if I'm going to get like that someday, too. Don't think you're so special, Keziah, just because you have to look after your grandmother. A lot of us have stuff like that to do. We just don't fling it around like it's the end of the world. You want attention, and I get that."

285

Still looking at her phone, Olivia tapped her thigh, caught in skin-tight leopard print pants. "I do a lot of things for attention. It's just who I am, and it's who you are, so get over it. Get over yourself."

*How do I respond to that?*

"Be thankful you get this opportunity," Olivia went on. "You get to live with your grandmother. You get to spend time with her, just like what I get to do. I thank God every day for blessing me with my family. Then, I take each day one hour at a time. You get what I'm trying to say?" Olivia lifted her gaze off the cell phone's glowing screen. "Do you?"

I *was* blessed. Every day I learned something new about Oma, whether it was my grandmother's favorite color, which varied day by day, or her favorite food, something else that varied depending on the hour. I got to spend this time with her.

"Yeah." I nodded. "I do get what you're trying to say." Olivia didn't want to be harsh, just truthful. She said what I needed to hear.

"I have to go outside, the reception in here sucks." Olivia snapped her phone shut. "See you later, Keziah."

"See you later," I echoed.

Out of everyone I'd met in New Winchester, I liked Olivia the best. Even if she was odd, she was also the most down to Earth person, and she got what I went through every day.

Maybe, if Oma was in a good mood, I could invite Olivia over sometime.

\*\*\*\*

I found Domenick in the kitchen, arguing with a man who looked just like him, only thirty years older.

"I hate marble cakes," Domenick said. "I told you I hate marble."

"Your mom loves marble. She's the one who picked it up," his dad said.

"But I hate marble!"

"It's not the end of the world," his dad shot back.

I pulled the gift card out of my purse and hovered in the doorway. *Your dad's right. It isn't the end of the world.*

"Where do you want the cake?" his dad snapped.

"What does it matter what I want?" Domenick turned away and faced me. "Hey." His face reddened. "Kez, you made it!"

"Yeah." I hated the way his dad wracked his gaze over my body, as if appraising me to sell. "Here, this is for you. Happy birthday."

"Thanks!" He accepted the card and patted my arm. "I'm glad you could come."

I thought of his dad glowering in the background, and the classmates who didn't remember my name. I thought of how Olivia had called me antisocial.

"You know," I offered a smile, "I'm really glad I could come, too. There's someone I'd love for you to meet."

"Really?"

His dad had his back to us as he fiddled in a silverware drawer, so I took Domenick's hand. "My grandmother."

\*\*\*\*

287

"I can't believe she really came," Domenick said as we weaved through bodies to get to the living room.

"Today's one of her good days."

"Right." Domenick said the word as if he understood.

It felt good to have his hand wrapped around mine. Domenick, warm and solid.

I felt safe with Domenick, a sensation I hadn't realized I missed. When was the last time I'd actually felt safe?

Back in the city? No, in New York City, I felt anxious because Phebe was my responsibility. I loved my little sister, but sometimes I wanted to hang out with Tiffany during the day when she was off from school or skipping. Even though my sister wasn't an annoying brat, I knew Tiffany resented the younger presence.

The last time I'd felt safe was when we had all lived in New Winchester.

Domenick and I rounded the hallway to enter the living room.

The couch was empty. I froze, but Domenick kept walking, jerking to a halt when I didn't budge.

"Kez?"

"Where is she?" I yanked my hand free of Domenick's. "Oh my gosh, no, I left her on the couch! Where is she?"

I ran to the couch and picked up one of the toss pillows before throwing it on the floor, even though I knew Oma couldn't hide behind it.

"Domenick, she isn't here. Oma isn't here!"

"Kez, calm down. Chill." Domenick grabbed my arm. "She probably just went to the bathroom."

"I told her to stay right here. She wouldn't have gone to the bathroom." I turned in a circle. The faces of strangers blurred together. No one glanced over. I looked at the plant Oma had thought was a Goat Child, and I wished I spoke vegetation, so I could ask it where my grandmother had gone.

"Keziah, she's got to be here. We'll find her. Calm down."

"No, it's a big house." My voice shook.

In my mind, I heard Mama screaming, *How immature can you be? You know how Oma is. How on Earth could you have left her alone in a strange house?"*

"I can't believe it." My legs gave out, dropping me onto the couch. I hid my shakig hands beneath my thighs. "I can't believe I just left her here. I'm so stupid."

"Hey," Domenick called to a man standing nearby. "Did you see the woman who was sitting on the couch?"

"What? No. Happy birthday, Dom. Hey, where's your dad?"

Domenick didn't answer as he moved to a woman, asking her the same question about Oma. As she shook her head, I bolted off the couch to ask a different man.

"Excuse me, sir! I left my grandmother sitting on the couch, and now she's not there. Did you see where she went?"

"Uh, no." The man eyed me.

"Honey, I saw her."

I whipped around to face another man. "You did? Where is she now?" Domenick slid his hand over my back.

The man popped a mini bagel into his mouth. "The poor woman was bored. She can't hear well, can she?"

"No, she can't. Where is she?" My heart hurt as it beat faster.

"I showed her the balcony. It has a lovely view of the lake."

"You...you took her *outside*?" The colors in the room brightened. "Where is the balcony?" A roaring built in my ears. The room spun. *No, I won't faint. Oma's fine.*

"Over here, come on." Domenick tugged me toward the doorway.

"I knew it would give her something interesting to do," the man said. "She said all the noise was bothering her ears, poor thing. It's nice and quiet on the balcony. I was just out there myself a little while ago."

I wanted to punch him. *How dare you take my grandmother off somewhere?*

"Here it is." Domenick led me toward two glass doors covered by sheer white curtains and balanced by two oval tables on either side. Fake pink flowers sprouted from the skinny necks of vases on the tables. A woman stood beside the table on the left eating a mushroom puff .

"Kathy," the man called to the woman. "Remember the old lady I led out there? Is she still there, or did she come back in?"

She's still out there, Ed."

I broke away from Domenick to grab the brass handles on the doors. They moved soundlessly, and I yanked them open, stepping into the chill winter air.

The balcony was empty.

"Oma?"

Snow fell from the clouds above. Light spilled out of the windows and from the room behind me, but otherwise, the night was dark. Across the lake, yellow glows lit up the darkness, lights from other houses.

"*Oma.*"

"Keziah?" Domenick emerged onto the balcony. "Keziah, where is she?"

"Oma!" From inside the house, a Rihanna song started.

A thin layer of snow coated the cement floor of the small balcony. One set of footprints wandered to the railing. They stopped at the edge, and never turned around.

I ran to the railing, grabbing it as I leaned over. Looking down, all I saw was the darkness of the lake.

"Keziah, come on, she must be inside," Domenick called, but his voice shook, and when he grabbed my arm, he trembled.

I couldn't stop shaking. The lake was so dark. I couldn't see any waves, but there had to be some.

Domenick wrapped his arms around me, yanking me against him. Words dried in my throat.

"But..." Kathy's voice trailed off. She pulled a cell phone from her pocket and punched three new buttons, then cried out, "911? Quick, we need a team of rescue workers. An old woman fell over a railing into Lake Winchester!"

*Fell over a railing....*

Only one set of footprints.

"*No,*" I whispered. "No, oh no."

"I'll go ask around," Ed called from inside the house.

Domenick rocked me, but I shoved him away. He let go without protest.

I leaned over the railing as far as I could and he grabbed me around the waist to keep me from tumbling. The lake was so black, so dark.

"*Oma!*"

\*\*\*\*

*I am five years old. The neighbor's cat leaves a dead squirrel on Oma's front porch. Oma buries the remains under the tree while I sniffle. Even though I hadn't known the squirrel, it was still a living creature that had a family.*

*"Life goes on," Oma says. "All we can do is pay it respect."*

*It doesn't make me feel better. I'm glad she gave it a proper burial, though.*

# Chapter 31

A crow circled before landing on the top branch of a spindly tree. Another crow followed, cawing before landing on a branch below the first. The tree hung in mottled shadows, everything dull from the thick, gray clouds above. The sun remained hidden, the rays that came through thin and wispy, encircling the world in fog.

Beyond, the city of New Winchester stretched. The houses blended into a hill of faded colors.

"Amen." The reverend closed his Bible. I looked away from the crows to stare at the ground beneath my feet, the grass dead and brown. The dirt would be muddy if it weren't frozen. My breath puffed in front of my lips.

I refused to look at the gravestone.

"She was the best grandmother." My cousin, Jim, sighed.

*How do you know? You didn't live with her. You didn't take care of her.* I clenched my hands into fists, fingernails biting into my palms.

"I remember how many friends she had when she was still able to come to church," the reverend looked at us as though prompting someone to supply another fond memory.

"When I was little, she would sit me on her lap and read to me for hours," Uncle Jan said. "I'll never forget those days."

*She used to do that with me too, when I was little.* Tears burned the backs of my eyes and crawled up my throat. A single droplet slid down my cheek. I didn't brush it away, savoring the way it froze on my skin in the cold air.

"It's amazing the snow melted for this," my aunt said.

*Is that your fond memory? That you're thankful the snow melted?* I squeezed my eyes shut as another tear fell.

"We'll always get to come here and speak to her like she's still with us," another of my cousins said. He had flown in with his family for the funeral.

I finally allowed myself to look at the stone. My grandfather lay beneath his side of the joint tombstone. Oma wasn't, though. The authorities had searched the lake, but they'd never found her.

"Things happen to bodies when they're in the water," a policeman told me. "Maybe she'll wash up."

I didn't want to think of my grandmother washing up in someone's yard. Uncle Jan and Mama had waited two weeks for the funeral, just to see if it would be the case.

It hadn't.

"I'll always miss her," Phebe said.

I felt everyone smiling and a surge of pride went through me. Even though Oma had never treated her as she should have, Phebe was sweet enough to offer those words, and she meant them.

Mama pressed Phebe against her front, hands resting on her shoulders. Although they held tissues in their hands, neither tried to wipe away the telltale signs of heartache.

"Keziah?" The reverend's gentle voice permeated my thoughts. "Would you like to share something?"

My lips parted. He nodded, encouraging me to spill my heart.

What could I say? How sometimes I had resented Oma, but I'd never stopped loving her, even when she yelled at me over something that didn't make sense? I could talk about how often she had played with me when I was little. How she had been my best friend until we had moved to New York City. I could talk about the times when I'd fed Oma lunch, and my grandmother had thanked me, or how, suddenly, the roles had reversed, and I was in charge of looking after her.

Dad rested his hand on my shoulder. "You don't have to say anything if you don't want to."

I would never see Oma again, and all the times I had thought wicked things stabbed my heart like poisoned needles. I would never get to laugh with her. We would never walk down to the café for breakfast. It would never be just the two of us again.

I tried to take a breath, but a sob lodged in my throat, and I shuddered. Oma was gone, yet it felt as though she was coming back. Only she was never coming back, and I missed her. There was nothing I could do about it.

*Oma.*

The reverend still nodded. Uncle Jan stared at the gravestone. My aunt looked at the other stones in the near vicinity. My cousins had downturned mouths. Mama was on the verge of hysterics, Phebe her link to reality, and Dad looked not only mournful, but also remorseful.

"Keziah?" the reverend prompted.

"She went to be with the Goat Children," I said.

\*\*\*\*

I dropped out of school to be homeschooled again.

"Are you sure?" Mama asked.

I could have a real high school graduation if I wanted, but I declined. My mother got a leave from her school, so she and Phebe lived in New Winchester, taking care of affairs.

Domenick had visited me a week after the incident at his birthday, but I'd been too embarrassed to talk with him much. I'd ruined his special day. I should have never left my grandmother on the couch. I should have never taken her at all. It was all my fault Oma was gone.

*My fault. It's my fault.*

Domenick and his parents came to the calling hours, and Ed sent a huge bouquet.

"It was an accident," Mama told them. "It was her time to go."

"It was my fault," I whispered. Domenick's family shouldn't feel guilty.

Olivia also came to the calling hours. She hugged me and slipped me a piece of paper with her number scrawled on it.

"Call me, sometime, okay? We can talk when you're ready."

"Okay." I put the paper in my purse, but I knew I would never call. I didn't know what to say.

Mrs. Naylor didn't try to touch me, and she didn't smile. The teacher held her hands over her heart. "Nothing will make you feel better, and I'm sorry we didn't get our Monday meeting yet. When you come back to school, my door's open if you ever want some place to sit."

*Sit, not talk.*

"Thanks, I'll probably take you up on that." I felt glad the journalism teacher moved on without further ado.

Meg never came to the calling hours. Neither did Marianna or Michael. He'd told Mama he was sorry when she'd first arrived in New Winchester, but otherwise ignored us. Good. Michael hadn't been what I'd thought at all.

Mama couldn't bear to go through Oma's clothes, so Phebe and I did it. We made two piles. The first went in the garbage. It involved Oma's underwear and socks. The second pile went to the Salvation Army.

We spent a week after the funeral going through everything.

"We can't keep it all," Mama said. "Only take what you really want."

Those items went into the spare bedroom. Everything else we put a price tag on. Uncle Jan said he didn't care, but my aunt spent a day taking everything she wanted—the antique furniture that fit in her van, handmade afghans, antique Christmas ornaments. I was glad I had thought to hide Oma's jewelry. It was mostly mine, anyway. Oma had given me the jewelry box that once.

"We shouldn't be doing this," I argued. "When Oma comes back from the Goat Children, she'll want her stuff." It felt right to say it, as though Oma would walk back through her door at any moment.

"Hush," Mama snapped. "I feel like Oma's coming back too, but denial isn't going to help anything. She isn't coming back. The Goat Children were just her fantasy."

I gave the charm bracelet to Phebe. "Oma wanted you to have this."

Phebe's face lit up, and she never took it off.

Mama hosted an estate sale. We sat at a card table in the living room watching people flit through the house, except the unused bedroom with its door shut.

It broke my heart to see people pick through Oma's trinkets, but I sat beside my mother throughout, knowing it hurt Mama just as much as it hurt me. Only Phebe seemed unaffected, grinning at the charm bracelet.

The sale lasted a weekend, and afterwards, we bundled everything into brown paper bags to take to the Salvation Army.

The house seemed hollow and empty, more so without Oma's presence. Every night, I cried beside Phebe, Mama on the other side of my sister.

As we scrubbed the house to put it on the market, I asked for the hundredth time, "Why can't we move to New Winchester?"

"You know your father works in the city," Mama said. "Moving back here just wouldn't be feasible."

"But I don't want to leave. I love it here."

"Your father—"

"He isn't my father!" I threw my wet rag at the wall and it hit with a *sploosh*. "Oma told me all about that."

Color drained from Mama's face.

"When were you going to tell me?" I ranted. "When I was an old maid? When I got married? *When*? He isn't my *father*. He's my *uncle*, and you're a *slut*!"

"Keziah," Mama gasped as I whirled away.

I almost crashed into Phebe as she entered the living room with a fresh bucket of hot water.

"Kez?" Phebe called.

I marched into the backyard, slamming the door behind me. I ran down the hill to my old swing set. Cold air nipped through my cardigan, one Oma had knitted in her youth. Snow sprinkled the wooden seat, but I sat on it anyway.

Oma wasn't really gone. She couldn't have fallen over the railing into the lake. The Goat Children had taken her.

The backdoor opened, and I looked up. Phebe, bundled in her winter coat, wandered down the hill. I leaned over to lift my sister onto my lap. Phebe clutched the chains, and we sat on the swing for a moment without speaking.

"I love you," I whispered. "You know that, right?"

Phebe nodded against my shoulder. "I know. I love you, too."

"Did you hear what I said to Mommy?"

"No." Phebe paused. "I just heard yelling."

I knew my sister wanted me to elaborate, but for now, I wanted the little girl to remain my sister, not a half-sister.

"What are Goat Children?" Phebe asked.

I smiled against her head. "They're warriors, and Oma's one of them."

I mentioned the enemies, otherworldly creatures that used their minds to force people to act against freewill, and to do whatever the enemy wanted. Like the Goat Children, once they surrendered that life and traveled to Earth, they lost their powers. I thought of the mailman I'd caught in Oma's house. Had he really been one of the enemies?

As late morning sunlight reflected off the snow, I told my sister all about the Goat Children.

\*\*\*\*

"I'll only say this once," Mama said. "Your…Tom never wanted to be a father. I don't think he even wanted to get married, but I pushed. I promised him an amazing life, and he went for it with me. He loved you, really, but he was never cut out to be a family man. He loved his church too much. He put that off for me. For us."

"So he didn't love us enough to stay," I said.

My mother paused, which became answer enough. The same thought must have crossed her mind as well.

"Tom has always loved us, but he couldn't hold us together as a family. When your uncle came into the picture, he took over Tom's role. He became a father to you, then a friend to me, and it only seemed natural to…marry him."

"Of course. It's always natural to marry your brother-in-law," I said sarcastically.

Mama pursed her lips. "I wouldn't expect you to understand. Ask Tom about it if you want, but do not upset…my husband over this. He loves you."

After that, Mama didn't speak to me again. It gave me time to sit on the floor of Oma's bedroom, on the smelly carpet my mother hadn't vacuumed yet, and reread the Goat Children notebooks.

Bodies disappeared when they joined the ranks. That was why Oma hadn't been found in the lake.

The first time Oma had joined, when she was a teenager, she had put on the bracelet from the Goat Children and announced she was ready. She had faced a mirror to do it, and they had spoken in her mind to tell her how she had to join.

The next day, she had climbed the tree in the yard and jumped. As she fell, she was transported and landed in their world.

I ran into the other bedroom for my purse and searched through the zippered pocket until I found the ring where I had put it during the packing. I slid it onto my finger. The metal chilled my skin. I took the mini-mirror from my purse and smiled into the glass. A fingerprint smudged the lower left corner.

Oma had written in one of the notebooks that the Goat Children made a difference, and that was why she loved being one of them.

It was time I made a difference in the world.

"I'm ready," I told my reflection in the mirror. "I'd like to join the Goat Children." I kissed the gemstone in the ring and waited, but nothing happened.

No otherworldly voice filled my mind. Oma didn't appear in the mirror.

"I'm ready to become a Goat Child!" I kissed the ring again. Still, nothing happened. I scowled and put the mirror away, but I left the ring on.

I was stuck going back to New York City. I wouldn't see Oma again.

****

The letter to Uncle Tom glared at me from the bathroom sink. I lifted my cell phone and punched the buttons, dialing the number I'd memorized off the Internet.

I leaned my head against the closed door and shut my eyes, each ring echoing through my mind. On the fourth, a man answered.

"Pastor de Forest speaking."

Words caught in my throat and I coughed. "Uncle Tom?"

Soft voices sounded in his background. "Keziah, is that you? I'm sorry about your grandmother. I hope you got the flowers I se—"

"Why didn't you ever tell me you're my dad?" My voice emerged harsher than I'd intended. "I know, okay? Oma told me, and Mama agreed."

"You spoke to your mom?"

I tried to find a similarity between his voice and mine, but he sounded too far away, too hollow.

"Why did you leave?" I covered my eyes with my hand. "Why didn't you tell me?"

He sucked in a breath.

"I'm your *daughter*."

"You know I love you." His voice trembled. "It was never a matter of that. I left because..."

"Because what, you didn't like Mama, or you didn't like having a family?"

"Your mom wanted me to get a different job, like be a banker or a store manager. I tried that kind of life, but I wasn't happy, and whenever I came home, I would always take it out on you guys." He sniffled.

*He's crying.*

"I'm not proud of that. We should have waited longer before getting married. Your mom and I had only known each other a few months before I proposed."

"Then you left us?" The heat turned on in Oma's house, blowing the toilet paper. The white squares waved at me like flags of truce.

"No." His voice softened. "Your mother had a lawyer draw up the papers. She gave them to me when I came home one day. I've always loved your mother, but not the way your...not the way my brother does."

"You almost called him my father." I rubbed my cheek.

"He had the glamorous life she always wanted. She and I decided a divorce was best. They stayed in New Winchester and I moved on. When you were three, we decided it would be better if you knew me more as an uncle and had only one father. I'd been out of your life too long. You didn't remember me more than phone calls and presents."

"You guys shouldn't have lied to me!" I slammed my fist into the floor.

"You're right. I'm sorry." He snuffled louder. "We never did it to hurt you. I'm here now, and you know. Come stay with me for a while, as long as you want. I'd love to have you here."

I sucked in a breath. "Really?"

"I'll send money for a ticket. Bus or train? Plane maybe?"

*I'll get to be with you, really get to know you. Escape from everything.*

Escape didn't solve problems.

"I'm sorry." I scratched my nails across my cheeks, savoring the pain. "I can't right now. Maybe later. I don't want to run away from things."

He blew his nose. "Call me anytime you want, Keziah. Ask me anything. I've always been here for you. I still am. That'll never change."

"Thanks. Bye." I squeezed the cell phone, wishing I could break it. Sighing, I skimmed the speed-dial screen until I found the number I wanted. The other line rang only once before a young man answered.

"Hi, Domenick? Do you want to go out to dinner tonight?"

\*\*\*\*

I waited at the front door, watching for his car to pull into the driveway. I hid on the stairs, letting him come to the door and knock, a privilege Oma hadn't allowed.

303

Domenick took my hand, to guide me from the house. "You look amazing."

"Despite the bags under my eyes?" I giggled so he'd know I'd meant it as a joke. I had changed my clothes twice before deciding on a gray sweater, black jeans, and silver boots.

"It's your personality." He took my arm to lead me off the porch. "It makes you shine."

I laughed as I climbed into his car. "My personality. How cliché."

"But sometimes cliché works." Domenic winked. "I got you to laugh, too." He plugged his iPod into the radio and selected a Blink 182 song.

"I haven't heard this song in ages." It changed to one of my favorites when Domenick pulled into the parking lot for *Vighesso's*. He left the car running until the song ended, and as we sang along to it, I didn't care how off-key I sounded.

We splashed through the slush puddles in the parking lot. When muck got on my boots, I didn't care, and I laughed louder. Domenick grabbed my hands and twirled me while I threw my head back.

I tugged him inside, and within the doorway, I pressed my lips to his. He didn't hesitate before he pushed me against the wall and kissed me harder. Maybe he could taste my racing heartbeat.

The door opened, and we broke apart, breathless, as a couple entered. They both smiled at us, and Domenick nodded back, but I remained dazed in his arms, savoring the strength of his grip. I rested my head against his shoulder before he drew me inside.

The waitress seated us at a booth and handed out menus.

"What would you and your girlfriend like to drink?" she asked Domenick.

*Girlfriend.* I couldn't stop smiling. I could be a real girlfriend, not a one-night stand like what Michael wanted.

"I'll have a Coke," he said.

"Me, too."

After she left, Domenick flipped through the menu. "I know you don't eat meat, so I'll avoid the chicken parmigana."

"You don't have to. No one ever does that. Just eat what you like."

"I would like to avoid it for you." He reached across the table to hold my hand, and my heart raced even more. When the waitress returned, he said, "I'll take the spaghetti with plain tomato sauce."

"Me too." Spaghetti suddenly sounded delicious.

"Talk to me," he said while we waited for our food. "You don't have to say what your feelings are, but talk about something."

"Okay." I drew a deep breath. "Let me tell you about the Goat Children."

He leaned forward to listen and nodded whenever I paused.

I finished with, "And I want to be one someday, just like Oma."

"You'd make a great one." He grinned.

After dinner, we strolled the mall, and he drove me home. He turned off the engine in my driveway and pulled me into his lap. We kissed and clawed at each other, and broke apart for breath. Sheltered within the glow of the streetlamp, we clung, and I savored his strength.

\*\*\*\*

I lay on the bedroom carpet wrapped in a blanket, my head resting on a single pillow, while Mama wept in the living room.

"Can I do anything to help?" came Phebe's gentle voice.

I squeezed my eyes shut. How long before Mama spoke to me again? I didn't feel bad for yelling, though. It was wrong of her to keep something like that from me.

It came to me, like a whisper.

*Jump off the roof, and we'll catch you.*

I sat up on my elbows to stare at the shadows on the wall. Outside, the light from the streetlamp cast odd images from the magnolia tree. A car drove by.

*We'll catch you....*

"The Goat Children," I whispered.

\*\*\*\*

Different words haunted me in the morning. *It's my fault Oma's gone. I shouldn't have taken her to the party.* Everyone had to think that when they looked at me. I saw it in their eyes. Uncle Tom probably thought it, too.

At the calling hours, I hadn't been able to stand it when people asked what had happened as if they didn't know.

*She fell off a balcony.*

*She did? What balcony? How did that happen?*

*Keziah took her to a party. She went to talk to a friend, and Oma wandered off.*

I'd been given one task—look after Oma, and I'd failed. Because of me, Oma was gone, and now I had to make things right. I had to go to Oma and take care of her. I had to go make a difference in the world.

"Hi." My sister washed the window in the front door. "Wanna help me?"

I glanced at the ring on my finger and slipped the cosmetic mirror from my purse into my pocket.. "Sure." I tore some paper towels off the roll on the floor before squirting them with cleanser. "I'll work on the windows upstairs."

"Okay," Phebe said. "I'll tell Mommy. She's cleaning the tub."

I kissed my sister's forehead. "I love you, Phebe."

"I love you, too," When she scrubbed the window, the charms on her bracelet jingled together.

I wandered up the stairs. The cleaning fluid on the paper towels made my eyes sting.

Upstairs, I shut the door and crossed the room to the window I'd used to break in the day I'd almost had sex with Michael. I left the paper towels on the floor as I slid up the glass. The desk was gone, the upstairs empty, so it was easy to climb through using my arms and knees.

Standing on the sloping roof, I turned my head to stare at the backyards stretching before me. No one was out. It hadn't snowed for three days, so the warm sun had melted everything on the roof. The tiles scraped against the soles of my combat boots.

I grabbed the upper roof and didn't feel more than a pinprick as the rough tiles tore through my skin.

*It's my fault Oma's gone.*

I slid one knee onto the roof and rolled to get both legs up. I stood, noting a tear in the knee of my green cargo pants. Something red shimmered on my skin. Blood. My palms bled. Somehow, I didn't care.

I walked across the roof to the edge. It sloped more than the other roof, so I moved with my arms held out. When my toes touched the end, I let my arms down.

"Hey!" A mailman waved from the sidewalk. "*Hey.* What are you doing? Get back!"

I kissed the ring. "I'm ready." Something, like a hand, touched my arm.

"Keziah," Mama called from inside the house. Faint, yet real.

"Hey," the mailman yelled again. "Get down from there. Help, somebody *help*. I think she's going to jump!"

"I'm ready." My voice echoed through my mind, and the invisible hand on my arm slid down to grasp my wrist.

*I'm so sorry, Oma, but don't worry. I'm going to make everything all better.*

"Stop it," the mailman screamed.

"Keziah!" Mama's voice came from outdoors.

Still smiling, I closed my eyes and stepped off the roof.

****

*I am seventeen years old. Oma is diagnosed with dementia. She cannot live alone anymore, so Uncle Jan wants to put her in a nursing home. I know Oma would hate that, so I volunteer to stay with her. She took care of me when I was little, so now it is my turn to take care of her.*

# Epilogue

The ground I lay sprawled upon was soft and startlingly white. It didn't look solid, more like threads of cotton bound together. I lifted to my knees, shaking my head to move the hair away from my eyes.

The skin on my palm was whole, unmarked. I sat on my heels and looked around, lips parting. Golden rays shimmered through the sky. Young women stood around me, all in their teens.

*Virgins.* The thought flickered through my mind as I stared at them. Each young woman wore a dark blue gown fastened at her left shoulder with a golden brooch shaped like the sun. The long skirts brushed the cotton-like floor, hiding their feet.

Behind them, I noticed a horse. No, not a horse. It was a Pegasus, and there were many more than one. The velvety coats on the animals were as white as white could be, and the horns jutting from their foreheads flashed with the colors of the rainbow.

These were the creatures the Goat Children rode, and curled to their backs must be feathery wings. The horns, I remembered, healed the worst of wounds, and the wings made them fly faster than a jaguar could run.

"I'm here," I whispered. "You...you are the Goat Children."

From the ranks of young women, one stepped forward. Her hair was cut short, curled, and a shining brown. Her green eyes sparkled, and her smile stretched wide.

I recognized the bone structure of the oval face, the prominent nose, and the deep-set eyes. I saw the same face when I looked in the mirror, and when I looked at Mama and Phebe.

The young women knelt to clasp my trembling hands to help me stand.

My legs wobbled, and she tucked my snarled hair behind my ears for me.

"Oma." Tears burned my eyes. "I missed you so much."

"Darling Keziah." My grandmother's eyelids drifted shut as she kissed me on both cheeks. "Welcome to the Goat Children."

THE END

# Acknowledgements

My maternal grandmother, who will always be Amma to me, has always been my best friend. She watched me while my mom worked, took me on vacation, and taught me manners. Not a day passes that I don't hear her voice in my head.

When I was around sixteen, I noticed that she was starting to forget things. When I told my family, they didn't take it to heart at first, but as the years progressed, the forgetfulness heightened. Many of the instances in this story are based on real interactions with my grandmother.

She had always encouraged me to love the written word. She bought me books every chance she got, and many of them she read to me. Amma loved my stories, so she would have me recite them into a tape recorder, and she would often write them down for me. She did this until I had my first computer, which she bought for me. Afternoons were spent at her house typing away.

My mom, uncle, and I took care of her for many years so that she could stay in her home. Eventually, though, she asked us if she could "go somewhere people take care of you." We researched nursing homes and found one we felt would be the best in the area.

After a few years of living there, my grandmother passed away. She wasn't sick, but she stopped eating, and nothing we could do would encourage her to eat again. My heart still aches for the loss of her, and every day, something reminds me of her. I like to think that now she isn't suffering from dementia, that she can be at peace with her loved ones that have gone on before.

I hope that this book will strike a chord with others who have lost someone to dementia. Remember the good times; remember what they would have done for you before the illness.

As always with any book, I must thank my critique partners for all of their assistance. Their keen eyes have helped to polish my work.

I wouldn't be an author without the support of my family. They are always eager to go to book signings with me and hear any book news I have. Their marketing ideas will forever be appreciated.

In the story, Keziah's family is not a reflection of mine. We all supported each other in taking care of my grandmother; we were a team. Keziah's family members are all completely fictional.

Speaking of family, the name Keziah is borrowed from my fourth-great-grandmother, Keziah Bennett-Kimber (1792-1858), and my sixth-great-grandmother, Keziah Mather-Lain (1749-1814).   Phebe is borrowed from my fifth-great-grandmother, Phebe Lain-Bennett (1770-1830). The last name de Forest comes from my ninth-great-grandmother, Rachel de Forest (1609-1643).

The biggest thanks of all is reserved for those who have enjoyed my other books. You don't know how much your messages warm my heart. I hope you enjoy this one too!

# About the Author

Jordan Elizabeth, formally Jordan Elizabeth Mierek, is known for her odd sense of humor and her outrageous outfits. Surrounded by bookshelves, she can often be found pounding away at her keyboard – she's known for breaking keyboards, too.

Jordan's young adult novels include ESCAPE FROM WITCHWOOD HOLLOW, COGLING, TREASURE DARKLY, and BORN OF TREASURE. GOAT CHILDREN is her first novel with CHBB. Her short stories are featured in over twenty anthologies. Check out her website, JordanElizabethMierek.com, for bonus scenes and contests.

Fun fact: In the author photo above, Jordan is wearing her grandmother's wedding dress.

Made in the USA
Charleston, SC
14 June 2016